THE BRIGHTONIANS

UNDER SIEGE

A NOVEL BY DAREN KAY

Grosvenor House
Publishing Limited

Front cover photography by Antony Edwards
heycanitakeyourpicture.co.uk

This book is published by
Grosvenor House Publishing Ltd
Link House
140 The Broadway, Tolworth, Surrey, KT6 7HT.
www.grosvenorhousepublishing.co.uk

A CIP record for this book
is available from the British Library

ISBN 978-1-80381-793-4
eBook ISBN 978-1-80381-794-1

For my Lockdown Legends: husband Gary, and good friend Rory, with whom I shared one of the most bizarre social science experiments the world has ever seen.

For the lives lost during the pandemic that triggered it.

And for those cut short by the previous one, which sadly received far less attention and urgency – and continues to affect people today.

Also, the reason why I will be donating all royalties from sales of the print edition of this book to The Sussex Beacon, the Brighton-based charity that cares for people living with HIV.

A FEW WORDS FROM THE SUSSEX BEACON

On 31st March 1992, the foundation stone was laid for what we are proud to say has become one of Brighton's much-loved charities, The Sussex Beacon.

Established in response to a major need from the Brighton and greater Sussex communities, during the AIDS pandemic of the 1980s and 90s, although the nature of care required has changed over the years, the need is just as great.

Thirty years on, our services promote independence and improve health & wellbeing via both Inpatient & Community resources – from our centre in Brighton, equipped with a 10-bed Inpatient Unit, therapy rooms and larger rooms for group work.

Even though HIV is now a manageable condition, providing support for people living with HIV remains as vital as ever. *This is especially true in light of the number of people now ageing with the virus.*

The services that we now provide include peer support, a drug and alcohol detox programme, crisis prevention, homelessness support, a women and families group and mental health support. More recently we have been placing an increased focus on tackling stigma, including self-stigma, with several campaigns taking place throughout the last year.

Thanks to advances in medicine and education, much has been done to reduce the number of people in the UK acquiring HIV. Yet, as I mention above, our role within the community is still hugely important. It is a shame then that despite this on-going need, over the last decade, many services similar to The Sussex Beacon have gone by the wayside, in part as a result of cuts in public spending.

It is why we are so grateful to the many thousands of people who have freely given their time and skills to help raise money for the charity over the years – and continue to do so. Like Daren, who is kindly donating all the royalties from the paperback sales of *The Brightonians Under Siege* to The Sussex Beacon.

Set mainly in the town, and flitting between 2020 and the early 80s, his novel is packed with characters and places many of you will recognise.

Indeed, our longest serving patron David Raven (aka Maisie Trollette) may very well have rubbed shoulders with real-life incarnations of characters like George, Odi and Pagan Pete. As may have one of our newest patrons Jill Nalder (of "It's A Sin" fame) who, having supported so many throughout the AIDS pandemic, continues to campaign, educate and inspire us all.

And now you can meet them too!

So, grab yourself a cuppa, seek out a cosy nook, and say 'Hello' to the cast of witty, bitchy, loveable, Brightonians, who have made our wonderful-city-by-the-sea their home.

Happy reading!

Scott Davidson (no relation to Grace in the novel!)
Fundraising & Communications Officer
The Sussex Beacon

FOREWORD

Brighton. There's simply nowhere quite like it. I'm not saying it's ALL good; my rose-tinted glasses aren't that powerful, but it's definitely unique. And you don't need to be queer to live here.

Although it does help!

Seriously though, if you embrace the unusual, admire the eccentric and feel strongly about personal freedom, then you really ought to visit. The dangerous thing about doing so is that you might find it's quickly followed by renting a removal van and starting a new life here by the seaside.

It's not the cheapest place to live now. But that wasn't the case in the 1980s and 90s, when many of us flocked here in search of something... different.

I arrived here in 1987: young, optimistic, and *almost* out. This was a matter of months before Section 28 of the Local Government Act banning 'the promotion of homosexuality' – a nonsense concept designed to induce fear and shame – became law.

Many a closet door was flung open in anger. Mine included.

Making us unmentionable in schools and local authorities at a time when AIDS was starting to decimate our communities was unspeakably cruel.

And whilst the physical impact of HIV/AIDS was restricted to a minority of the population. *Compared to COVID-19 which affected every single household in the country – and indeed the whole world.* For anyone old enough to have experienced the first pandemic, the second one brought back uncomfortable echoes of a grim time.

A gut-churning uneasiness. The feeling of being threatened. *Under siege, you might say!*

In this instalment of *The Brightonians*, we follow our quirky band of residents as they navigate their way around lockdown and the government's ever-changing regulation of our movements. We also flashback to the 1980s, when behaviours were forced to change too.

Yet despite being set partly against the backdrop of those dark times, *The Brightonians Under Siege* serves up plenty of light with the shade.

Although that may not be so surprising given that the main protagonist is a 73-year-old drag queen, keen to reminisce about gay leather bikers, wild fancy-dress parties and almost-forgotten sex codes.

As a historian, I particularly enjoyed Daren's mingling of fact and fiction. And just as in life, sometimes the most unlikely things turn out to be true. If you'd rather not know in advance, you might want to put your finger over the next paragraph to avoid any spoilers.

Why not come back here when you've read the book and see if you guessed correctly?

So, the gay discos on a fruit farm... completely true. A gay motorcycle fetish club where few members owned a bike… based on fact. A set of magical symbols carved into stone by Anglo-Saxon settlers… well, I'll leave that up to you to decide. Although a little search on the internet should give you a great big clue.

I'm not the first to say it, but the characters you will meet and adventures you'll enjoy evoke something of the warmth and humour of *Tales of the City* by Armistead

Maupin. Only this time it all takes place in Sussex, England. Well, most of it does – but I'm not giving anything more away!

Daren's warring socialites trying to out-manoeuvre and out-bitch each other are hugely entertaining. And his flashbacks transport us to some amazing locations and delicious moments in time.

Past or present, it's a joyous end of the pier roller-coaster of twists and turns. So, strap yourself in because the ride's about to start.

Alf Le Flohic

Historian, curator, archivist and author of MAGIC Farm and other Queer Tales.

As a leading expert on many aspects of queer history, Alf has contributed to countless magazines, news programmes and podcasts on the subject, and his own website gayhistory.co.uk is a treasure trove of information about LGBTQ+ heritage.

PREFACE

Why did this book need to be written?

It's a question often asked by agents and publishers alike.

And one that, in relation to my first novel, I always struggled to answer.

For me, *The Brightonians* was simply a celebration of my adopted city and its community – past and present. As much as anything, I wanted to write something that represented the confident queer people I knew who'd benefited from and embraced the 'gay' rights ushered in over the previous two decades. In the UK, at least.

But did the book 'need' to be written?

Other than as a record of the above, the answer is probably 'No!'

However, if you were to ask me the same question about *The Brightonians Under Siege*, then I would answer with an unequivocal 'Yes!' – for not only does it include queer histories which have only recently come to light, but it also celebrates the lives of those extraordinary people without whom the rights now enjoyed by most of our rainbow community wouldn't exist.

I am, of course, talking about our queer elders and siblings who bore the brunt of the AIDS pandemic and Clause 28: challenges which led to the founding of the LGBTQ+ movement we know today.

An intensely personal story, *The Brightonians Under Siege*, draws upon my own recollections of that dark period in order to try and explain why the fear and stigma created back then continues to impact many of us today, especially those living with the virus. Which is why I am so pleased to be able to use the book to raise money for The Sussex Beacon, a leading charity dedicated to helping people with HIV.

But please don't think this is a sad story. If anything, it is about the resolve, kindness and humour shown by people who feel they are under siege, whether that was the relatively specific groups affected by AIDS or the billions across the world who were forced to re-evaluate their lives as a result of the more recent COVID-19 pandemic.

And what about the mystic on the front cover?

Well, even before lockdown, I had a vague idea that I wanted the sequel to include a storyline which touched upon Brighton's long history with fortune-telling.

Of course, one thing I couldn't have predicted (except, perhaps, with the help of my fortune-teller!) was the arrival of COVID-19. But since I wanted the sequel to pick up from where *The Brightonians* left off, there was no way of avoiding it.

That being the case, I decided not only to make it central to the story but to use it to tell an almost-forgotten chapter of queer history; how the world responded so incredibly differently to COVID-19 compared to how it did to AIDS.

And also to explore how a city whose lifeblood is its social life would cope with being placed under house arrest.

The result is *The Brightonians Under Siege*.

The second book in the saga of warring socialites who will use every trick at their disposal to gain influence in their shared social circle.

Even if it means dabbling in the dark arts to do so!

Too early to reminisce about lockdown? Not on your nelly! Cut yourself a slice of banana bread. Mix a cocktail with whatever leftover liqueurs are gathering dust in the back of your drinks cabinet. And let the socially distanced party begin!

Daren

Author of two works of fiction and editor of a book on copywriting. Community Curator and 'sometime' guide of Queer the Pier *at Brighton Museum, an exhibition celebrating 200 years of queer history in the county. Long-standing volunteer at The Ledward Centre, the city's LGBTQ+ centre. And door-whore at queer-friendly-dress-fancy-soul-salon, Fever Club.*

ACKNOWLEDGEMENTS

First and foremost, I want to thank queer historian, in both senses of the words, Alf Le Flohic, for his painstaking research into our community's rich heritage. Most notably on this occasion for Hazelpits – the farm in Kent that once upon a time hosted gay discos in its barn – and the biker fetish club, the Sussex Lancers, both of which are heavily referenced in the novel and covered in detail on Alf's website – www.gayhistory.co.uk

Indeed, it's fair to say that without Alf's determination to celebrate these queer histories – and his generosity in letting me in on what he has discovered – this book would have been a totally different fish.

Secondly, I'd like to thank my friends Luke & Shaun in Malta and Caroline & Nathan in Spain for letting me set up shop in their beautiful homes in order to write and finish the first draft of the novel.

Invaluable, too, was the input from my husband, Gary, who I met at an AIDS benefit at the Father Red Cap in Camberwell in 1994 when he was working for the Landmark South London AIDS Centre. As Services Support Manager there from 1988–1997, he was a vital source of information about the virus and of the impact it had during that period. For similar reasons, I'd also like to give a mention to some older members of our community whom I got to know via Brighton & Hove Older and Out, the Sussex Gay Liberation Front and The Ledward Centre, for their recollections of the crisis. Details around funeral arrangements were an area of particular note and poignancy.

To find out what some of my Beta readers thought about The Brightonians Under Siege, *take a look at the short reviews I've included in the next couple of pages. Testimonials from people who live way beyond the borders of East Sussex, including New Zealand and the USA.*

As with my first novel, I'd like to thank Rachel Reese and Emma Cusdin from Global Butterflies for reading the chapters that talk about Grace's transition and her reunion with George after 15 years. As a cis-gendered gay man, I make no attempt to be inside Grace's head at any time in the novel, but to exclude transgender people from a story set in Brighton would not be a true representation of our wonderfully vibrant city-by-the-sea and its LGBTQ+ community and allies. Likewise, with *The Brightonians,* I'd also like to thank Diane Naughton for checking Izzy and Maria's Spanish, and David Harkins for advising on Cameron's Highlands dialogue. For Adam's Northern Irish brogue, I had my dear departed and much missed friend Graeme in my head throughout.

And moving beyond the words, I specifically want to acknowledge the people behind the stunning jacket in which the novel is clothed, that has once again been designed by my incredibly talented friend, award-winning artist Sarah Arnett, whose work is synonymous with Brighton, especially the Royal Pavilion, with whom she has worked. In addition to this, I am absolutely thrilled to have been able to draw on the skills of photographer Antony Edwards, who is also the model for Pagan Pete on the cover. Two Brightonians whose artistry I admire. So, thank you both for bringing the magic and mysticism of *Siege* to life in photography and design.

Their contact details are with the photo and design credits at the front of the book, so do have a butcher's if you get a moment.

Thank you once again to Grosvenor House Publishing for their professionalism and handholding along my journey with this and my first novel and to copy editor Jenny Warren, who likewise applied her gimlet eye to both.

And with my first novel in mind, I'd like to thank shops and retail outlets in the city that stocked and celebrated *The Brightonians,* including City Books, Kemptown Book Shop, Waterstones, i360, Brighton Museum, Bookmakers, Paxton & Glew, the Queery, The Sussex Beacon and Nice 'n' Naughty. And organisations and people who helped me promote it, including film-maker Danny Turvil and actor Hugh Ross for making my 30-second promo film, Torsten at Fagbreak PR, David at Marlborough Productions, Nathan and Justin at Inkandescent, David and Kitty at the i360, John at the Queens Arms, Miss Jason, Davina Sparkle, Father Andrew at St. Mary's, Duncan at The Ledward Centre, Alex, Nigel & Nat at Gaydio, Sarah and Kathy at BBC Sussex, Anna at Brighton Book Club, Andrew at Latest, Chris and Alex at ScenemagazineUK, the team at The Brightonian, Jed and Katrin at The Whistler and Andrew (Queer.I.Am) and Ruth (Kitty Fisher) for interviewing me on their wonderful podcasts.

And last of all – though given the main thrust of the novel – certainly not the least!

I am immensely proud to have been able to collaborate with The Sussex Beacon, referencing the charity several times in the story and using the book to help raise money for the incredible work they do.

Thank you all! I salute you.

WHAT FANS OF *THE BRIGHTONIANS* THOUGHT OF *UNDER SIEGE*

Think 'Tales of The City' only gayer, boozier,
and with posher accents.
This novel packs in enough Brighton history,
mystery, and bitchery to meet your
daily nutritional requirement for snark, secrets,
and even a dash or two of sweet sentiment.

Chris Hunter, Creative Director

A page-turner from start to finish; The Brightonians Under Siege is clever, canny and oh-so caustic in places. Daren brings out the lighter side of lockdown in Brighton in the most ingenious ways – matched with being a highly entertaining way to make a serious point.
A true tale of the unexpected.

Nikki Gatenby, Author of *Superengaged*
and *Better Business on Purpose*

Having been on Brighton's first Pride march in 1973, Daren's novel reawakens wonderful memories of gay life in the hometown of my youth. A delight to read. I loved it!

David Maplesden, Real Estate Agent
and former member of the Sussex GLF

The juxtaposition of the AIDS and COVID-19 pandemics illustrates the importance of love and humour in communities under siege. How wonderful to return to the cavalcade of Brightonians as they career through a new adventure. More please.

Gary Moyle, Hospice Fundraiser 2002–2023 and Support Services Manager at the Landmark South London AIDS Centre 1988–1997

Wiley old drag queens, gay leather bikers, wild fancy dress parties and almost-forgotten sex codes. What's not to love!

Alf Le Flohic, Queer historian and author of *MAGIC Farm and other Queer Tales*

I didn't know I wanted a flashback to the lockdown until I read this hilarious tale that follows a cast of charming, conniving and sexy characters as they navigate the twists and turns of living life to the full in a pandemic.

Rory Smith, advertising strategist and ceramicist

As one of those on the famous anti-Clause 28 march through Manchester in 1988, I know only too well how much my queer friends felt under siege at that time. But as the novel illustrates, it was also a decade packed with fun and adventure, so it was great to be reminded of those heady days.

Matt Lee, Entrepreneur and club DJ

Poignant, witty and Oh Em Gee!
Daren's love affair with
Brighton shines brightly throughout
this charming tale of a city in lockdown.

Antony Edwards, Photographer

I could not put it down. On finishing, I felt an
overwhelming tender sadness.
Drawing parallels between the two pandemics
is a salutary message whilst at the same
time wonderfully capturing the bitchiness and
bravery, the fear and fierceness,
exhibited by communities that feel they are under siege.

Victoria Jakobs, Property Developer, mum and
political activist against hate speech

I've always been fascinated by fortune-tellers and their
craft, so it was thrilling to visualise the story of Pagan
Pete and his premonitions about the two pandemics.
I hope I've done justice to the magical Sarsenic
Sigils with my cover design!

Sarah Arnett, Award-winning artist and designer

The story captivated me from the off – finishing
it in just one sitting! Combining humour and
intrigue with more serious issues dealt
with sensitively. Highly recommend.

Andrea Deakin, Housing rights
campaigner and LGBTQIA+ ally

Fans of The Brightonians will not be disappointed with this absorbing sequel, crammed with local colour and featuring many of the same entertaining characters, this time coping with one of the most surreal experiences of our time.

Brian Wade, TV presenter and interior designer

A deft sequel to Kay's joyful debut which continues to immerse the reader in a slip-stream of Brightonians past, present and (almost) everything in between. With great flare Kay summons up the riotous South Coast gay scene of the 80s and sensitively portrays the hardships of the AIDS pandemic. At its core is a great warmth and affection for Brighton which can't fail to draw you close to the story he artfully weaves.

Ed Kluz, Artist and author of
The Lost House Revisited

The best thing about this book is that I could recognise the hard truths and wallow in the nostalgia without feeling down about it all. This book is an absolute joy, about people living their best, crazy lives and squeezing every bit of love and pleasure out of it, despite everything. Genius.

Jenny Warren, Editor
Quote given by special dispensation since all royalties from the paperback are going to The Sussex Beacon

PROLOGUE

Thursday 23rd January 2020 – i360 – Lower King's Road, Brighton

I've been watching over this city for centuries.

Gliding over its pebbly beaches.

Looking down from its rooftops.

And whilst the old place has witnessed many changes over the years, the view I see before me today is much the same as it ever was.

Yes, the huge iron skeleton, marooned in the waves ahead, is relatively new.

As are the three-armed beasts on the horizon.

But the sea in between and the sky above are almost exactly as they were when the people who gave this stretch of land its name, stepped ashore here over a thousand years ago.

Fearsome warriors about whom the fortune-teller, sitting in a wheelchair below where I now perch, is well-versed.

That's because the tools of his trade are cards inspired by the magical symbols which were etched into stone by those ancient folk.

But whose fortune is he about to tell?

Apart from me, the old man is completely alone.

Still too early for the hordes of day-trippers that are drawn daily to this end of town by the doughnut-topped observation tower on my right.

Yet if the seven cards our fortune-teller has just laid out are anything to go by, he definitely has someone in mind.

Lifting his head, he stares into the distance towards the remaining pier.

Is the subject Brighton, herself, perhaps?

If it is, the blank look with which he greets the first two cards – a jester and a farmer – gives nothing away.

But wait. The third one stops the old man in his tracks.

Judging by his scowl, I fear that the picture of a wolf climbing up the side of a dome-topped tower does not bode well.

Clearly rattled by what he has seen, the next two cards, he turns in quick succession.

First up is a mermaid.

And after her, a sword.

Whatever their meanings, the sight of them causes our fortune-teller to shake his head from side-to-side.

Almost at the end of the row, he takes a deep breath and turns the penultimate card.

It is the image of a thorn-covered branch.

What little colour the old man had in his wrinkled cheeks drains to the same ashen grey as his moustache and beard.

There is now just one card left.

Yet before he has the chance to turn it over, a gust of wind wraps its icy fingers around the card and throws it whirling dervish-like into the air.

But do not think that our wheeled fortune-teller is so easily beaten.

Quick as a flash, he chases the maverick card until it is within his grasp.

Held tightly against the old man's chest, the image is hidden from my prying eyes.

The look of horror on his face, however, says it all, and moments later he is off down the promenade.

What fortune has been foretold for the city? We will have to wait and see.

Certainly, it seems that the Brightonians who call it home are about to experience a testing new challenge.

But to reveal why our mystic is so concerned about the reading, I must first fly you to a place far, far away from here.

The past.

And to this most curious of seaside resorts, almost four decades earlier…

Chapter One

Black Friday

Friday 3rd August 1984 –
Whispers Club – St. James's Street, Brighton

'Fee, fi, fo, fum! Do I smell the blood of a leatherman?' cooed George Gibbons into the darkness at the bottom of the cellar steps.

'Well, why don't you troll on down and find out?' goaded a theatrical voice from below.

'OK. As long as you're decent,' added George coyly.

'Good God! I hope not, dearie. This harness will have been a complete waste of money if I am!' came the reply.

The camp ripostes, George recognised as belonging to his friend Brian – or the Dowager as he was more commonly known on account of his less-than-common upbringing and wealth.

The basement he was gingerly descending into, however, was less familiar to him.

Belonging to a pub situated halfway up a road known locally as Vaseline Alley – on account of the number of gay-friendly hotels in the area – it was the latest venue for the Friday night get-together of the Sussex Lancers motorcycle fetish club.

'Ugh!' sniffed George, as the Dowager came into view. 'It is a bit whiffy, actually! What *is* that smell?'

'Just a spot of damp, dearie. It'll soon disappear once the poppers come out!' bellowed the club's maître d'. 'Help yourself to the buffet. My quiche is to die for!'

As George's eyes adjusted to the half-light, he could see that the party had already started. To his right were four men dressed in leather jackets and peaked caps. The nearest two, friends of the Dowager, who together as a trio were affectionately known as The Three Muskaqueers, were deep in conversation. Seeing George, they broke off temporarily to smile at him. The other couple – younger and both wearing chaps – were too embroiled in some heavy petting to notice his arrival.

And at the far end of the room, near a table in front of a small stage on which was placed a selection of sandwiches, vol-au-vents and sausage rolls, were the two friends George had arranged to meet there: Peter Sissinghurst and Odi Olafson.

'Well, look what the cat dragged in!' cried Pete from his wheelchair.

Clearly there was a less precarious entrance to this subterranean lair, thought George to himself. *Or perhaps his friend had made it downstairs on his bum?* But before he could enquire…

'Hey, Georgie Boy. So glad you could make it. Pete said you might put in an appearance. I know it's not really your kind of thing,' added Odi, the handsome surgeon from Copenhagen who, in keeping with the dress-code, was wearing snug-fitting leather trousers and a matching waistcoat.

Already sporting the 'clone' look when they'd first met four years earlier, judging by the attire of the club's other members, it seemed to George that by the late summer of 1984, fashion had finally caught up with the Dane.

'Yes, you're right,' agreed George. 'Bit on the butch side for me, but the Dowager said she'd waive the dress code as you're only in town for a few days.'

'No Gracie?' asked Pete, stroking his thick black handlebar moustache.

'Sadly not, she's gone up to London for a meeting with some of her miners,' replied George, referring to the gang whom their friend Grace Davidson had met through the Lesbian and Gays Support the Miners group; one of the more unusual alliances formed as a result of the strike, which had just entered its sixth month.

'*Dole* Not Coal!' shouted the Dowager, who'd followed George down to the end of the room.

As a man of some means, he was a natural Tory and made no secret of his adoration for Mrs Thatcher. Though whether feelings would have been mutual was highly questionable, given what the Dowager had planned for later. Certainly, if the poster advertising the act was anything to go by, male stripper, Dick Whippington, wasn't exactly someone you'd describe as 'conservative'.

After taking a seat at the table, George focused his attention on Odi and Pete – and their leather biker gear.

'Aren't you roasting in all that get-up?' he asked, fanning himself with a beermat.

'Mmmm? It depends on who turns up!' sniggered Pete.

Acknowledging the double entendre with a snort, George moved on to why he'd gatecrashed the event that evening. In short, to find out more about an ominous card reading which fortune-teller Pete had drawn that week, which he said would be of interest to them all.

About the future of Brighton, in fact.

'So, what's this prophecy of doom you called about?' enquired George, rolling his eyes at Odi, who was leaning against the wall next to the table.

'Oh boy, I wish I'd never given you that book on runes,' exclaimed the Dane, his comment suggesting this was the first time he'd heard about Pete's recent premonition.

'Except I don't use runes, as well you know. My cards are based on the Sarsenic Sigils. The magical symbols of the Saxons, not the Vikings,' protested Pete. 'Although it's a bit spooky we're having this discussion in a pub called Whispers.'

'Is that right, oh wise one. How so?' asked Odi, with a mischievous glint in his eye.

'Well, because in Old English, the word 'rune' can be translated as a mystery, a secret or… a whisper!' explained Pete.

'Yes, well, whatever you use, let's get on with it before the stripper turns up,' said Odi impatiently.

'Good idea,' agreed Pete. 'I think we'll all need a bit of light relief after this.'

Slipping his hand into a canvas bag slung over the back of his wheelchair, he retrieved a slim deck of cards held together by a rubber-band.

'From the reading I did for Brighton earlier this week,' said Pete, laying all but the last one face up in a row on the table. 'I do it for the town most months. Usually nothing to write home about, but this one's really got me worried. For all of us!'

George looked at the pictures on the cards.

Given the preamble he'd just heard, it didn't take a genius to guess that what they foretold wasn't great, but to his untrained eye, what stared up at him appeared to be little more than a series of charming illustrations.

Evidently, in the world of the Sarsenic Sigils, looks could be very deceptive.

'So, what do they foretell?' asked George, eager to know the dark intent behind the pretty pictures.

'Well, the first one represents 'the past',' replied Pete, tapping on the image of a rather fey-looking youth in a green tunic and orange tights. 'Known as *The Scop*, in Saxon society he was the main source of entertainment. A bit like a court jester or a fool. Poet, storyteller and comedian all rolled into one.'

'A bit like Larry Grayson?' suggested George.

Ignoring the heckle, Pete lit a cigarette and continued to explain the meaning of the first card in the row.

'The Sigil Card bearing *The Scop* suggests pleasure and adventure, which was why people started coming here in the first place, wasn't it?'

'I suppose so,' agreed George.

'And this one represents 'the present',' continued Pete, pointing to a beardy man in a brown tabard, clutching a bushel of straw in one hand and carrying a large trug of fruit in the other.

'Phwoar! You wouldn't kick *him* out of bed, would you, dearie?' chuckled the Dowager, between mouthfuls of quiche, on his way back from the buffet.

'Not with a basket that size, I wouldn't,' agreed Odi.

Again, the interruption did nothing to deter Pete from practising his craft.

'Bedwig. Named after the Saxon word for barley, he's associated with agriculture and is a sort of fertility god. His sigil stands for prosperity and happiness.'

'Mmmmm… I'm certainly feeling happy right now,' said Odi, screwing the top back onto a small brown bottle.

Alerted to the pungent fumes of amyl nitrate, George glanced over at his friend, whose attention seemed to be more focused on the naked buttocks of the chaps in chaps, who were helping themselves to sausage rolls and vol-au-vents from the table on the stage.

In an effort to coax Odi away from the bare behinds by the buffet and back to buff *Bedwig* on the card, George humoured Pete's interpretation with one of his own.

'Well, Brighton's no Costa del Sol, but it *still* pulls in the tourists. Especially the gay ones. Sounds pretty rosy so far.'

'So far yes, but look…' instructed Pete, tapping the third card in the sequence, which featured a ferocious-looking wolf climbing up the side of a tower.

Topped with an onion-shaped dome similar to the one that adorned the Royal Pavilion, flying overhead was a large bird, which, according to Pete, had a vulture-like reputation for picking clean the corpses of fallen warriors on the fields of battle.

'They're waiting for the inhabitants of the tower to surrender… or die,' continued Pete, sucking on his cigarette and exhaling a large cloud of smoke. 'More often than not, *The Wolf Sigil* card is interpreted as meaning disruption, abandonment and the end of friendships.'

'But what does it represent?' asked George as the nicotine haze dissipated.

'The future!' exclaimed Pete dramatically.

So much so that Odi's attention was at last drawn back to the cards.

'And the next one?' asked the Dane, looking down at the table.

'The fourth card is the thing we must overcome,' replied Pete, tapping on the image of an androgynous looking creature sitting atop a lily pad in the middle of a pond. '*Nicor*, a river spirit, whose sweet music was said to be so enchanting that people would drown themselves trying to reach its source. A bit like a merman or a siren.'

Pausing for a moment, Pete turned to George and looked him squarely in the eye.

'Think about it. Men lured to their deaths by desire. Doesn't that sound like this 'gay virus' we keep hearing about?'

But before George could answer, one of the chaps in the chaps got in there first.

'Oh God. It's really scary, isn't it? A friend of mine from San Francisco was over last month. He said it's all anyone ever talks about over there these days. Apparently, they're trying to shut down the bathhouses to try and stop it from spreading. Some are even blaming it on poppers!'

With the smell of Odi's amyl still lingering over the table, an uneasy silence descended upon the group.

Of course, George had heard about the strange virus which mainly seemed to affect gay men. And he also knew that several people had been diagnosed with it in London. But knowing no one personally, he'd tried to put it to the back of his mind. Especially as there was so much confusion relating to how you got infected.

The last comment being a case in point.

'Poppers! Really? They'll be blaming it on the boogie next!' quipped George, glancing over at Odi. 'What do you think, Doctor?'

'Ooh, a doctor! Sexy *and* smart!' said the other chap in the chaps, a skinny lad with cherubic blond curls.

'Well, it's not my area…' began Odi. 'But I do think we need to be more careful. Wearing a rubber for a start. And I know they're working on ways to treat it. But until then, just pray you've been lucky and hope they find a vaccine pretty soon.'

'Or we could see what the cards have to say,' suggested blondie's chum, pointing at the fifth one in the formation, which featured a menacing-looking sword.

'*Ironstone*,' said Pete before dropping his cigarette butt into the dregs of beer at the bottom of his pint glass, causing a single plume of smoke to spiral above their heads. 'The rock containing the metal from which the Saxons made their deadliest weapons.'

By this point, George had decided that life in olden times was looking increasingly unappealing. After a good start with the camp comedian and the fuckable farmer, the last three cards seemed to show an unhealthy preoccupation with fighting and death.

'But what does it mean?' he asked.

'*The Ironstone Sigil* suggests that a battle is approaching,' began Pete. 'Yet armed with the right weapon, it is one which can be won. And the fifth card in the reading denotes the best course of action. So, if it's about this virus…'

'A cure. The right weapon. Surely the best course of action is to find a cure?' cried the blond boy who'd been flirting with Odi, his outburst attracting a couple more people to the huddle around the table.

'Well, that's definitely how I would interpret it, but the sixth card, representing the obstacles we will face, isn't quite as appealing,' replied Pete. 'Look!' he instructed, pointing to the next image in the row. '*The Blackthorn Sigil*, with its razor-sharp thorns, suggests that the journey will be a painful one with many setbacks.'

'Razor-sharp thorns? No, that doesn't sound good,' said one of the new arrivals. 'Especially when you come across them in the bushes up at Duke's Mound. You should have seen the scratches I got on my backside the last time I went cruising up there!'

'Ha! One prick you'd definitely want to avoid!' added someone else.

'But that's just it,' continued Pete once the sniggers had died down. 'The thorns of this tree were often used by witches to pierce wax dolls. So, a more literal interpretation could suggest some sort of wound. Like that skin condition doctors in London are seeing more and more people with. Kaposi's sarcoma, I think it's called.'

'God yeah. I remember watching a TV documentary about it last year,' interjected one of the newcomers. 'Beautiful young men in California with purple blotches all over their bodies.'

'Yeah, well, it's not just America anymore. Or London even. My next-door neighbour told me he'd seen someone on the nudist beach this week with them on his back,' said Pete before lighting another cigarette.

As George digested this news, his thoughts turned to friends he'd not seen for a while. Especially anyone who'd seemed a bit under the weather the last time they'd met. No one sprang to mind. Though in fairness, he wasn't entirely sure what symptoms he ought to be looking for. Weight loss? A cough? Purple blotches? Feeling a sudden desire to give himself a once-over with a hand mirror, he tapped the final card in the formation, which, unlike the others, was placed face down on the table.

'So, what about this one?' he asked, with a sense of foreboding.

'The seventh card represents the outcome of the reading,' replied Pete, turning it over to reveal the image of another wolf. 'That's why I've kept it covered until now.'

George stared gloomily at the final card. The animal was three or four times the size of the one climbing up the tower and munching on the hand of a man who could be seen in the right-hand corner.

'*Fenrir the Wolf*,' said Pete, gravely. 'Though originally created by the gods themselves, as the wolf grows bigger, they fear that he is getting too powerful and hatch a plan to restrain him. Basically, a trick involving three increasingly robust chains. *But the wolf has brains as well as brawn!* And after breaking the first two with ease, on seeing the flimsy-looking third one, he suspects skulduggery and agrees to be bound in this chain only if one of the gods places their hand in his mouth.'

Breaking off temporarily to take a drag of his cigarette, after exhaling another one of those noxious clouds, Pete returned his attention to the final card.

'Step forward Tiw, the God of War,' he continued, tapping on the unfortunate fella in question. 'Of course, this final chain, being made with magic, is impossible to break. So, on realising the deception, *Fenrir* exacts his revenge by chomping down on Tiw's hand.'

Ouch! thought George to himself, almost as gripped by the story as was the hand in the wolf's mouth. But as fascinating as it may have been, he was still rather anxious for Pete to finish so that he could get home and begin a full body search.

'Which in the context of the reading means what exactly?' asked George, in an attempt to chivvy his friend along.

'Well… because *Fenrir* represents something that ultimately cannot be controlled, not even by the gods… in the context of the reading…' began Pete before being interrupted again.

'Fuck! You think it means that this 'gay cancer' is gonna become so massive it'll be impossible to control?' asked blondie.

'Well, it's one interpretation, yes…' replied Pete.

'Jeez!' cried someone, in a tone which suggested they were far from convinced.

Indeed, from mutterings nearby, it sounded like the sceptic wasn't alone in his view.

Not that this deterred Pete, who, like the good zealot he was, had a counterargument up his sleeve for just such cynicism.

'Oh, I know what you're thinking. What a load of old nonsense!' he said, turning to the row of naysayers standing behind him. 'But I reckon there's gonna be a lot of people out there re-evaluating their position on God and suchlike before we get through this. So why not look for guidance in the same way our ancestors did? I mean, just because the Pagans weren't as good at writing stuff down as the Christian monks, it doesn't mean that what they believed was any more ridiculous than the Second Coming or the Parting of the Waves, does it?'

'Second coming? I should be so lucky. Haven't had my first one yet,' shrieked a voice in the crowd which, like *Fenrir the Wolf*, had grown monstrous in size.

'And I can't remember the last time someone parted *my* waves!' howled another, prompting more laughter, until a real-life god appeared at the other end of the cellar.

Just as muscle-bound as *Bedwig*, the Saxon god of fertility, but in a leather harness and brandishing a riding crop, it was clear that the evening's entertainment had arrived.

The reading over, George said his goodbyes and prepared to make his exit.

Which he would have done had his escape route not been blocked by the gyrating fleshy buttocks of male stripper Dick Whippington.

Ah well, thought George to himself, *my appointment with the hand mirror can wait until tomorrow.*

Chapter Two

2D or not 2D? –
That is the question!

Thursday 23rd January 2020 –
George's flat – St. James's Street, Brighton

'Aaaaaaaaaaargh!' screamed George in the direction of the shadowy figure at the foot of his bed.

Clearly, the 40 years that had passed since the fateful reading in the basement of Whispers gay club had done little to dampen the old man's penchant for the dramatic!

Yet despite sounding like the hysterical heroine in a black-and-white horror movie, the cause of his outburst wasn't a gigantic gorilla or a blood-thirsty vampire.

No.

It was something far more frightening.

Himself!

Or rather, it was the life-sized cardboard cut-out of his drag queen alter-ego, Bette y'Sweet Ass, dressed in a rhinestone-encrusted green evening gown and pouting at him suggestively over a Martini glass.

'Oh, dear Lord,' gasped George, as the fingers of his right hand walked tarantula-like across the top of his bedside table and brushed against his spectacles in the spot where he always placed them before going to bed.

At least some things are still as they should be, he thought to himself; the cardboard cut-out a stark reminder of how much the rest of his world had been turned upside down recently.

Reassured that he wasn't about to be attacked, George switched on his bedside lamp and turned towards his alarm clock.

Quarter to ten.

'No rest for the wicked,' he said to 2D Bette. 'Almost time for my close-up!'

Or more accurately, it was almost time for his call with Cameron McIntyre, the smooth-talking Scottish adman who'd hired George as something called a 'brand ambassador' for one of his agency's booze accounts which was in desperate need of a refresh, a make of gin called Rakewell's that had last been popular in the 1960s.

Convinced that Bette would be hugely appealing to a new generation of hipsters in thrall to all things drag, Cameron was also the reason for the promotional stand which would soon be gracing supermarkets and off-licences throughout the land.

Pulling himself up into a seated position, George scanned the scene in front of him.

Eyes slowly adjusting to the light, with the aid of his spectacles and the scarlet hue cast by the lampshade, more details of his bedroom intruder gradually came into view.

'Rakewell's! The Gin that made the 60s Swing!' claimed the tagline which was hovering over Bette's beehive wig like a swarm of rcturning bees.

'Oh gawd! What have you got us into now!' muttered George to his drag queen persona.

But no sooner had the words left his lips than the phone in the hall began to ring.

'Hold your horses, dear!' cried the old man, easing himself out of bed and feeling for his slippers on the floor. 'I'll be with you in a couple of shakes!'

Indeed, whilst his gait hadn't been what you might have called 'swinging' since the decade famed for it, despite the extra demands on his time, the recent developments did seem to have given him a new lease of life. And, certainly, he had more spring in his step of late.

So, with unusual vitality for a septuagenarian, George pulled on his dressing gown and made his way towards the ringing.

'Good morning, sir. You're an eager beaver today!' he sang into the receiver.

'Ah, George daaaarlink, soooo sorry to call you at this hour…' began the voice.

But rather than hearing the Highlands brogue he'd been expecting, George was greeted instead by the sultry tones of Brighton Museum curator Isobel Pitt, which despite her ardent Anglophilia, still carried a hint of her native Spanish.

'Oh! Izzy!' exclaimed George, a little taken aback.

Not by the fact she was phoning him.

As he was one of the main sources of information for a book she was writing about Brighton's queer history, Izzy had called to pick his brains quite a few times over the last couple of months.

In fact, having lived in the city all his life, George had been a veritable font of knowledge on the subject, being able to draw upon a chequered past which, before taking to the stage as Bette y'Sweet Ass, had included a brief stint as a teenage porn star, membership of the Sussex Gay Liberation Front, and playing a key role in the town's response to AIDS and Clause 28.

More bizarre, though, was why a middle-aged straight woman from Spain was so fascinated by the queer underbelly of his hometown.

In a nutshell, the source of her interest was a collection of homoerotic movies from the 1960s, which she'd found in her attic. And whilst George was under no illusion whatsoever that the films he'd made as a teenager were little more than soft porn, if Izzy was convinced that they were of huge significance to local queer history – and perhaps even to British cinematography itself – then who was he to argue!

So, given his pivotal role in her research, the voice at the other end of the phone was not unusual.

The time of the call, however? Now that *was* a cause for concern.

'Sorry, dear. I was expecting Cameron,' began George. 'He usually calls for his pound of flesh around now!'

'Ha, I bet he does!' huffed Izzy, dismissively.

It was no secret she and Cameron didn't get on.

In fact, it was no secret they loathed each other with a vengeance and were almost permanently at each other's throats.

Having made both their acquaintances only fairly recently, George wasn't entirely sure of the reason for this mutual dislike, but as far as he could ascertain, it had something to do with the amount of influence each commanded within their shared social circle.

Of course, as a recent émigré from London, Izzy still had some distance to go before she would be in a position to overtake her adversary. But if the way she'd capitalised on being in possession of those old movies was anything to go by, George thought it would be wise for Cameron to watch his back!

'Well, I won't keep you then, darlink. I just wanted to ask you a question about Grace Davidson,' said Izzy.

'About Gracie?' repeated George in order to buy himself more time to digest her request.

And more specifically, to brace himself for whatever she wanted to know about his recently departed friend.

As Britain's first-ever transgender MP, there was plenty on the internet about the Brighton politician who'd passed away peacefully at the grand old age of 84 the previous October. That being the case, George guessed that Izzy's request could mean only one thing.

She'd finally uncovered the secret about Grace which had lain hidden for almost 50 years.

Just then, bang on 10am, a bleeping sound in George's ear announced the person he *had* been expecting.

Saved by the bell!

But before George had a chance to click Cameron on to the line, another demand for his attention presented itself: his door buzzer. Pressed frantically over and over again, the loud vibrations ricocheted off the walls of his narrow hallway.

'So sorry, Izzy, there's some lunatic at my front door. I'm going to have to see who it is,' said George, abruptly ending the call and reaching for his intercom button.

Yet as he did so, a new thought came to him.

What if it really was some crazy person who'd just randomly chosen his bell?

There was certainly no shortage of odd bods at his end of Kemptown. So, ignoring the noise for a little while longer, he walked back down the hall to the bay window in his kitchen.

A favourite spot from where to observe the comings and goings of his neighbourhood, George had no trouble spying on the street below without being seen.

Except, perhaps, by the large seagull on the roof opposite which, like Mother Nature's CCTV, seemed to be closely monitoring his movements at that particular moment.

Ignoring his feathery stalker, George looked down to the cause of the commotion at his front door: an elderly gentleman in a wheelchair.

'Well, I never!' exclaimed George as he released the catch on the sash and thrust his head into the freezing January air; the screech of metal and wood causing the seagull to erupt into a fit of cackles and the surprise visitor to look up at the window.

'Pagan Pete! You old charlatan!' shouted George. 'What on earth do *you* want at this time of the morning?'

Chapter Three

Dragging up the past

Thursday 23rd January 2020 – Golden Square – Soho, London

'Blood and sand!' cursed Cameron, realising that his call had gone straight through to voice mail. 'Where could the auld fella be, I wonder? Probably overslept again!'

Och! I thought children and animals were a handful!

Perhaps he should add geriatric drag queens to the list of performers with whom one should never work!

Ah well, there wasnae anything particularly pressing which needed George's attention. The main reason for the catch-up had been to tell him about the venue they'd hired for Rakewell's relaunch party in a few weeks' time.

Called the Rococo Piccolo, just off Piccadilly Circus, it had been a popular haunt of the 'in-crowd' during the Swinging Sixties, so it would be the perfect backdrop for a brand hoping to recapture some of the pizzazz it had enjoyed back then.

What's more, it had a huge screen on which to play George's homoerotic movies, that with the backing of a local historian had been sold to Cameron's booze client as rare examples of British 'art-house' cinema and were now part of the campaign to make Rakewell's 'cool' again.

Yet most exciting of all was the celebrity he'd booked to host the event: Irish comedian and popular chat show host, Liz O'Hara.

Ah well, I can put it all in an email later.

Besides which, there were plenty of other people Cameron needed to contact that morning.

Next up was someone he'd have willingly added to the list of those with whom one should never work. He was, of course, referring to the aforementioned historian, Isobel Pitt.

Having a number of friends in common, Cameron and Izzy, or Bottomless Pitt as he called her on account of her willowy figure, had crossed cocktail sticks on several occasions since her move down from London two years earlier and their feuding was widely known.

Caused in no small part by her incessant chatter about the fabulous dinner parties she used to hold and the countless artistic soirées she was now missing out on, Cameron had quickly concluded that Izzy viewed Brighton as some sort of cultural backwater, desperately in need of new leadership to guide its inhabitants from their philistine ways.

Not on my watch, lassie!

Residing in the city for almost a decade, Cameron had worked tirelessly to assemble his 'court', and there was absolutely no way he was going to allow Bottomless Pitt to swoop in and make herself queen.

Indeed, given the animosity which existed between them, her involvement in the relaunch wasn't exactly out of choice.

No! The reason for this necessary evil, as Cameron put it, was because George's *dirrrty* movies had been found in the house she'd inherited from a relative, and so he needed her permission to use them.

Thankfully, the deep pockets of the drinks company had been very persuasive in getting everyone on board.

George for the princely sum of £25,000 and a slice of the profits from the spin-off merchandise. *Though Cameron suspected the gravitational pull of the spotlight was the thing which had actually sealed the deal.* And for Izzy, the funding of a book about the homosexual *demi-monde* that had existed in Brighton since at least the 1960s, with particular focus on the gay porn industry in which George had once been involved.

Allowing her a minor role at the Rococo Piccolo was purely a gesture of goodwill on his part to get her over the line.

Or rather to get her to sign on the dotted one!

And given that the shindig was just the first of many events being planned to put Rakewell's back on the map – *none of which, after the one in Soho, would include Bottomless Pitt!* – in the grand scheme of things, letting her join George on stage for the interview with Liz O'Hara was a concession worth making.

In fact, his client had already briefed the agency on the campaign to reintroduce Rakewell's to the Asian market, which was due to kick off in Singapore in a couple of months.

Reminded of this, Cameron looked at his phone. 10.30am. As well as Izzy, he also needed to call the woman who handled the gin account at his agency's Beijing office, who'd shortly be arriving in the UK for a full briefing.

Anytime between 9am and 11am, she'd said in her email. If he called now, he'd probably get her before she finished work for the day.

He dialled the number and crossed his fingers. After a few echoey beeps…

'Hello, Yang Wei speaking,' said a voice at the other end.

'Oh, hello, it's Cameron McIntyre from the London office. We chatted over email last week. I just wondered if you had any more details about your trip.'

'Ah, Cameron. So good to hear from you,' replied Yang after a short delay. 'I can't wait to meet you in person. I haven't been to London for ages. Not since Chinese New Year in 2018.'

'Oh aye! The celebrations in Soho are amazing. So vibrant. We never miss them,' lied Cameron, typing *Chinese New Year 2020* into his search engine. 'What is it this time?' he added, recalling a party he'd attended in Brighton the previous January where everyone had been asked to wear something to mark the Year of the Pig.

'Rat!' said Yang. '2020 will be the Year of the Rat!'

'Oh!' was all Cameron could muster before adding, 'Aye well, there's nae shortage of those over here...'

The deafening silence which greeted his retort was not encouraging, until...

'Yes, especially in advertising!' howled Yang.

Phew! thought Cameron, realising that the delayed reaction was owed to the distance of the call – not his gag. Indeed, remembering the photo of Yang on the agency website – a large woman with a Cheshire Cat smile – the laughter he heard at the other end of the line sat well with the snapshot of her on her profile.

'Aye, though hopefully no at *oor* agency!' added Cameron with renewed confidence. 'So, you'll be heading over here somtime after your New Year's celebrations?' he asked, noting from his search that the Year of the Rat was just two days away.

'Yes, I'll be spending it with friends in Hong Kong this year,' replied Yang. 'A few days there and then straight to London. I'm aiming to be with you in the first week of February. And after that, I'll be heading to Singapore to check out venues for Rakewell's relaunch at this end.'

'Excellent, I'll block out the 3rd and 4th and book something fancy in Chinatown for your last evening,' said Cameron, typing *Chinese 5-star restaurant Soho* over his previous search.

'Oh please… if it's all the same to you, I'd prefer something a bit more… mmmmm… you know… when in Rome and all that,' requested Yang.

'Nae problem, I've just the place. OK. I know it's late over there, so I'll say goodbye for now and confirm dates in an email. See yous in a few days. Happy New Year!'

Conversation over, he was about to send the promised reply when his attention was drawn to a headline on his screen, which had no doubt been triggered by his recent searches.

Deadly virus causes chaos on mainland China – Wuhan Province locked down.

Intrigued by its dystopian tone, Cameron clicked on the link to find out more.

He had a vague recollection of an article he'd read over Christmas about some new strain of flu that was causing concern out there, but having heard nothing about it since, assumed it'd all been sorted. *And hadn't he just been talking to someone from mainland China*?

Surely, Yang would have mentioned it if it had been anything to worry about.

Wouldn't she?

Chapter Four

Spanish Inquisition

Monday 3rd February 2020 – Royal Pavilion Café – Brighton

A couple of weeks later, someone else with China on their mind was Izzy.

Not the events unfolding in Wuhan that had interested Cameron, but the Chinoiserie interiors of the long entrance hall to the Royal Pavilion. Or at least an interpretation of the Orient by the early 19th-century interior designers employed by George IV to transport his guests there as they entered his fabulous pleasure dome.

Featuring hand-painted pink wallpaper, fake 'bamboo' seating and heavily gilded coving, it was both garish and beautiful in equal measure. Yet as striking as it might have been, the lavishly decorated corridor was not the reason for her visit that morning. Rather it was the café on the floor above, which, boasting a terrace that overlooked the Palace gardens, was arguably the most delightful place in Brighton to enjoy a cup of tea.

Chinese or otherwise.

Assuming, of course, you were prepared to face off the odd seagull, for whom it was also a popular lunchtime destination.

Yet since it was still winter and the terrace closed, the view today would be locked behind the French windows and, in all probability, only visible after wiping away the condensation which frequently clouded the glass during the early months of the year.

Even so, it was a vista that Izzy knew well, for as a curator at Brighton Museum, a short stroll from the Pavilion, she had her 'own' table in the café, which she defended with she-wolf ferocity should any pitiable tourist try and sit there.

Seeing her lunch guest arrive, she told her face to smile and rushed forward to greet him.

'George, daaaarlink… so glad you could squeeze me into your busy schedule, what with all your 'ambassadorial' duties,' she fawned, just loud enough for the guard to hear and hopefully misinterpret her little joke.

'Sorry, dear? Oh yes… ambassadorial duties… very droll!' replied George, taking a moment for the penny to drop.

Whether the man at the entrance had fallen for her little ruse, Izzy couldn't say, but the deep bow he gave as he unhooked the rope suggested that he was hedging his bets as to what kind of dignitary George may have been.

Thrilled at her deception, she turned around and led the way up the cast-iron bamboo-railed staircase to her 'throne-room' upstairs.

In the few minutes it took to reach the café and order their lunch, George filled her in on what being the 'brand ambassador' for Rakewell's Gin had involved since they'd last spoken.

'Oh yes. They've definitely had their pound of flesh these last few days. I was up in London doing some radio ads on Monday and Tuesday. Something called a podcast on Wednesday. And then a photo shoot on Thursday and Friday. I don't know what for exactly. Bette just looks into the camera and pulls a few faces,' he said, talking about his drag queen alter-ego in the third person, as he often did.

'Sounds exhausting, daaaarlink!' exclaimed Izzy, as they arrived at 'her' table.

'Yes, I was completely shattered when I got back on Friday night,' concurred George, dabbing his forehead with a mustard-coloured handkerchief he'd had in the top pocket of his jacket. 'But it was so lovely to be up West again. And I also got shown around the venue for the relaunch party. The Rococo Piccolo on Piccadilly Circus. Very swish!' he added, placing his hanky on the table.

Cameron had called Izzy about the upcoming event in the West End, so this wasn't exactly news to her, but keen to let George know that she was on the inside track, she filled him in on the finer details of her role on the night.

'Ah yes, he's asked me to join you on stage to talk about the remastered films and their importance to cinematography. Apparently, they've got some famous comedian to interview us both!' said Izzy, with a sniff of disdain.

'I know! Exciting, isn't it?' gushed George.

But as eager as the old man clearly was to talk about the upcoming relaunch party, Izzy was more focused on picking up where she'd left off a few days earlier, before they'd been rudely interrupted by George's early morning visitor.

'So, as I was about to ask before the commotion at your front door….' she began, before the old man jumped in.

'Oh gawd yes, the day Pagan Pete turned up on my doorstep!'

Thrown by the unusual sounding name, she stared blankly at her lunch guest.

'You know. The fortune-teller who has a spot next to those rusty old pilings at the bottom of the i360,' explained George.

Still none the wiser, Izzy decided to make an intelligent guess.

'Ah, the mysteries of the tarot. How exotic!' she said, placing the tips of her fingers on her forehead in a way which she hoped suggested mysticism.

'Sorry, dear, would you like an aspirin?' asked George, seemingly mistaking her communion with the spirit world for a mild headache.

Dropping the act, Izzy assured him that she was not in need of any immediate First Aid and urged him to continue.

'But no, not the tarot, dear. Pagan Pete tells fortunes using the Sarsenic Sigils,' said George.

Now this was getting embarrassing. As a renowned historian, she ought to have at least heard of the Sarsenic Sigils, even if she had no idea what they were.

Sadly, she knew neither and reluctantly decided that this was one of those rare occasions when her desire for knowledge was greater than the one to appear superior!

'*Sarsenic Sigils*, darling?' she asked softly.

'Yes, dear,' confirmed George. 'Symbols carved into sandstone boulders. A bit like Viking runes but peculiar to Sussex. He's even written a book about them. *Unlocking the Magic Code of the Anglo-Saxons*, or something like that, by Peter Sissinghurst. Pagan Pete is just his 'stage name'.'

Despite having to acknowledge her ignorance on the subject, Izzy was utterly captivated by what she was hearing. But before she had a chance to ask more about these fascinating symbols from the past, her lunch guest returned to more recent events.

'In a right state, he was!' continued George. 'About a reading he'd just had.'

'Gracious! Who was it for?' asked Izzy.

'Not who, dear! The reading was for Brighton!'

Had this been anywhere else in Britain, the punchline would probably have been described as a 'damp squib'.

But in Brighton, where the mere mention of the city was greeted with respect and awe by its inhabitants, the reaction was one of horror.

'Oh no!' gasped Izzy. 'But why was… Pagan Pete did you say his name was, darlink? Why was he so concerned that he felt you needed to know about it right away?'

'Because I was there the last time he drew the same sequence of cards,' began George. '1984, it would have been. The year we first heard that someone in town had died of AIDS.'

'AIDS!' cried Izzy, just as the waitress arrived with their drinks.

A little embarrassed by her outburst – *not exactly becoming for an academic like herself* – she helped to decant the contents of the tray in an attempt to hasten the girl's departure.

Satisfied they were alone once more, Izzy returned to the discussion about Pagan Pete's premonition. *Albeit with a bit more decorum!*

'The reading foretold AIDS?' she asked quietly under her breath.

'No dear, of course not!' replied George, shaking his head. 'But it was around then that more and more of our friends started to get sick.'

'Ah yes… dark times,' agreed Izzy.

Having been a teenager in the early 80s, she was well aware of the horror about which George was talking.

'Oh, it was, dear. It hit Brighton very hard. There were more cases in London, of course, but down here, the scene was smaller – more close-knit. You only have to listen to the list of names that are read out during the candlelit vigil on the New Steine each year for World AIDS Day to realise how many people we lost,' said George, stroking the mustard-coloured handkerchief.

Had the square of fabric belonged to someone he'd known back then?

The faraway look on his face seemed to suggest that he was teetering on the edge of one of his regular trips down memory lane. But jolted by the sound of a seagull landing heavily on a metal table on the terrace, all of a sudden, he was back in the room.

'It's this coronavirus-thingymajig. Pete's convinced it's all going to happen again,' he added, glancing, or so Izzy thought, at the handkerchief.

'Oh, yes. I read something about it just this morning. Though I'm not sure we need to worry. They can't bang on about Brexit anymore, so they're putting the fear of god into us all with stories about this awful virus. Scaremongering, I call it!' she said dismissively before pouring some milk into her teacup.

'Don't be so sure, dear. It's putting the willies up lots of my other friends, too,' exclaimed George just as the girl returned with their food order.

Perhaps meeting in the Pavilion Café hadn't been such a good idea after all!

Reminded of how apt the old man was to fall into the fruity vernacular of his drag queen persona, Izzy attended to her pot of Earl Grey with only slightly less diligence than if she'd been performing a Chinese tea ceremony, until she was sure the girl was out of earshot.

As she did so, she became aware, from the hubbub around them, that the lunchtime crowd was starting to arrive. Noting this worrying development, she decided she'd better move on to the reason for her inquisition.

In short, to grill her guest about his friend Grace Davidson, the recently departed politician who'd once represented Brighton Kemptown at Westminster and was the UK's first ever transgender MP.

'Anyway..' began Izzy, once the coast was clear. 'As I said when I called. The reason I wanted to talk to you was…'

'Something about Gracie, wasn't it, dear?' interrupted the old man.

'That's right… well… as you know, I've been doing a lot of research into the city's queer past, including those 'art-house' movies in which you were involved…' continued Izzy, cautiously picking her way through the minefield that was George's past. 'Well… anyway… the person you said was the driving force behind the whole thing…'

'Yes, dear?' he encouraged.

Despite rehearsing this part of her 'inquisition' several times, now she was in front of the old man, she found herself unable to say the name out loud.

Thankfully, George came to her aid.

'Michael Mancini?' he asked calmly.

'Um… yes,' replied Izzy, a little thrown by his apparent keenness to fill in the gaps.

Indeed, far from being surprised, he seemed better prepared than she was herself, and before she was able to gather her thoughts, he was off again.

'To be honest, dear, I suspected this was what you wanted to talk to me about when you phoned,' said George. 'I knew it would only be a matter of time before you'd put two and two together. Or rather before you'd put Grace and Michael together.'

'Oh!' exclaimed Izzy, somewhat disorientated by the theft of her thunder as George continued to steal the show.

'I mean, I know Grace could be quite vague about her life before she transitioned, but she never tried to erase it. A quick search online will tell you that her parents were Italian immigrants…'

'Maria and Guido Mancini!' interjected Izzy excitedly.

'That's right, dear,' confirmed George before pausing to take a sip of tea.

Seeing her chance, Izzy quickly wrestled back control of her 'thunder'.

'Yes, I thought the name rang a bell, so I did a bit of digging. And despite the large number of Italians who emigrated to Britain in the 50s, there was only one Mr Mancini listed in the 1961 census. A Michaelangelo Mancini at an address in Brighton. The only child of Maria and Guido. So, I felt sure it had to be the same person.'

'And the rest, as they say,' began George, returning his cup to its saucer, '…is *her*-story!'

'Quite!' agreed Izzy. 'Though after that, I hit a bit of a dead end. I don't suppose making homoerotic movies was something you shouted about in the 1960s!'

'Or something you'd tell the tax man about either!' exclaimed George. 'As you know from your research, all that 'under the counter' stuff was a nice little earner. And no prizes for guessing what she needed the money for. Still expensive today, I bet. But back then, surgery like that would have cost a small fortune.'

'Dangerous, too, I expect,' suggested Izzy.

'Yes, dear. It took a special kind of bravery. But she was a tough old bird, our Gracie,' said George, polishing off his sandwich while Izzy continued summarising her findings.

'Of course, there are one or two articles on the internet about Grace's time in San Francisco campaigning with Harvey Milk. And loads about the incredible work she did in Brighton during the AIDS crisis and afterwards as an MP, but…'

Once again, Izzy found she was lost for words.

Thankfully, her lunch guest knew exactly where she was going.

'Yes, I know. In fact, I suppose the only thing people *don't* know about our Gracie is that she was the one behind those pornos!' chuckled George before reaching for the treacle tart he'd ordered with his sandwich. 'Until now that is!'

Though a little riled by his description of the 'art-house' movies, the old man's final comment did, at least, suggest that he was OK with her including these new revelations in her book. Certainly, it seemed he had no strong objections.

So, deciding she'd got what she wanted, Izzy prepared to wrap up her 'inquisition'.

But just as she was about to do so, George suddenly returned to this less documented aspect of Grace Davidson's past.

'Though that wasn't where I met her again after all those years,' he said, reaching for a paper serviette to wipe the crumbs off his lips. 'Brighton, I mean.'

'Oh?' enquired Izzy. 'So where did you…?'

'Kent!' replied George. 'In a barn, would you believe? Summer of 1980, I think…with Pagan Pete of all people!'

'Gosh!' exclaimed Izzy.

'Mmmmm… yes,' he teased before lowering his voice to a whisper. 'Of course, back then, it wasn't for Paganism that Pete was best known!'

Sensing from his smirk and the secretive tone that there was an amusing anecdote on its way, Izzy poured the remaining hot water into her teapot and leaned in a little closer.

'Please, do go on, darlink,' she begged.

'Oh well, if you insist…' began George, cheekily.

And for the next few minutes, lunchtime crowd or not, Izzy sat entranced as the old man divulged the unusual circumstances of his reconciliation with Grace Davidson.

And the thing for which Pete had once been famous.

Chapter Five

Ghosts and Gods

Saturday 9th August 1980 – Hazelpits Farm – Kent

Cool, dull, and wet.

Like most of the summer that year, the first few days of August 1980 had been notably lacking in sunshine, and trips to the beach few and far between.

That being so, the decision to swap the seaside for the countryside for a couple of days had been an easy one for George and Pete to make.

Especially as the event to which they were driving was being billed as the Party of the Year.

Not so surprising then that after nearly two hours of intermittent drizzle, the realisation they were finally at their destination was a cause for some excitement.

'Look! Look!' shouted George, pointing to a floodlit pond in front of a large farmhouse. 'It's beautiful. Like a fairy grotto!'

'Fairy grotto! I bloody well hope not! Butch queens only for me tonight,' replied Pete, pulling up opposite an opening in the hedgerow.

'Very funny,' said George, with a sigh. 'I'm not here for that anyway. I just fancy a boogie and a laugh. I'll leave the rumpy-pumpy to you. And your serpentine sausage,' he added, referring to his friend's notoriously large appendage.

So famous, in fact, that he was known on the 'scene' as Python.

'Well, they're playing your song, so we best get a wiggle on,' urged Pete, turning the car onto the mud track which led into the farm.

As they got closer, George could also hear the insanely catchy chorus of Kelly Marie's monster hit, 'Feels Like I'm in Love'.

'Bugger! They better play it again. I've been learning the moves and everything,' he said, referring to the dance routine that the singer's male backing dancers had performed on *Top of the Pops* that week.

In truth, George had been far too distracted by the crotch area of their tight-fitting trousers to remember the finer details of the performance. Though he did seem to recall some jazz-hands and a bit of leg-crossing. He'd also been drawn to Kelly's gold-coloured bowler hat. So much so that he'd hunted one down in the North Laine that morning and was planning on it being his crowning glory later. It had cost him more than the 7-inch record, but as the evening was the last big blow-out before Christmas, he'd decided it was worth the expense. And besides, they'd no doubt be spinning the year's other anthems – 'D.I.S.C.O.' and 'Dance Yourself Dizzy' – so he was sure to get his money's worth out of it on the dance floor.

But where was that exactly?

As a first-timer, George was as much in the dark as the rest of the farm was that evening, which, apart from the lake, seemed to be rather poorly lit.

Fortunately, Pete was a regular at Hazelpits and confidently led them towards the place from where Kelly

Marie had been regaling everyone with her feelings of being in love.

George couldn't remember the last time he'd been so giddy. In fact, the gay discos at a farm near the small village of Headcorn in Kent had become the stuff of legend amongst his friends in Brighton. With lots of revellers travelling from London and some even from abroad. Certainly, the raucous din he could hear suggested that the event was as popular as ever. But what was the cause of the grunts and sighs which were coming from the nearby bushes? George was pretty certain that Hazelpits was a fruit farm, so it couldn't have been livestock.

He was about to ask Pete, when the door of the building to which they were heading suddenly swung open and lit up the ground in front of them.

'Python, the old tart! You're here at last. We thought you'd been arrested for soliciting…' screamed a slim figure in the entrance.

'Again!' guffawed a second, appearing by his side a moment later.

Temporarily startled by the light, it took George a few moments to fully take in the two silhouettes, and by the time his eyes had adjusted, Pete was already engaged in some enthusiastic hugging with both men, though perhaps lingering a little longer on the second chap.

Feeling somewhat abandoned, George placed his bowler hat on his head and made his way over to the trio.

'Sorry I'm late, I had to pick up that virgin you ordered!' howled Pete, nodding in George's direction.

Virgin! Whilst it was true that he hadn't taken advantage of the sexual freedoms ushered in by the 70s as much as his friend had done, it was quite a few years since he'd been accused of being one of those!

'Georgie Boy,' said Pete. 'Say 'Hello' to Hazelpits royalty!'

Having just turned 34, it was a long time since he'd been a 'boy' either. But deciding that there was nothing very 'royal' about the fellas to whom he was about to be introduced – *other than them being a couple of old queens* – he decided he was in good company.

'This is Jeff,' announced Pete, placing his hand on the shoulder of the one wearing brown plaid trousers and an orange tank top.

'Pleased to meet you, Georgie Boy,' said Jeff camply.

'And this is Odi,' added Pete.

'Nice bowler!' said the second man, with a slight accent which sounded like German.

Broad-chested and shirtless under his black leather waistcoat, he reminded George of a Tom of Finland drawing. Although the mustard-coloured handkerchief he was wearing around his neck was somewhat at odds with the tough-guy look.

'Thank you! Nice erm… hanky…' mumbled George as he shook Odi's hand. 'One virgin as ordered! Where do you want me?'

'Well, I think the bar's a good place to start,' suggested Jeff. 'But come back soon. We love a Hazelpits virgin, don't we, girls!' he added, wrapping an arm around the other man's shoulder.

Damn! They're a couple, thought George to himself.

'Yes, we do. And with a face like yours, there'll be no shortage of people waiting to relieve you of your cherry!' added Odi. 'It is a fruit farm after all!'

'Oh, stop it,' chastised Jeff. 'He's only just got here. Go grab yourself a drink, and we'll see you in a bit. You'll be in good hands. No one knows their way around an orgy better than Python. Later gay-tors!'

And with that, they were gone.

'Welcome to Hazelpits!' bellowed Pete before heading through the door of the barn. 'Let's get pissed.'

Pushing their way through the crowd of sweaty bodies getting down to the pulsating disco beat of Lipps Inc's 'Funkytown', a few moments later they arrived at the bar, a trestle-table piled high with enough wine, beer and spirits to rival George's local off-licence in St. James's Street.

'Let's have a voddy. I think we've got some catching up to do!' cried Pete before shouting their order to the bloke behind the table.

While the barman rustled up the drinks, George turned his attention to the heaving dance floor. More than a little aroused by the bare chests jostling before him, he was keen to find out what his friend knew about the beefy stranger with the accent.

'So, what's the lowdown on the Muscle-Mary at the door?' he asked.

'Danish. Odi is short for Odin, as in the Viking god who lived in Valhalla,' replied Pete, handing the barman a pound note for their drinks.

'Viking god is right! Did you see those guns? And his grip. Thought I was gonna lose circulation in my right hand! Jeff and Odi? They sound like children's TV presenters,' scoffed George as Pete passed him a paper cup filled to the brim with ice.

'They're not together. Odi lives in Copenhagen. Just comes over for the discos,' explained Pete, dipping two fingers into his drink and smoothing down each side of his thick black handlebar moustache with the sticky wet liquid. 'And with a bit of luck, he'll soon be cumming over me!'

As this was accompanied by one of his trademark guttural laughs, George wasn't sure whether Pete was joking or not, but it certainly explained the lingering embrace he'd witnessed earlier.

'Right, I'm off for a roll in the hay,' announced his friend before necking his drink in one go and throwing the empty cup over his shoulder.

Even though George was a Hazelpits virgin, he knew that 'rolling in the hay' wasn't a quaint euphemism but a reference to the hayloft, which on party night doubled as the darkroom, the hottest spot for *rolling in the hay* with any number of strangers.

'Enjoy yourself. Don't do anything I wouldn't do, Georgie Boy!' shouted Pete as he pushed his way back in the direction they'd just come.

Ha! Well, that doesn't leave much off limits!

Though as he'd said earlier, he wasn't there to fuck. He was there to *funk*. And since, thanks to the extended 12-inch remix the DJ was playing, Lipps Inc. were still singing about the town famed for that very thing, George took a large gulp of his drink and started to dance.

But no sooner had he done so than he felt someone squeeze his behind. Assuming that Pete had forgotten something, he was about to tell him to cut it out when...

'Hello again, how's my virgin doing?' enquired an accented voice which George now knew to be Danish.

It was the Odi chap he'd taken a shine to at the entrance of the barn.

Temporarily thrown by the return of the Viking god, George let out a little piglet squeal.

'Cherry still intact,' he replied, aware he was turning the colour of one.

Thankfully, it didn't seem to deter his admirer, who responded by taking hold of George's belt and pulling him into his heavenly aura; so close, in fact, that George could feel the bristles of Odi's moustache as he whispered in his ear.

'Great, because I think you look good enough to eat!'

Heart in his mouth, George had just about plucked up the courage to say that he'd be happy to satisfy Odi's hunger when the Dane made another announcement.

'But first let me introduce you to my friend.'

Removing his hands from George's belt and stepping back a little, he turned to a woman in a black jumpsuit – like the one worn by Kelly Marie on *Top of the Pops*.

She was dancing with her back to them, and in the few seconds it took her to respond to Odi's tap on the shoulder, George also noted that she was wearing a bowler hat like the one he'd picked up in the North Laine.

Yet coming face-to-face with the glamorous disco diva, that wasn't all he recognised.

There was something about the smile which gave him the distinct feeling they'd met before. But despite racking his brains, he couldn't quite place her.

Thankfully, Odi took the lead.

'Gracie. This is the peach I told you about,' he said.

'Georgie?' exclaimed the woman. 'Oh, my giddy aunt. Is that really you?'

If being propositioned by a handsome Viking had left George grasping for words, hearing a complete stranger say his name caused him to lose his ability to speak entirely.

But was she a stranger?

Her voice was definitely familiar.

Suddenly it came to him.

The stylishly dressed woman was not *only* a friend of Odi's.

She was also a ghost from his own past!

Someone he'd not seen for 15 years.

And now he knew why.

Overwhelmed by what his eyes and ears were telling him, George dropped his drink and stumbled backwards.

'Well, for all our sakes, let's hope he doesn't bruise like a peach!' said Odi, catching George and guiding him over to a couple of hay-bales a few feet away, where they were joined moments later by their mutual friend.

'Can you give us five minutes, dear?' asked the woman as she made herself comfortable on the makeshift sofa.

'Yes, of course. I'll go to the bar. Looks like you could both do with a stiff drink!' suggested the Dane, grinning from ear-to-ear.

'Oh, don't worry about Georgie here; he's hardier than he looks! But yes, that would be very much appreciated,' she conceded.

Whilst George's fainting-fit threw into question his supposed *hardiness*, once he'd got over the initial shock, he breathed deeply and turned to face his long-lost friend.

'It's so good to see you again…' he began, trying to recall how Odi had introduced her.

'Grace. Grace Davidson,' she said, perceptively aware of his discomfort. 'Not exactly how I'd planned to introduce you to my new self. But here we are!'

Eyes the same sparkly blue as he remembered, she looked kindly at him and stuck out her right hand.

But this wasn't an occasion for formalities. Ignoring the polite offer, George flung his arms around her neck.

And in return, she gently stroked his back.

Grace by nature as well as by name.

Introductions over, George sat back and made himself as comfortable as he could on a seat made of dry grass.

Still struggling to take it all in – not least because the last time he'd seen her was on the set of a soft porn movie – George tried his best to think of something to break the silence.

'Well, at least I now know why you disappeared,' he blurted out at last.

'Yes, sorry about that!' she said, smiling. 'To be honest, I just figured it would be better for everyone if I slipped away quietly. You know how people were about these things back then?'

'What? In the Dark Ages, you mean?' replied George with a smirk.

'Mmmmm, I suppose the world's changed quite a bit since the 1960s,' agreed Grace, glancing over at the dance floor, the backdrop of their reunion being an excellent example of the point she was making!

Feeling a bit more relaxed, George decided it was time to approach the elephant in the barn.

'So, where *did* you go?' he asked tentatively.

'Copenhagen,' replied Grace.

'Like Christine Jorgensen!' exclaimed George, remembering the name of the former GI who'd become a household name after her transition in the 1950s.

'Exactly,' confirmed Grace. 'It's how I know Odi. He was a junior surgeon at the clinic where I had my operation. I didn't go there straight away, though. Had a few adventures before then. And there's been plenty more since!'

Indeed, given the length of time which had elapsed since they'd last met, it was clear that their catch-up was going to take more than the five minutes Grace had requested. So, for well over an hour, George sat transfixed while his old friend filled him in on everything from her operation in

Denmark to her time on the campaign trail with gay politician Harvey Milk!

Certainly, it made George's membership of the Sussex Gay Liberation Front seem a little tame by comparison.

And even harder to believe that the last time they'd sat down together, he'd been a teenage porn star!

Chapter Six

Battle of the Bulges

Monday 3rd February 2020 –
Plato's Gym – Kemptown, Brighton

More than 50 years on from those heady days when George had 'starred' in a bunch of homoerotic soft porn movies, it would be fair to say that the lives of queer people in Britain had changed considerably.

And though the road had not always been a smooth one, on the whole, most would agree, it had been a change for the better.

For evidence of that in Brighton, you needed to look no further than the gym located a few hundred yards from St. James's Street, where you could find any number of loud and proud members of the city's vibrant LGBTQ+ community living their true, authentic lives.

Of course, over the same period, the country itself had changed immeasurably, too. Especially with regard to her neighbours. A relationship which at the beginning of February 2020 had just experienced the biggest shake-up for almost half a century.

PM celebrates getting Brexit done flashed the headline on the digital monitor in the entrance to Plato's Gym.

After almost four years – and three prime ministers – it seemed that the government was finally able to honour the result of the closely contested referendum and break away from the European Union for good.

Or bad.

Depending on how you'd voted.

Which for the prime minister and his supporters, was most defiantly the former, believing Britain's exit would lead to the dawning of a new Golden Age. No more pandering to lawmakers in The Hague. No more kowtowing to Eurocrats in Brussels.

And that wasn't all. It would also mean millions of pounds a day being redirected to the NHS. An end to those pesky Continentals hot-footing it across the channel to steal British jobs. And most importantly of all, no more sleepless nights worrying about the shape or length of our bananas and cucumbers.

That had been the claim anyway, according to whichever newspaper, door-drop or bus-side advertisement you believed.

Though in all honesty, irrespective of how people had cast their vote four years earlier, by the time Prime Minister Boris Johnson climbed the podium in the Painted Hall at the Old Naval College in Greenwich to announce that he'd 'got Brexit done', most Britons just wanted to move on; to get back to a time when politics was duller than ditchwater, and the front pages were reserved for headlines about cheating celebrities and UFOs.

Someone who happily counted himself amongst this group was George's downstairs neighbour, Ollie Simpson. Not least since, as a personal trainer at the gym, he'd had to endure similar updates to the one he'd just seen on the digital screen for what seemed like an eternity.

As such, the headline about Boris's speech barely even registered before his attention was drawn to something that was of far more interest to him.

'Oh Em Gee!' he screamed. 'It's massive!'

'What is?' asked the middle-aged man who Ollie was training.

'The package the delivery guy has just dropped off!' replied Ollie, 'Sorry, mate, I think you'll want to see this.'

Placing the heavily weighted bar back into its cradle and lifting his head to see what all the fuss was about, it didn't take the bearlike presence of Adam Moxon long to confirm Ollie's prediction.

'A fella with a huge packet?' growled Adam in his Northern Irish drawl. 'Have we met!'

Known amongst his friends for his bawdy sense of humour, it was the predictable response from someone who could find sexual innuendo in the most innocent of everyday objects. *That being the case, the mention of a large package provided little in the way of a challenge for him!*

'Ha! You crack me up,' lied Ollie with a fake laugh.

Whilst 'sexy daddies' like Adam were the kind of blokes Ollie often went for, after an hour's personal training session, the constant flow of *dad* jokes, reduced his appeal considerably. But since the Irishman was paying him £40 an hour, Ollie felt he should humour his client with the occasional LOL.

'Want to help me unwrap it?' he asked, walking briskly over to the parcel without waiting for an answer but confident that it would have involved some lewd play on words.

Whatever might have been his reply, Adam wasn't far behind him, and with both of them on the case, Ollie with a pair of scissors and the Irishman ripping at the tape with his bare paws, the delivery was released from its bondage in no time.

'Holy shit. Get a load of that grin. I look like I'm on happy pills!' giggled Ollie as he got acquainted with the life-size image of himself smiling back at him, his teeth shining more brilliantly than ever against his ruby-red lips, his light brown skin looking smoother and more glowing than it had done in years.

The large package was, of course, the promotional stand he'd had made to help him recruit more clients at the gym.

Dressed in the skimpy blue shorts and tight-fitting white vest he'd worn at the Olympics over a decade earlier, the outfit was accessorised with the bronze medal he'd won for his prowess on the parallel bars. And even though these days he was more likely to be seen hanging around the bars in St. James's Street, Ollie was still in pretty good shape for 35 and could easily pass for younger.

Especially after a bit of TLC, as was the case with the retouched photograph of himself at which he was now staring.

In keeping with the wardrobe, the headline running along the bottom of the stand in large type read: TRAIN LIKE AN OLYMPIAN. And in smaller lettering underneath: *with Bronze Medallist Ollie Simpson!*

Remembering how he'd cringed when his friend Cameron had suggested the line, seeing his two-dimensional self in front of him now, Ollie was pleased that he'd been persuaded to mention being a former member of Team GB after all. And also that he'd dug out his old kit for the photo shoot!

Adam, on the other hand, seemed more focused on a *member* of a different kind.

'Holy shit. The bleedin' state of ye! Forget happy pills. Looks like you've popped a few blueys,' he roared.

Typical of him to go straight to the crotch!

Though he wasn't wrong. The bulge in the doppelgänger's shorts did look pretty big!

'That'll definitely drum up more business!' cackled Adam.

'I hope so. I'm still paying off Christmas,' replied Ollie. 'And Valentine's Day is less than a fortnight away.'

Knowing that the mere mention of the occasion would have confirmed bachelor Adam recoiling like a vampire from garlic, the barb was well-aimed. By contrast, Ollie couldn't have been more excited about the approaching date. For the first time in ages, he actually had someone to share it with, and the sight of heart-shaped balloons in shop windows filled him with joy rather than dread for a change. In fact, the only discomfort he felt when thinking about spending the day with his boyfriend, Drew, was a tightness in his underwear, which at that moment was in danger of making his actual bulge resemble that of his lookalike's.

'So, what do you think of the headline?' asked Ollie in an attempt to shift the focus of the discussion.

'Fair play. About time you *bigged-up* your… ahem… Olympic medal. It's your unique selling point, after all,' replied Adam.

'Yeah, that's what Cameron said. *And it is true.* No one can accuse me of false advertising,' added Ollie.

'Aye. As long as none of your ex-shags see your packet!' laughed the Irishman, walking behind the stand and placing his hands over Ollie's groin like a footballer in the line-up for a free kick. 'Seriously, mate. What have you got down there?'

'Nothing! It's just my push-up pants,' protested Ollie, reaching for his mobile and opening up his camera. 'Hang on a sec, that'll make a great shot for my socials. Say cheese…'

'Sleaze!' snarled Adam before returning to the front of the stand – and to his specialist subject. 'Wonder-pants, eh?'

‘Hey. Don’t knock ’em till you’ve tried ’em,’ replied Ollie.

‘No need for enhancements down here, pal,’ said the Irishman, groping his privates and winking in Ollie’s direction.

As he did so, the alarm on his watch beeped the end of their training session.

‘Feck! Better make a move,’ shouted Adam, as he marched off to the changing room downstairs. ‘Same time next week?’

Temporarily distracted by his client’s buttocks as they jostled for space in his tight green nylon shorts, after a moment or two, Ollie turned once more to the stand.

In truth, his choice of underwear for the photo shoot had been by design rather than by accident. Situated just a hop, skip and forward-roll from the gay village, Ollie was keenly aware who his target audience was. Not that Adam needed to know that. And hey! *What’s a pair of push-up pants between friends?* Especially when they’re Friends of Dorothy!

‘Now where shall I put you?’ he asked his 2D self under his breath while scanning the corridor which ran from the staffroom to the stairwell at the far end of the gym.

Spying an empty space just in front of a row of vending machines, Ollie picked up his stand and walked over to the chosen spot.

Territory staked out, he retrieved his phone from his pocket, opened up his social media account and uploaded the photo he’d just taken. After choosing a filter which made the hair on Adam’s face, head and arms look even thicker than it actually was, he typed GRIN & BEAR @platosgym_brighton with @adamgmoxon #brightonbear #bearweekend #brightonpride #pride #dilf #bulge

Pleased with his wordplay, he returned the phone to his shorts. That’ll teach him, he thought to himself as his mobile clinked against the pound coin he’d felt in his pocket earlier.

Ah! Just enough for a protein bar.

But before he could fish it out, his lunch money slipped through his fingers and rolled under the machine.

'Bollocks!' said Ollie under his breath.

Ordinarily, he would have walked away, but skint as well as hungry, if he wanted to eat, he had little choice but to climb behind the snack dispenser to see if he could retrieve his coin.

And as if this wasn't humiliating enough, once there, he heard a gaggle of voices which he recognised as belonging to the trio of older gay men who often trained together and had a comfortable camaraderie about them which suggested they'd known each other forever. Hidden out of sight in the cavity behind the machine, Ollie decided to save himself further embarrassment by waiting it out until they moved on.

That had been the plan, at least.

'Ooh… I say! Vada the dolly basket on the feele omi ajax! Looks as stiff as the rest of her!' exclaimed one of the voices.

'Who knew Bette's neighbour had such a big one!' cried another.

Unfortunately for Ollie, instead of moving on, it became clear that his promotional stand was ticking all the boxes for his target audience. What Cameron had called – ironically as it turned out – low-hanging fruit!

'Bette's neighbour?' asked a third voice.

'Yes, dearie. Lives underneath her,' replied the first one, whose voice was a little deeper than the other two.

'I bet she does!' squealed the second.

'*She?* Are you sure?' asked the third.

'Oh aye, she's a mauve one and make no mistake,' confirmed the one with the baritone.

Fuck! They're using that queer language which George is always banging on about. *If only I'd looked it up like I'd meant to.* But then he had an idea. He wasn't going to let this free 'market research' pass him by. Quietly slipping his mobile out of his pocket, he quickly found his voice memo app and pressed record.

'You only have to vada her mince!' agreed the second voice.

How rude, thought Ollie. He knew the meaning of mince, and it didn't take a genius to guess what mauve implied. *Am I that obvious?*

'Didn't know she was an Olympic medallist, though,' added the deeper voice.

'Or that she had an Olympic-sized cartes!' said the second, laughing.

'Ooh stop it, Doris, she's chicken,' chastised the third one.

'At our age, dear, they all are!' sighed the voice Ollie guessed belonged to the one they'd called Doris. 'Lovely riah! What's left of it!'

Assuming from the last comment that they were talking about his hair, despite being rather hurtful, it wasn't entirely without justification. Sporting a closely cropped style since his late 20s, the afro from his youth was a distant memory. Though he was still a long way off being bald. That was just mean!

'Bona eek and bod, though,' continued Doris. 'I'd definitely be up for a session or two if I wasn't living on the national handbag. How about you, Dowager?'

'Taking down her particulars as I speak, dearie!' replied the chap whom Ollie now knew was called Dowager. 'I'll drop her a line when I'm back from Key West next month!'

'Ooh 'eck, ladies, do you know who she reminds me of with those shorts and that medallion?' cackled the third man.

Ollie waited with bated breath for the fatal blow to his ego.

'Pagan Pete!'

The name sounded familiar, but he couldn't quite put his finger on where he'd heard it before.

The other two, however, knew exactly to whom their friend was referring.

'Yes!' cried Doris. 'At one of those fancy-dress parties at Hazelpits. Heroes and Villains, wasn't it? Early 80s, I reckon.'

'The one where Bette came as Lady whats-her-chops on that bloody mule,' recounted Dowager. 'And we did our little homage to Flash Gordon.'

'Oh God!' began Doris. 'That was the night it happened, wasn't it? Pete's accident.'

'Oh yes! Right in the middle of our dance routine,' added the third man, followed by an eruption of laughter which seemed a little out of kilter with the remark that had caused it.

'Still going strong though. Bumped into her only the other week on my morning troll along the prom. Shouted something about needing to see Bette and then sped off as fast as her wheels'd carry her,' said Dowager, once he'd recovered from his fit of giggles.

Wheels? thought Ollie to himself.

Suddenly, it came to him.

The fortune-teller who sets up shop beneath the i360. The one who uses a wheelchair. That's who he reminded them of.

But having no idea what Pagan Pete had looked like in his youth, Ollie didn't know whether he should be flattered or insulted. *Perhaps George has some photos of him from back then?* Making a mental note to ask his neighbour when he got home, Ollie tuned back into the conversation on the other side of the vending machine.

'How intriguing. I wonder what was so urgent?' enquired the voice with no name.

'Well, apparently she's had that reading again, dearie,' replied Dowager.

'What? You mean 'that' reading?' asked Doris.

'Mais oui, mais oui, ducky. No flies,' confirmed Dowager.

'Then you better book a few sessions with Miss Olympic here before it's too late,' said Doris.

'Aye, and her dolly basket!' added the nameless voice, causing one final communal shriek before they finally began walking away from the stand.

Hearing the laughter fading down the corridor, Ollie stopped recording and crept out from behind the snack dispenser. Confident he was alone, he inserted the rescued coin into the machine and grabbed his selection from the tray at the bottom.

'Packed with fruits and nuts,' he said, reading the ingredients. 'Yep, sounds about right!'

Chapter Seven

Chinese whispers

Monday 2nd March 2020 – Golden Square – Soho, London

What with the constant rounds of meetings for the upcoming event at the Rococo Piccolo, the first few weeks of the Year of the Rat had been rather full-on. So much so, in fact, that by March, Cameron still hadn't caught up with Yang Wei, his colleague in the Beijing office, to find out how she'd got on in her mission to find a venue in Singapore for the Asian relaunch of Rakewell's Gin.

He glanced at his phone. Eleven o'clock already. If he was quick, he'd probably catch her before she left for the day.

Thankfully, someone picked up and, after a short silence, filled the void with a tentative *'Hello?'*

It was clearly not the exuberant Miss Wei whom he'd had the pleasure of entertaining the previous month and who had indeed turned out to be the barrel of fun that her photograph on the agency website had suggested. Damn, thought Cameron, I've missed her. Or perhaps she's in a meeting. Finishing off the dregs of his coffee, he looked out of the window of the café he'd decamped to that morning and hoped for the best.

'Hello…' he said, mirroring the tone of the greeting at the other end of the phone. 'It's Cameron McIntyre calling from

London. Can I speak to Yang Wei, please?' he continued, in his best Queen's English, knowing that colleagues in the Beijing office sometimes found his native Scots a wee bit tricky to decipher.

'I'm so sorry, Mr McIntyre,' began the voice. 'Yang's no longer with us.'

'Oh!' replied Cameron, somewhat thrown by this unexpected news. But mainly he was annoyed. He'd already briefed her on the relaunch. *I wonder where she's gone.* But before he could ask, the person at the other end of the phone suddenly burst into tears.

Was his English accent that bad?

'She passed away last night,' announced the weeping colleague. 'Corona.'

'Shit!' gasped Cameron.

'Yes, I know. We couldn't believe it either. The whole agency is in shock,' continued the voice. 'She started feeling ill after her London trip and was rushed to hospital a few days ago.'

'Oh God! I'm so sorry,' was all Cameron could muster.

'Yes. Yang was such a…' began the woman, pausing to blow her nose.

The word that came to Cameron's mind was 'lush' – but he was pretty certain Yang's colleague had another character trait in mind.

'…lovely person.'

'Aye, a ken,' agreed Cameron, falling into Scots as his thoughts began to wander to far greater concerns than being understood. Recalling that the virus had broken out in some place on mainland China called Wuhan, he tried to remember what Yang had said about it. From memory, she'd hardly mentioned it. But just as he was digesting the news that Yang had gone to a place rather more permanent than a competitor, an even darker cloud appeared on his horizon. Fuuuuuuck! He'd spent lots of time with her when she was in London. Fuck. Fuck. Fuck.

Keen to find out what he could about the thing that had killed his colleague, he offered the woman his sincerest condolences and informed her that he had to be away!

Minutes later, Cameron was back in his office. Door closed and blinds drawn, he called his PA and told her to cancel all his meetings for the rest of the day, making it crystal clear that he wasn't to be disturbed.

But he was disturbed.

Distraught even.

Whilst the death of Yang Wei was tragic, the fact that he'd only recently been in her company was the most worrying aspect for Cameron.

Did she already have corona when she arrived in the UK? Could he have caught it off her? And how would he even be able to tell if he had done?

The harsh truth was that he knew virtually nothing about this scary new virus. A situation which was about to change. Safely barricaded in his 'panic room', he poured himself a large whisky and got to work.

Like most ad-folk faced with a stressful situation, Cameron became almost robotic in his response. True, the situation was more upsetting than a client throwing their toys out of their pram, but the approach to the problem was much the same: arm yourself with the salient facts and take decisive action. With that in mind, he spent the next few minutes glued to his mobile and laptop.

His mobile, trying to get through to his surgery in Brighton.

His laptop, searching the internet for anything he could find on corona.

The most pertinent of which was an article dated 30th January, which said that a woman from Wuhan Province had tested positive after arriving in York to visit her son at the university there.

30th January! That was over a month ago.

How this gem had managed to pass him by, he didn't know. Although it had to be said, at the time, the newspapers were still getting their knickers in a twist over the final days of Brexit. Especially those which had thrown their weight behind a campaign to raise cash to speed up repairs to Big Ben so that the iconic timepiece could mark the UK's exit from the European Union with its celebrated chimes. Or 'Bung a bob for a Big Ben Brexit bong' – as new Prime Minister Boris Johnson had coined it.

Of course, the nugget of information Cameron gleaned from the story about the Chinese woman was that there was definitely a test he could take.

Mmmm... I wonder if I can get one done privately, he thought to himself as he took a swig of whisky. Reassured by this possibility, Cameron pulled up his desktop calendar to check the dates of Yang's visit and wrote down the relevant intel on his notepad.

Hong Kong to UK – 2nd February
Office – 3rd & 4th February
Supper – 4th February
London to Singapore – 6th February
Died – 1st March

After scanning the page for a moment or two, he took a deep breath and underlined the last word and date. *But what did it mean?* He clicked back into his search engine and entered – 'how long coronavirus symptoms from infection'. Scribbling down '5-6 days', he quickly went back to the search box and typed – 'how long coronavirus symptoms to death'. Presented with a much longer article – detailing, amongst other horrors, shortness of breath, sepsis, organ failure and cardiac arrest – he found what he was looking for and added 'average 18.5 days' to his pad.

Desperately trying to erase an image of Yang in her final hours, Cameron studied the data from his recent searches.

So, he thought to himself while anxiously chewing the end of his pen. If she'd got it in Hong Kong, she could still have been symptom-free when she arrived at the office.

Fuuuuuuuk!

There was a very real chance that she'd given him the virus!

Fuck, fuckety fuck, fuck!

Topping up his whisky, Cameron took another deep breath and stared again at his notes. *But it was over three weeks since they'd had supper together.* That was way more than the 5-6 days between infection and symptoms. And he'd certainly had none of the ones listed. Not even a cold, in fact.

Feeling a little calmer, Cameron saw that it was much more likely Yang had been infected in Malaysia or on her way back to Beijing. Certainly, it explained why she'd shown no signs of ill-health while she'd been in London.

Removing the pen from his mouth, he jotted down this new information.

Infected – 6th February
Symptoms – 11th or 12th
Add 18 days – 1st March

Underlining the final date, the day of Yang's death, Cameron sighed deeply.

Oh aye! That makes much more sense.

Hugely comforted by the most likely scenario being that Yang had picked up coronavirus thousands of miles away and sometime after meeting him and his work colleagues, Cameron reached for his tumbler of whisky and swallowed the whole lot.

Who knew that forensics was such thirrrsty work?

Returning the glass to its coaster, he was suddenly aware of a voice coming from his mobile. It was his surgery. But instead of speaking to the receptionist, he cancelled the call and searched instead for the number of one of his Harley Street contacts.

Aye, well. Better safe than sorry!

Chapter Eight

Hanky Panky!

Monday 2nd March 2020 – Royal Pavilion Café – Brighton

Since her last visit to the Pavilion Café, Izzy's research into Brighton's queer past had come on in leaps and bounds.

After her suspicions had been confirmed that former MP Grace Davidson had been the driving force behind the movies she'd found in her attic, George had also introduced her to Hazelpits, the farm in Kent that in the late 70s and early 80s had been the venue for a series of gay disco nights which had drawn crowds of revellers from across the globe.

And on top of all this, there was the halo effect the project was having on her curatorial reputation, too.

At a time when museums everywhere were debating the thorny issue of representation and relevance, shining a light on the queer history of her recently adopted city had done much to establish her as a 'mover and shaker' in her relatively new position.

Yet there was another reason for Izzy's good mood that day. It being Monday, her place of work was closed to the public, so she'd been able to get on with her research without any visitors to the museum clogging up the corridors or disturbing her with their chatter.

As a result of this happy solitude, she'd spent a very productive morning going through the papers and magazines which had been sent over from The Keep, the building that housed the county's archives.

And what a trove of treasures it had turned out to be.

For a start, there was a stack of radical magazines from the 60s and 70s which contained references to the activities of groups like the Gay Liberation Front, Lesbian and Gay Switchboard and the Campaign for Homosexual Equality.

And from the 80s and 90s, there was a batch of newsletters that had been created specifically by gay men and lesbians.

Aimed at the growing numbers of queer people who'd made the town their home, most articles in these were focused on the prejudice facing the community and the fight for equal rights, with mentions of AIDS and Clause 28 gradually gaining more space from the mid-80s onwards. Though it wasn't all queer content. There were also features about other *causes célèbres* of the period, including nuclear disarmament, the legalisation of cannabis, support for striking miners, and concerns around conservation – like the discovery of a hole in the ozone layer above Antarctica.

But most thrilling of all, in the context of recent revelations about the city's former MP, was an advertisement for *Gracie's Palace*, Ms Davidson's hotel on the New Steine, that, in addition to boasting a Teasmade and a trouser-press in every room, proudly listed a hairdryer as well!

Initially bemused by the mention of this particular 'mod con', after perusing the photos which peppered the magazine, it occurred to Izzy that the back-combed hairstyles which were popular during the period would probably not have been possible to achieve without the aid of an awful lot of hot air.

And several cans of lacquer!

Indeed, it was a wonder the hole in the ozone layer hadn't been discovered above Brighton rather than the South Pole! mused Izzy as she wafted over to 'her' table at the far end of the Pavilion Café, where lunch guests – sister Maria and her wife Meena – were already seated.

After the required amount of air-kissing and a smattering of appreciative cooing about how well they all looked, Izzy took their orders and relayed them to the girl at the counter.

Noticing it was the same waitress who'd been on duty when she'd met with George, and reminded of the fruity language the girl may have overheard on that occasion, Izzy was especially friendly. Even leaving a tip in the saucer at the till!

Peace offering deposited, she sauntered back to her 'throne' and made herself comfortable for the audience with her subjects.

'¿Que pasa?' enquired Maria, who, unlike Izzy, happily flitted between her native Spanish and her heavily accented adopted language – often in the same sentence.

In truth, despite being close, the sisters couldn't have been more dissimilar.

In the parlance of the period that Izzy had been researching that morning, Maria was a *butch dyke*, boasting short greying hair, stocky physique and a wardrobe which consisted mainly of combat trousers and black T-shirts.

For her part, Izzy was tall and willowy. And though also fond of dark colours, her preferred *ropa del dia* consisted principally of long black 1920s style dresses for socialising, squid-ink kimonos and kaftans for relaxing, and slate-grey houndstooth and herringbone tweed skirts and jackets for work.

In fact, such was Izzy's passion for the funereal, husband Ken had once joked to friends that opening the door to her walk-in wardrobe was akin to gazing into a bottomless pit. An unwelcome reminder of the cruel nickname she knew that Cameron called her behind her back, the raven look she'd given her husband on that occasion put paid to the comparison ever being repeated!

This love of obsidian also extended to Izzy's hair colour, which rarely hinted at her true age of just over 50 years.

And something else kept in check, of course, was her native tongue.

Even when talking to Maria.

'Never better, daaarlink. The project I told you about just gets more and more interesting. I really think 2020 is going to be my year,' replied Izzy before filling them both in on the fruits of the morning's research and Grace Davidson's involvement in the 'art-house' movies.

'¡Que asombroso!' exclaimed Maria when Izzy finally paused for breath. 'She was behind the whole thing!'

'Wow! You'll have to apply for a blue plaque at this rate!' added Meena.

Izzy was pretty sure that her sister-in-law was joking, but why not?

And wouldn't the unveiling of it make the perfect setting for her book launch?

Yet, as the thought gained traction in her mind, it occurred to her that there was an even greater reason why she should give it serious consideration. In short, getting one over on Cameron McIntyre, who, despite all the help she'd given him on the Rakewell's relaunch, still kept her at arm's length, repeatedly thwarting her attempts to make inroads into the circle of Brightonians whom she'd met through her sister, and of which he appeared to be at the centre.

It was time to step up the offensive. How she exploited the discovery in her attic could play a key role in her campaign to snatch Cameron's crown. Yes, the affair in Piccadilly might provide a minute or two of content for the social media feeds of London's 'influencers' – or Soho-cialites as he'd pretentiously referred to them on his call the previous week – but the story behind the films was so much richer than a knees-up in the West End. Once the 'circus' was over, it would be her time to shine. Petitioning for a plaque to commemorate this important aspect of local queer history might just be the ticket to garner media interest in her research. And with Davidson now associated with the movies, getting approval ought to be a doddle.

Deciding it was certainly worth further consideration, Izzy added 'Blue Plaque' to the 'to-do' list in the back of her diary and swallowed the last of her Earl Grey. That done, and with no other news to impart, she made a great show of packing up her things until her subjects got the hint that the audience with their queen was drawing to a close.

Preparing to leave, she was about to treat her sister to a rare 'Hasta luego, cariño'– when the waitress from before appeared at the table with something in a brown paper bag.

'Sorry to interrupt, madam, it's just that we found this on the floor after your last visit,' she said, handing over the suspect package.

Not sure exactly what to expect, Izzy laid it carefully on the table and peeked inside.

'Ah!' she cried, with schoolgirl elation. It was the mustard-coloured handkerchief George had been stroking while they'd been talking about the AIDS crisis. 'Dear Georgie's hanky! Bless the forgetful old thing. Thank you, darlink. I'll make sure it's returned to him safely,' said Izzy, slipping it into her handbag.

The fact was she'd been wanting an excuse to talk to him some more about those outrageous goings-on at the farm in Kent. This would do perfectly. Noting her good fortune, she was reminded of what she'd said earlier to the girls about 2020 being her year and even managed a small regal wave in the direction of the waitress as she made her way out of the café.

Chapter Nine

The last days of disco

Tuesday 3rd March 2020 – St. James's Street, Brighton

As a consequence of his promotional stand - or erection as Adam kept calling it - Ollie had been inundated with new clients over the previous month.

Exploiting his Olympic medal had clearly paid off!

Although if feedback from the 'focus group' was anything to go by, it was as much to do with the prominent bump in his shorts as it was to do with any talent he'd once displayed on the parallel bars.

Of course, 'focus group' was probably stretching it a bit. But the conversation between the trio of older gay men at the gym which Ollie had secretly recorded – and translated from Polari into English – confirmed that he'd been right about his target audience.

Thinning riah (hair) or not, his dolly basket (nice bulge) and bona bod and eek (great body and face) had reeled 'em in good and proper. And he'd finally got around to learning a bit of Polari, too, which he looked forward to trying out on his upstairs neighbour when he saw him next.

But what did the old fellas mean by 'that' reading?

And then there was what they'd said about him reminding them of a young Pagan Pete. At somewhere called Hazel's

Pit in the early 80s. He knew that George had definitely been there on the night they were talking about. Though the mention of a mule was a bit odd. *Was it a rarely used Polari word, perhaps?* Truth to tell, the recording he'd made on his phone was a bit echoey in places. But there was no mistaking the laughter which had been triggered by the memory of Pete's accident.

What could possibly have happened that would merit such a response?

With so many unanswered questions, Ollie was eager to talk to George about it all. Especially anything to do with 'that' reading.

Fortunately, his neighbour was relatively easy to steer down memory lane, so enquiring if he had any photos of Pagan Pete from back then would be a good way to get him onto the subject.

That being the case, noticing when he came out of the supermarket that George's kitchen light was on, Ollie decided it was time to pay him a visit.

As it seemed, so did his boyfriend.

'Look,' said Drew, releasing his right hand from one of the two heavy bags of shopping he was carrying and pointing to the old man's bay window. 'Let's go and see if he can shed any light on what the blokes at your gym were talking about.'

'Good plan,' agreed Ollie, also laden down with two equally weighty carriers.

Given the closeness of the supermarket to his flat, the size of the haul was unusual. Ordinarily, Ollie only bought groceries as and when he needed them. But after seeing a number of videos on social media of people panic-buying toilet paper and other 'essentials' as a result of this new virus everyone was talking about, he and Drew had thought it best to stock up.

Though judging by the clanking and crunching sounds they were making as they entered Ollie's kitchen, it seemed that the only 'essentials' they could be accused of panic-buying were Sauvignon Blanc and crisps.

'We can bribe him with chipsticks and cheese puffs,' joked Drew as Ollie made space in his cupboards for the supersized shop.

Bags unpacked and items stored, ready for the much mooted 'end of days', they each grabbed a packet of crisps and made their way to the floor above.

'Helloooo…' cried Ollie, tapping on his neighbour's door. 'Anyone home?'

'Come on through!' shouted a voice from within. 'It's not locked.'

Sharing a communal staircase, Ollie and George had been friendly for over two years. But since the unravelling of his neighbour's past – most notably his brief career as a gay porn star – Ollie had become even closer to the old man, regarding him as a sort of queer pioneer.

And since Drew had virtually moved in downstairs, he'd also got to know George pretty well.

'Coming, Mommie Dearest,' cried the Welshman, referencing the famous movie about Hollywood legend Joan Crawford, which they'd all watched together, recently.

Entering the lounge first, Ollie suddenly came face-to-face with another *legend*: the cardboard cut-out of Bette y'Sweet Ass, proclaiming the virtues of Rakewell's glorious past and leaning, appropriately enough, against George's 1960s cocktail bar.

'Oh! Sorry, I didn't realise you had company!' said Ollie, laughing.

'Oh yes. Cardboard Bette. What do you think?' asked George.

'Terrifying!' exclaimed Drew.

'I know,' agreed the old man. 'I did have her in the bedroom, but every time I woke up, I thought I was about to be attacked. She's much happier over there with the booze!'

'Really? She looks rather *board* to me! Not to mention a little flat-chested!' said Drew with a snigger before adopting a more reverential tone. 'Seriously, though. You look stunning.'

'Even better in the 'flesh',' agreed Ollie. 'Cameron showed me the artwork on his laptop last month. In fact, he's had one done for me, too.'

George looked rather bewildered.

'Not of *you*. Of *me*. For the gym. To drum up a bit more business. It's partly the reason I'm here,' explained Ollie.

'Oh no, dear. Let me stop you right there. There's absolutely no way you're getting me on a treadmill!' cried George.

'Ha. Don't worry, that's not what I meant,' reassured Ollie.

'Thank gawd for that. So, to what *do* I owe this pleasure? I've been so busy with my 'ambassadorial' duties, I've hardly seen hide nor hair of you both,' said George, waving a bottle of Rakewell's at them from behind the cocktail bar. 'G&T, anyone?'

'Yes please,' replied Ollie. 'But don't worry. I'm not gonna ask you to dig out your leg warmers. It's to do with something I overheard a group of old fellas at the gym chatting about.'

'Old fellas?' enquired George.

'Yes, friends of yours, I think. Acquaintances, at least, as one of them knew that I lived in the flat below you. I thought I heard the names Dowager and Doris.'

At the mention of this, a huge smile crept across George's face. 'Ah yes, The Three Muskaqueers. Doris, Deidre and the Dowager. The last one on account of her sizeable trust fund.'

'Ah right, I see. Well, anyway, they were admiring my new advertisement and…' began Ollie, quickly deciding to omit what else they'd been admiring. '…and one of them said that I reminded him of Pagan Pete. In his youth. A fancy-dress party at some place called Hazel's Pit. Heroes and Villains, I think they said the theme was. I just thought you might have some old photos.'

'Ha. I think you mean Hazelpits. It's a farm in Kent. Though *Hazel's Pit* does have a certain ring of truth about it. Heroes and Villains Party, you say?' enquired George.

'Yes, I'm pretty sure that's what I heard,' confirmed Ollie. 'The same night as Pete's accident… apparently…'

'Oh God, of course,' acknowledged George, followed by a little chuckle.

Bloody hell! First the men at the gym, and now George!

'They said something about my shorts and medallion. I'm bigging up my days on Team GB,' added Ollie.

'Amongst other things…' sniggered Drew under his breath.

'Sorry, dear. What was that?' asked George, taking an ice cube from a pineapple-shaped bucket.

'I said, yes, I'd love a gin,' replied the Welshman, a little louder.

Thankfully for Ollie, in addition to George's impaired hearing, the old man was already too lost in his memories of Hazelpits to pick up on Drew's wisecrack.

'Well, what there is from those days will be in the Charles and Diana album,' said George, pointing to a bookshelf which ran along the wall opposite the cocktail bar.

'The showroom dummies in Nice 'n' Naughty?' asked Drew, referring to what the locals called the two sexily clad mannequins that regularly featured in the window display of the 'adult' shop on St. James's Street.

'No, dear. The actual Charles and Diana. Far left. Union Jack on the spine.'

Perusing the line of various sized and coloured albums, the photographic record of his neighbour's personal memory lane, it didn't take Ollie long to locate the one which George had described. Glancing at the cover as he passed it to the old man, he noticed that it did indeed feature an image of the tragic princess and the future King of England.

Diana, shy and demure, in a blue jacket and white neck-scarf. Charles, in a grey suit, looking decidedly awkward. Knowing how it all ended, it seemed obvious from the photograph that their marriage was doomed from the start.

'Grace met her once, you know,' said George. 'Some AIDS benefit or other. Lovely woman, she said. Nice teeth, apparently. Sad eyes, though.'

Ending these telegram-like observations with a sigh, the old man opened the album and began turning the ring-bound pages to a soundtrack of tuts and 'oh gawds'.

'Aha! Here we go. Heroes and Villains Party. Hazelpits. Summer '82,' he cried before passing it to Ollie.

The thin sheet of plastic film that held the photos in place reflected the light and made viewing rather tricky, but before he could drink in the debauchery of 'Heroes and Villains Party. Hazelpits. Summer '82', George tugged the album out of his hands.

'Oh, give it here, dear. They're hardly Mapplethorpes!' he exclaimed, peeling back the transparent sheets with a crackle and picking the photos off the pages beneath. 'Let's go into the kitchen. You'll be able to see better in there.'

Moments later, all three of them were seated around the table in the bay window which looked onto St. James's Street. In the glare of the overhead light, the fuzzy images in the photos gradually came to life.

'Oh God. Is that him?' asked Ollie, pointing at a bloke in shiny blue shorts, long sports socks and not much else. Except for a gold medallion nestled between a mass of dark chest hair.

'Oh yes. That's Pete alright,' confirmed George. 'As Victor Hugo. You don't hear much about him these days, but in the 70s and 80s he was quite famous. With the gays, anyway. One of the regulars at the notorious New York nightclub, Studio 54. Former escort, Warhol model, party animal. He was particularly well known for his outrageous costumes. And sometimes, for the lack of them! Like the ensemble Pete had thrown together that evening.'

While George was talking, Ollie studied the toned and tanned figure in the photograph. He could see what the old fellas at the gym had meant about the resemblance between himself and the fortune-teller in his younger days. Quite flattering, really. And though outside of Movember, Ollie rarely grew a moustache which came anywhere close to the bushy handlebar that Pete was sporting, if he'd not shaved for a couple of days, his own five o'clock shadow was cast darkest above his top lip.

Yet there was one more thing they had in common to which Ollie couldn't help being drawn. *Or rather it was a particular characteristic that the cardboard cut-out version of himself had in common with the gentleman in the photograph!*

'Jesus! Leaves nothing to the imagination, does it!' he cried, tapping Pete's crotch with his finger.

'Oh yes,' agreed George, picking up the theme. 'He was never shy in *that* department. So much so, in fact, that back then, he wasn't known as Pagan Pete. His nickname was *Python!*'

As funny as this was, Ollie was keen to move on from the talk of large packages. What's more, there was the question of the mysterious reading. Hearing George's reference to the fortune-teller's 'stage' name, he saw his opportunity to steer the discussion in that direction.

'Actually, there was something else your friends at the gym mentioned. A card reading which Pete had rushed over to see you about,' said Ollie.

'Yes, that's right!' gasped George. 'Apparently, he almost sent the Dowager flying, he was going so fast!'

'Oh no! But why the urgency?' asked Ollie, as seriously as he could, given the image with which he'd just been presented.

'Well,' began George. 'It wasn't just that the reading predicted such terrible things. It was more to do with what happened the last time he dealt this same sequence of cards.'

'What was that then?' asked Drew.

'In a word, dear. AIDS!' replied George, pausing to take a gulp of gin and tonic. 'It was around the time we started to get concerned about it. 1984, I reckon. A couple of years after these photos were taken,' he added, looking down at the table. 'Which is why Pete's so worried. He's convinced that it's all going to happen again. You know, with this coronavirus!'

Ollie glanced sideways at his boyfriend. Whilst the videos of shoppers fighting over loo rolls and bags of dried pasta had been the reason for their recent trip to the supermarket, he'd actually found the whole panic-buying thing mildly amusing.

The mention of AIDS, however, made fears surrounding this new virus much more real.

Not sure what to say next, he returned his gaze to the photographs in front of him. Thankfully, the faded images came to his rescue.

'Fuck! Is that you?' he said to George, pointing at a chap with a blond moustache and matching beard, wearing a winged helmet.

'Sadly not,' replied the old man.

'Hot!' added Drew.

'Yes. That's Odi, short for Odin. Like the Viking god. Gorgeous, isn't he…' agreed George wistfully.

Had he been an ex-lover? Certainly, the sigh and the way the old man was looking at the photo suggested that he and Odi had been close. But rather than falling into melancholia, George picked up a photograph which had been hidden by the others on the table and began laughing.

'No, dear. This is me, with Eeyore!' he said, holding the snap of a figure in a nude bodysuit and long wig, sat on the back of a donkey. 'My tribute to Lady Godiva, the noblewoman who rode naked through the streets of Coventry on a white horse.'

'Oh Em Gee!' cried Ollie, suddenly realising that he'd heard the old fellas correctly.

'Mule' wasn't a Polari word, after all. They'd been talking about an *actual* donkey!

'Ha. No half measures with you lot, were there!' laughed Drew. 'And who's that in the silver breastplate and pageboy wig, the one holding Eeyore's reins?'

'The woman dressed as Saint Joan? That's our Gracie!' replied George.

'Wow. She looks amazing!' gushed Ollie, instinctively using the adjective which was almost always used to describe the former MP.

Reminded suddenly of Izzy's recent discovery about Davidson and the old pornos, news of which had quickly made its way to Kemptown, Ollie was about to ask George about it all when his eyes were drawn to a tall man in a red vest carrying a long gold-coloured sword.

Flanked on either side by two men dressed like Roman gladiators but with huge, feathered wings, Ollie immediately recognised them from the 80s film inspired by the Flash Gordon comic books. Not least because the handsome lead in the movie had been one of his first-ever crushes. And come to think of it, were the muscle-bound Hawkmen the reason why, in later life, he was attracted to 'sexy daddies'?

But more than Flash and his feathery friends, Ollie knew the identities of the men themselves.

'Fuuuuck! It's The Three Muskaqueers,' he screamed, recalling what George had called the old blokes from his gym.

Looking at the photos spread across the table, Ollie couldn't help wishing he'd been around back then. It all seemed like so much fun. But as thrilling as it was to be given this window into the past, there was still one question that remained unanswered.

What had happened to Pete which led to him using a wheelchair?

Ollie knew from the old fellas at the gym that the accident had occurred during their dance routine.

But why did everyone seem to find the circumstances surrounding it so hilarious?

With George still lost in mists of nostalgia, Ollie knew it was now or never.

'Obviously these photos were taken before Pete's accident…' he began.

'Yes,' confirmed George, taking the bait. 'In fact, if my memory serves me right, it happened just after The Three Muskaqueers had started their dance routine.'

'Jeez. That's one floorshow I'd loved to have seen,' enthused Drew.

'Yes, you would have, dear. Brought the house down,' said George, pausing.

'Literally!'

And just like that, he was off down memory lane.

Chapter Ten

Accidents will happen!

Saturday 14th August 1982 – Hazelpits Farm – Kent

'Oi. Eeyore, cut that out!' demanded George, tugging the end of his long black wig from the mouth of the donkey on whose back he was balanced. 'You can have your carrots as soon as we're given the green light.'

Throwing the tresses over his shoulder and adjusting his figure-hugging nude bodysuit, George stroked the animal's mane and readied himself for their ten minutes of fame.

With himself dressed as Lady Godiva, the scene was made just a little bit more surreal because holding Eeyore's reins was a woman impersonating Joan of Arc.

'What's the song again, Gracie?' asked George, looking down at his friend.

'Happy Birthday!' she replied, rolling her eyes.

'Yes! I know that. I mean, which one? Stevie or Clare?' he clarified.

'Well, knowing Jeff, I think we best listen out for Clare's version,' replied Grace.

Just then, the hi-energy dance track coming from the room in front of them was replaced by the plinky-plonky sound of a glockenspiel and the little girl vocals of Altered Images' Clare Grogan.

Right on cue, the heavy curtains over the door were pulled back, and the reason for the fancy-dress costumes explained.

The 'Heroes and Villains Party, Hazelpits, Summer '82' was in full swing.

'Hold tight. We're going in!' announced Grace, gently pulling the donkey's reins and cautiously leading it into the throng of sweaty revellers. Thankfully, the promise of a carrot supper did the trick, and the animal famed for its stubbornness strolled nonchalantly into the crowd with a grown man on its back. An entrance made all the more remarkable given the almost deafening volume of cheers which were generated by the sight of Lady Godiva on a white-*ish* donkey: the result of several canisters of lavender-scented talcum powder.

Through his fringe, George could just about make out the raised area in the corner where the DJ was working his magic. And few feet along from this was the Birthday Boy himself – Odi Olafson – dressed, perhaps not so surprisingly, as his namesake, complete with winged helmet and golden beard. Of course, whether you considered Odin to be a hero – or a villain – depended on where you stood on the subject of theology. But from George's elevated position on the back of Eeyore, something about which no one could argue was that the theme had been an inspirational one; spotting Ming the Merciless, Wonder Woman, Cruella De Vil and Neil Armstrong, amongst the sea of bobbing heads around him.

Yet before he had a chance to pick out any more heroes, heroines or villains, he found himself being propelled in the direction of the stage, from where Odi was pretending to pull him in on an invisible rope.

Bathed in a shower of tiny lights from the glitter ball above his head, the Dane looked every inch the Viking god after who he was named; the fake beard that now accompanied his golden moustache making him look even more heavenly than he usually did.

Certainly, the wafts of talc released whenever one of the partygoers patted Eeyore's rump was enough to convince George that he really was floating on a cloud towards his personal Valhalla. *Albeit one which was lavender-scented and rather claggy.*

Indeed, given the noise and the powder, it was a miracle the poor animal hadn't bolted straight for the nearest exit.

Perhaps, he too was enraptured by the celestial vision beckoning them forward. That or the generous handfuls of carrots which Saint Joan was still feeding him as the trio made their way across the dance floor. Whatever the reason, moments later, George found himself being lifted onto the stage by Odi.

Who was the most relieved – Eeyore or Lady Godiva – was anyone's guess. But George was more than happy to swap beast for beauty.

'Many happy returns, you gorgeous man,' he cried, kissing the Birthday Boy on his cheek.

'Oh, Georgie, you never cease to amaze me! And that outfit. Wow! You look absolutely gorgeous!' enthused the Dane.

'Well, I hope the Lady hasn't *turned* you,' purred George in mimicry of Mrs Thatcher's now famous line about not changing direction, which, since Britain's victory in the Falklands War earlier that year, had been lurching increasingly to the right.

'Ha! Don't worry, Georgie Boy, I'm definitely not for turning. At least until I hit the hayloft!' howled Odi.

'Thank goodness for that. Be a shame to disappoint your fan club!' replied Lady Godiva.

It was true, for not only was George just as smitten with his Viking as he had been when they'd first met, there were plenty of men on the dance floor hoping for a birthday kiss from the Dane that evening, too. Including Pete, who, according to the mustard-coloured handkerchief which Odi usually wore in the right-hand back pocket of his jeans, had the thing he wanted most of all on his special day.

That is to say.

A big dick!

Part of the code which enabled men to 'flag' their sexual peccadillos or physical attributes, with further information given by whichever back pocket the wearer chose to display it, there were at least 12 different coloured handkerchiefs altogether. Far too many to remember them all, but from what George could ascertain, the most popular was dark blue. Worn in the left pocket, known as Greek Active, it meant that you wanted to fuck; in the right pocket, that you wanted to *be* fucked. Not quite as common, but just as easy to remember, were yellow hankies, which signified that you were into water sports. Worn in the left pocket, meaning you liked to wee on your partner; in the right, that you preferred being weed on. And most notably of all, as far as George was concerned, was mustard – Odi's choice – which was to do with cock size. In the left pocket, meaning that you *had* 8 inches or more; in the right, that you *wanted* 8 inches or more.

It was perhaps no huge surprise then that at Hazelpits, as in the pubs and clubs of Brighton, there were more mustard hankies worn to the right than to the left!

One member of the elite group of men who displayed a mustard hanky in their left pocket was, of course, Python Pete.

Reminded of his well-endowed friend, George glanced down to see if he could spot him in the pit of sweaty dancers below.

He shouldn't have been too difficult to locate if he had been since he was dressed as Victor Hugo from Studio 54, naked except for long sports socks, skimpy blue running shorts and a gold medallion. Oh, and a pair of silver roller skates, which gave him a few extra inches.

In height.

Where the hell was he? Surely, he wouldn't have headed to the hayloft already? The Three Muskaqueers hadn't even done their act yet.

Unable to spot Pete in the crowd, George was about to ask Odi if he'd seen him when the music was interrupted by the piercing squeal of microphone feedback and an announcement from the DJ box.

'Ladies and… *lesbians…*' began the voice while someone fiddled with knobs on the mixing deck and lowered the volume of the track which had been playing. 'Thank you so much for making our Heroes and Villains Party one of Hazelpits' best themed nights yet. We really couldn't have done it without you. So, thank you, thank you, thank you. Kiss, kiss, kiss.'

There was a short pause for the expected wolf whistles and cheers.

'And special thanks to Grace, Georgie and Eeyore the donkey. *Who knew that Gracie had such a great ass!*'

Once again, the DJ waited a few moments to allow for an appreciative ripple of laughter.

'But most importantly of all, I want to give a shout-out to our Birthday Boy. Hazelpits' very own Viking god, Odi Olafson.'

Not so surprising, given the Dane's popularity, the whistles that accompanied this last announcement were loudest of all.

'OK, OK, simmer down, everyone. There's plenty of him to go around. *Or so I've been told!* But before we give him the bumps, there's one final surprise for you all,' teased the DJ.

On cue, the lights were extinguished and, apart from a single beam directed on the glitter ball above Odi's head, the barn was plunged into darkness. In the sudden gloom, the crowd simmered down to an expectant hush of shuffling feet and whispered chatter.

Thankfully, they didn't have long to wait.

After a few seconds, the familiar drumbeat from the title track of the recent Flash Gordon movie could be heard in the background while the DJ finished his own intro.

'So please. Put your hands together and make some noise for Hazelpits' answer to Flash Gordon and the Hawkmen!'

Music turned up loud enough to rival the din of the requested applause, a pool of light appeared in the space where George and Grace had made their entrance with Eeyore a few minutes earlier.

No dumb animals this time. Instead, the spot was occupied by The Three Muskaqueers.

Quicker than a police raid at a 1960s gay club, the dance floor cleared, and the superheroes made their way to the centre of the room with a performance that would have given Hot Gossip a run for their money.

Synchronised arm gestures. Catwalk-worthy strides. Rehearsed to within an inch of their wigs, the moves were flawless. And as for the song itself, with little chance of matching Freddie Mercury's vocal range, the Muskaqueers had decided to lip-synch to the original track, which turned up to full volume seemed more high-pitched than ever.

Especially, as it turned out, to poor Eeyore, who'd been tied to a pole beneath a raised area of the hayloft where Pete was at that very moment engaged in some particularly energetic lovemaking.

In fact, the jarring 'hee-haw' of the animal's bray was most likely the last thing he and his rumpy-pumpy partner heard before the donkey, unable to bear the noise coming from the barn any longer, kicked away his pole and caused the lovers to plummet to the floor with an almighty...

Crash! Aaaaaaargh!

Yet despite the racket caused by Eeyore's escape, this was not the sound which caused the DJ to call a halt to The Three Muskaqueers' intergalactic space battle dance routine.

No!

Rather it was the ear-splitting screams of the unfortunate couple whose earth had well and truly been moved by the mule's break for freedom.

And also the reason why the 'Heroes and Villains Party' would, from then on, always be remembered as the evening at Hazelpits that had ended with a bang.

Just not the one Pete had been expecting!

Chapter Eleven

Shhhh... it just got real!

Wednesday 11th March 2020 –
The Rococo Piccolo – Piccadilly Circus, London

Hearing about Yang Wei's death had knocked Cameron for six.

Especially for a day or two afterwards when he'd feared that she might have given him the virus during her recent visit to the UK. *Thankfully his test had come back negative.* So, by the day of the relaunch party for Rakewell's Gin, he was in suitably good spirits.

Yes, a handful of guests had emailed to say they could no longer make it; news at the weekend that Northern Italy had gone into lockdown no doubt contributing to the jitters. But since O'Hara, George and Izzy were contractually obliged to show up, and the vast majority of the guests were at the end of the age spectrum deemed to be less at risk from infection, Cameron was confident that the Rococo Piccolo would be packed to the rafters.

In fact, apart from a few bottles of hand sanitiser, as far as the venue was concerned, it was business as usual. Especially after calls for the Cheltenham Gold Cup Weekend to be cancelled had been dismissed by the new government as the death throes of the Nanny State they'd just deposed.

I mean, now we've got our country back, nae Johnny Foreigner virus would dream of threatening our borders. Would it?

And as long as everyone washed their hands for as many seconds as it took to sing two rounds of Happy Birthday, it was a case of keeping calm and carrying on.

So that's exactly what Cameron intended to do. After he'd washed his hands for the 100th time and arranged for a company cab to take him, Alex and Adam back to Brighton after the relaunch event.

A work 'do' was one thing, but there was nae need to risk the Petri dish of germs which passed as the late-night commuter train if he could avoid it.

Especially since, unlike the Brexiteers, he wasn't nearly as confident that the English Channel was the barrier to corona as some of them seemed to think it was.

Can't be too careful, Cameron thought to himself as he looked for signs of ill health in the illuminated mirror of the dressing room which had been reserved for Liz O'Hara.

After making sure all was in order, he glanced at his wristwatch. 5.30pm. Just time to check on George and Izzy before their celebrity interviewer turned up. Other than that, there wasn't much else for him to do. His minions' hands were on deck making last-minute adjustments to the seating and catering. The PR wing of the agency was handling the press, radio, TV and social media. And the tech guys had checked and rechecked the audiovisual equipment in the auditorium. As a consequence, his only job after meeting and greeting Liz O'Hara was to escort Rakewell's CEO to his table and laugh at his jokes until the show began.

Oh, and look gorgeous, of course.

No worries on that score, thought Cameron to himself as he admired his reflection.

Just then, there was a knock at the door.

'Cameron, Ms O'Hara is here,' said a voice behind him. One last look in the mirror and seconds later he was experiencing the unusually warm handshake of Britain's favourite chat-show host.

Unusually warm because, despite the unseasonably mild March they'd been enjoying, the Irish comedian had on a pair of fake-fur mittens! But being used to the eccentricity of the rich and famous, Cameron passed this off as a loveable quirk and began the sycophantic greeting he'd rehearsed earlier.

Ms O'Hara, so great to meet you. Congratulations on your success at the TV awards last week. How many is that now? Three? Four? Incredible,' gushed Cameron, referring to the gongs she'd picked up over the past year for her uber-popular chat show, '*Shhh... it just got real!*'.

'Thank you, four including last week's, I think,' replied the star.

But rather than seizing the opportunity to talk about herself, O'Hara appeared to be more interested in Rakewell's 'brand ambassador'.

'Is your drag queen here yet? I'd like to say 'Hello' before we go on stage.'

He was about to answer when out of one of the smaller dressing rooms appeared Izzy.

Wearing a long black silk dress which made the most of her lithe figure, and her hair swept up in a bun, she reminded Cameron of Audrey Hepburn in *Breakfast at Tiffany's* – only Spanish and in her fifties. In fact, though it pained him to admit it, he couldn't deny that she'd scrubbed up rather well.

Imagine his delight then when Liz O'Hara enveloped Izzy's left hand with both fur-mittened paws, addressed her as Bette, and said how much she was looking forward to interviewing such an esteemed drag artiste!

Despite the expertly made-up face, there was no disguising Izzy's horror.

Mistaken for a 73-year-old drag queen! I'll be dining out on this one for quite some time! thought Cameron gleefully.

O'Hara, on the other hand, realising her error, looked almost as mortified as Izzy.

Seeing an opportunity to earn some Brownie points with his special guest, Cameron dived in to rescue her from the embarrassment caused by her mistake.

'Och, Liz,' he interjected. 'You're such a hoot. Nae wonder y'keep winning all those awards. Let me introduce ye tae Isobel Pitt, the historian who discovered the 'art-house' movies we'll be showing tonight.'

'Isobel, so pleased to make your acquaintance. Hope you didn't mind my little joke. You look amazing,' said O'Hara, noticeably relieved to have been thrown a lifeline. It was also evident from Izzy's grimace that she *did* mind. Especially in front of Cameron. But regardless of the obvious discomfort caused by O'Hara's faux pas, she managed to summon up one of her schoolgirl peals of laughter and said how much her sister loved the Irish woman's show.

Corridor calamity over, both women retreated to their respective dressing rooms to lick their wounds, and Cameron made his way to the auditorium in the hope of finding someone who'd appreciate the anecdote.

He was in luck.

'Hello, ladies!' he shouted in the direction of Alex and Adam, who, judging by the volume of their laughter, had been enjoying the free bar for quite some time already.

‘Hey, girl, hey!’ screeched Alex, acknowledging Cameron with an empty Martini glass. ‘Get us another round in while you’re up, will you, doll?’

‘Aye, go on, these kicktails have cocks like mules,’ slurred Adam.

Thankfully, as it got closer to 7pm, their cackles were drowned out by the boisterous crowd of young socialites who largely made up the guest list.

Noting that it was almost time for the main event, Cameron scanned the room for his client.

No sooner had he begun to do so when…

‘Cammy! Cammy!’ hollered someone nearby. ‘I said we’d find him up here, didn’t I?’ continued a loud voice with an American accent which Cameron recognised immediately as belonging to Rakewell’s CEO, Don Hunter, a chisel-jawed, blue-eyed jock of a man whom Cameron disliked as much as the uninvited shortening of his name. And just behind him was Bunny Goldman, the more likeable client services director of his agency’s New York office, who, contrary to the qualities of the animal after which she was named, was ferociously smart and uncompromisingly tough.

‘Donald! Bunny!’ cried Cameron in their direction. ‘So pleased tae see you both.’

At least it was half-true, he mused, as he vigorously shook the old goat’s hand and air-kissed the rabbit’s cheek.

‘Well, you’ve certainly attracted the Soho-cialites!’ said Bunny, referencing the word Cameron had invented to describe the cool-hunting urbanites at whom their campaign was aimed.

‘Yeah, well done, Cammy, me old mucka!’ bellowed Hunter in his atrocious mockney before lowering his voice and gesturing to his left and right at the fashionably dressed hipsters milling around him. 'Looks like you've managed to get the gays, too!'

A nod to the CEO's opinion about whom *he* thought was Rakewell's key demographic.

'Aye, there'll be slim pickings on Old Compton Street tonight!' replied Cameron.

But before Hunter could respond, a voice from the sound system announced that the evening's entertainment was about to begin, and Cameron was spared any more small talk.

Conversations cut short; a polite calm fell across the auditorium as guests made their way to their designated tables and the MC continued his introduction.

'She's sassier than a seagull. Saltier than a sea dog. Please put your hands together and give a warm Rococo Piccolo welcome to everyone's favourite Brighton Belle. The one. The only. Bette y'Sweet Ass.'

Kickstarting the show with a rendition of 'Hey! Big Spender', Bette looked a million dollars herself in the green rhinestone-encrusted evening gown that guests would recognise from the promotional material which was all around them at the venue. After that came a few minutes of Bette's bawdy stand-up routine, followed by a cover version of a song which was currently riding high in the charts. Sung in Bette's inimitable warble, it bore little similarity to the original tune but seemed to go down well with the youngsters in the room.

Opening numbers sung, it was time for the interview with Liz O'Hara.

Still dressed as his drag queen persona, George stepped down from the stage and made his way over to a sofa on which Izzy was already seated.

No doubt encouraged by the adoration of the crowd, George quickly settled into the role of national treasure, responding to O'Hara's gratitude for his presence with the riposte:

> *'Oh, don't thank me, dear. Thank my doctor—and the pills she gives me! I'm surprised I'm here myself!'*

Cameron breathed a sigh of relief. His gamble had paid off. Rakewell's had been pulled back from the brink of obsolescence. And the relaunch was on track to being a complete success. Noting the appreciative smiles on the faces of Bunny and the old goat, he made himself comfortable to enjoy the rest of the show.

With the films used as reference points, over the next few minutes, Ms O'Hara asked George about the saucier side of 60s Brighton, providing more opportunities for him to demonstrate his forte for camp innuendo and bitchy putdowns.

His comment, for instance, about stopping off for *'a quick one'* after a day's sunbathing, followed swiftly with – *'A drink, you dirty lot!'* – got a huge laugh. And almost as good was the one about 1960s gay bars not being as 'obvious' as they were nowadays – *'No rainbow flags or half-naked barmen. More's the pity!'*

Indeed, George – and Bette – were lapped up by the audience of millennials with the same fervour that they embraced forgotten treasures like vinyl records and books; that is to say, like new discoveries.

To Izzy, the comedian directed questions of a more academic nature, the importance of the films to cinematography and queer history, and also the recent revelations about Grace Davidson. A section that, if less entertaining than Bette's bit, did at least reaffirm the 'art-house' credentials of George's *dirrrty* movies – *the 're-imagining' of which Cameron was, in truth, no more convinced about than the 'star' of them was himself!*

So, all in all, the evening could hardly have gone better. And after a couple more songs, by 10.30, Cameron was able to shake off Bunny and Donald and hunt down Adam and Alex.

Someone else with an exit strategy, it soon transpired, had been Ms O'Hara. Sneaking off just minutes after the interview, according to Cameron's personal assistant. *Fucking VIPS!* Cameron said under his breath as he made his way to the comedian's dressing room.

But once inside, he began to doubt what he'd been told. *Had the celebrity left the building, after all?* An immediate assessment of the debris suggested otherwise. The designer jeans and jacket she'd been wearing were slung over the back of a chair, and several personal items such as make-up brushes and lip balm were strewn across the dressing table.

Intrigued by the apparent aftermath of a rapture, Cameron walked towards the abandoned clothes and paraphernalia. Reaching his destination, he spotted a hand-written note shoved under a bottle of hand sanitiser.

On closer inspection, he realised that it was addressed to him.

Cameron. Thanks for the gig. Sorry about the mess. Hope you can find a good home for the clothes. Might need a wash! See you on the other side. XXX Liz O'Hara.

Odd thing to do, leaving her clothes like that, thought Cameron. And what did she mean by 'the other side'? Perhaps she *had* experienced a rapture after all! But before he had a chance to solve the mystery, the answer revealed itself.

OFFICIAL. IT'S A PANDEMIC! – shouted the headline splashed across the newspaper on which the note was placed.

Fuuuuck! He'd been so consumed by the relaunch event he'd not seen the latest bulletin about the virus.

Cameron glanced around the room.

The discarded clothes and make-up brushes.

The hand sanitiser and paper towels.

The missing host of the multi-award-winning TV show '*Shhh... it just got real!*'.

Well, lassie, it certainly has done now!

Chapter Twelve

Getting to the bottom of it all

Mother's Day 22nd March 2020 – Brighton

Following the announcement that the coronavirus was now a pandemic, less than two weeks after the relaunch event at the Rococo Piccolo, like the rest of the country, Brighton was preparing to hunker down.

Last suppers had been eaten. Last orders called. And the day before National Lockdown being Mothering Sunday, one suspected that quite a lot of people in the city would be spending the last few hours of freedom with their extended families.

One exception to this was Izzy Pitt, who, at around the time when most mothers would have been relaxing on the sofa surrounded by flowers and chocolates, was setting off to visit a 73-year-old ex-porn star turned drag queen who'd once tripped the light fantastic on the dance floor of a pop-up gay nightclub at a fruit farm in Kent.

Yes, thought Izzy to herself, *these were indeed strange times!*

An observation further supported by her reaction to the sound of someone sneezing in the street behind her.

Panicked by the noise, Izzy hurriedly unlocked her car and got inside. Once there, she looked furtively in the rearview mirror to see who the perpetrator of this potential

Weapon of Mass Destruction could have been. Noting it was Mrs Pike from No.173, she tutted loudly and fastened her seat belt.

Ordinarily not a cause for concern in the leafy suburb which hugged the city's main cemetery, but as worries about the pandemic grew – every sneeze, cough and sniffle was now greeted with the same response as gunfire in a war zone might have been.

'Cover your mouth, daaarlink, at least,' chastised Izzy from behind the virus-proof windows of her SUV.

One more check in the mirror for unidentified explosive devices. *Or old ladies with bad coughs.* And she was on her way.

Although the official purpose of Izzy's mission was to return the mustard-coloured handkerchief that George had left at the Pavilion Café, with the lockdown coming into force the very next day, it would also be her last chance to talk to him face-to-face about Hazelpits.

And given the mounting concerns about the virus, she was now keener than the colour of the soon-to-be-returned hanky to find out more details about Pagan Pete's prophetic reading, too.

Arriving a few minutes later in the car park of the supermarket at the bottom of St. James's Street, she made the snap decision to stock up on a few basics while she was there. But met by a mob of hysterical shoppers as she came out of the lift, she aborted her plans to kill two birds with one stone and decided to go straight to George's flat instead.

Almost running into a squabble of seagulls fighting over a tray of chips as she left the store, a new thought suddenly entered her head.

If only she'd had an actual stone in her handbag!

Since the only thing she had in there was George's old hanky, she scurried away, leaving the birds to fight over their supper unharmed. All except one rather large gull, who'd followed her across the road and was now eyeing her up and down.

Fearing that her murderous thoughts had been read by the bird, she reached for George's buzzer and began pressing it manically.

Luckily for Izzy, her insistent jabs were answered, and her fears of befalling the same fate as Tippi Hedren quickly dissipated.

'Hello, Izzy. Do come up, dear,' crackled the voice at the other end of the intercom.

Although even inside the flat it seemed she was still not completely safe!

'Lavender crème or marzipan?' enquired George, reaching for a box of chocolates on the coffee table and waving the almost empty tray in her face. 'Take both, dear. I'm not particularly fond of either.'

Clearly, there were plenty of flavours of which he had been fond! thought Izzy to herself as she stared at the last two remaining soft centres.

Recognising the box as being from the same fancy London chocolatier as the one she'd received in the post the previous day – a 'thank you' for her help with the Rakewell's relaunch – she also noticed that it was at least twice the size as the one which Cameron had sent her!

'Ha! Me neither, darlink. I've already had my fill today, anyway,' she replied.

'Oh yes, it's Mothering Sunday, isn't it? Josh spoiling you rotten, I bet,' said George, referring to Izzy's son, as he poured two teas from the pot he'd just brought in.

'Like a queen!' she fibbed, painfully aware that her Mother's Day cupboard was barer than Mrs Hubbard's.

Though it wasn't entirely untrue as far as Izzy was concerned. For although Josh had *spoiled* his mother with neither chocolates nor flowers – not even so much as a card – her son had given her the greatest gift of all. His presence. And for the next three weeks at least, he and boyfriend Kwan would be riding out the expected storm in the Pitt family home.

Thinking about her Mother's Day gifts – or rather the lack of them – Izzy suddenly remembered the premise for her visit and retrieved the parcel containing George's handkerchief.

'Oh, thank you, dear. What a dizzy old queen I'm getting these days. I only realised that I'd lost it when I saw the original owner wearing it in an old photograph. I was so happy when you told me at the Rococo that it had been found in the Pavilion Café,' he said, placing the folded square of fabric on his lap.

'An old photograph?' asked Izzy, intrigued.

Of course, she'd suspected that the handkerchief had belonged to someone from his past, from the way he'd been stroking it when he'd been reminiscing about the friends he'd lost to AIDS. But the mention of a photograph was an exciting new development.

'Yes, dear. Around the same time as those discos at Hazelpits. I had a load of 'em out to show Ollie a couple of weeks back,' said George, reaching for a photo album on the coffee table. 'Some old dears at his gym said that he reminded them of Pagan Pete. In his younger days, of course.'

'Oh, I see. I'd love to…' began Izzy.

Nudging up as close to the old man as she felt she could, given the reason for the impending lockdown, in the next half an hour or so, Izzy was introduced to Pete, Grace, and The Three Muskaqueers at the Heroes and Villains Party.

With a little help, she recognised George. But who was the gorgeous blond hunk who, after the Viking outfit, turned up as some sort of naval officer at what the old man remembered as the Titanic Party? Another infamous theme night at Hazelpits, made even more memorable, apparently, by a terrific thunderstorm which caused the usual pitch-black anonymity of the designated darkroom to be interrupted every few seconds by flashes of lightning through the hayloft skylights.

'Oh yes, red cheeks all round that night, I can tell you,' said George, giggling at the memory and turning to a spread featuring a group of men dressed in leather biker gear, which included the trio he'd called The Three Muskaqueers – and Pete, whom Izzy noticed was using a wheelchair.

'Let me guess. *Grease*? Or maybe *The Wild Ones*?' she suggested, assuming the photographs of the men in peaked caps, adorned with chains and studs, had been taken at another of those outrageous costume parties in Kent.

'Gawd no, dear!' replied George. 'That's a meeting of the Sussex Lancers. A motorcycle fetish club. Men who liked men who liked bikes. Or rather, men who liked men who liked to dress like they liked bikes. I don't remember many of them actually owning one!'

'Oh!' exclaimed Izzy.

But before she had time to digest this new information…

'Fuck!' cried the old man.

'What!' shrieked Izzy, assuming that George had spotted something disturbing.

'FUKC. The Federation of UK Clubs,' explained George, tugging a piece of paper out from beneath the album's plastic sheeting and waving it in front of her. 'It's what they used to put on their flyers and posters. The Sussex Lancers were just one of several affiliated motorsports clubs which existed across the country.'

'Ah, I see,' replied Izzy before returning her gaze to the photographs.

'Oh God. I'd forgotten all about those chaps,' said George, taking a closer look at a photo he'd removed from the plastic sleeve.

'Who?' asked Izzy, expecting to be introduced to a couple of Sussex Lancers.

'Not who, dear. Chaps. Bottomless trousers!' replied George, handing her the photo for inspection. Thrown a little by the word 'bottomless', the pert posteriors at which she was now staring did wonders to take her mind off the word and its associations.

'Ah, I see. Like what cowboys used to wear,' she suggested.

'Yes. Though without the leather jockstraps, I expect!' added George.

'Indeed,' agreed Izzy.

And that's when she saw it: the mustard-coloured handkerchief she'd just handed back to George. More than that even, she recognised the man in whose back pocket it was shoved. It was the handsome blond again.

'Oh, my goodness,' she said. 'Is that your handkerchief?'

'Yes, it is. Of course, back then, it belonged to this fella here. A Danish friend of mine called Odi,' replied George, stroking the man's face. 'But it wasn't just a hanky. It was a sort of code, letting people know what sort of sex you were into. We used to call it flagging. There were loads of different colours.'

FUKC. Chaps. Colour-coded erotic semiotics. It seemed like George was speaking another language.

'How fascinating,' said Izzy warily.

Not sure whether her nerves could cope with whatever the different colours might have denoted, she quickly shifted the focus on to the one in the back pocket of the handsome blond.

'And mustard? Odi's handkerchief?'

'Well,' began George, his mischievous grin causing deep ridges to appear in his old cheeks. 'In the right pocket, it means you want a big one. And in the left, it means you've got a big one to give.'

Feeling her *own* cheeks start to redden, she decided not to pursue this line of chat any further and steered the discussion back to the men in the photograph. And to one man in particular: Pagan Pete. Drawing attention to the fortune-teller would, she hoped, provide her with an opportunity to ask about 'that' reading.

'So, I see that Pete's using a wheelchair,' she said, laying the trap.

'Yes, dear,' confirmed George before retelling the tale of Pete's fall from the hayloft.

'Oh no. Poor thing. How awful!' sympathised Izzy, secretly looking forward to relaying the story to her husband.

'I know. Although the accident is why he started reading the Sarsenic Sigils in the first place. It all began with a book about Viking runes which Odi gave him while he was in hospital. It had just been something to help Pete kill a bit of time, but when he discovered that the Saxons used something similar right here in Sussex, there was no stopping him,' said George. 'Took up fortune-telling not long afterwards. In fact, if my memory serves me right, these photos were taken on the night he first told us about the reading he thought was about AIDS. The same one he had the other month, which he's convinced is to do with this coronavirus.'

'Oh yes, the one you mentioned over lunch…' encouraged Izzy, placing a little bit of *queso* next to the trip wire. 'Can you remember what it said? The reading?'

'Of course, dear. Like it was yesterday. It was quite a big night for the Lancers, you see,' continued George, edging ever closer towards her trap. 'The first meeting at a new venue. In the basement of a pub on St. James's Street. Whispers, I think it was called.'

Snap!

Finally, she was going to get to the bottom of the mystery that had enticed her across town.

Chapter Thirteen

Day One in the Big Sister House

Monday 23rd March 2020 –
George's flat – St. James's Street, Brighton

Parking himself down in exactly the same place on George's sofa where 24 hours earlier Izzy had learnt about the lively gay scene which had existed on the South Coast in the 1980s, Ollie plumped up a cushion and propped it behind his back.

Though definitely no stranger to his neighbour's flat, the reason for the extra care he was taking to make himself at home was that for the foreseeable future, 'home' was exactly what it would be. Or at least an extension of his own home on the floor below. Indeed, since he and Drew had decided to throw their lot in with George for the duration of the restrictions, it was probably the first of many evenings Ollie would be spending there.

A situation which, for all its bizarre overtones, had become commonplace across the country as family members and friends decided with whom they would like to be locked down. Some driving through the night to be with their chosen loved ones. Others scrambling onto planes in order to get back to Blighty before the whole world entered into a weird social science experiment the like of which had never before been seen.

In fact, anyone who'd ever wondered how long they'd last in the Big Brother house was about to find out. And whilst in this version there would be no Diary Room or any chance of voting off fellow housemates, the potential for arguments over the minutiae of domestic living promised to be pretty similar.

Also making himself at home at George's place was Pete, who, as part of this frenzy, had taken up the offer of keeping his old friend company until things returned to normal. Though why it had ultimately been decided that he should move into George's second-floor flat on St. James's Street, rather than both of them moving into the fortune-teller's more wheelchair-friendly accommodation just up from Hove Lawns, wasn't entirely clear until it transpired that Pete's flat only had one bedroom and George had refused point blank to sleep on the sofa.

Of course, there was also the prospect of being holed up with a fitness instructor and a handsome ex-army officer, which may have ultimately swung things in George's favour!

But whatever the specifics of the deal, as day one of lockdown drew to a close, all four of them were gathered together for the much-publicised address to the nation.

Hearing the newsreader announce that the prime minister would be arriving shortly, Ollie had just enough time to position himself within reaching-distance of a bowl of crisps on the coffee table before the plummy voice of Mr Johnson filled the room.

'Good evening. The coronavirus is the biggest threat this country has faced for decades – and this country is not alone. All over the world, we are seeing the devastating impact of this invisible killer.'

Like millions of Britons across the country, they all listened intently to the promise of difficult times ahead.

So much so, in fact, that aside from the sound of munching and the PM's announcement, the only noise which could be heard was the occasional ha-ha-ha cackle of seagulls in the sky above.

Though even they seemed more subdued than usual as Mr Johnson talked through the various steps that were being taken to fight the disease.

'From this evening I must give the British people a very simple instruction. You must stay at home,' continued the PM, presumably from his relatively new home at No.10 Downing Street.

'Because the critical thing is that we must stop the disease spreading between households.'

Reminiscent of a costume drama set in plague-ridden London, an image of the Chancellor of the Exchequer, Rishi Sunak, daubing a red cross on the door of his neighbour's house while Foreign Secretary, Dominic Raab, rode past on a horse-drawn cart yelling 'Bring out yer dead' suddenly entered Ollie's head.

Why these two particular MPs came to mind was owed to a novel version of 'Snog. Marry. Throw off a cliff!' which he'd played recently, that required him to make his choice from whatever group of men had been written down on the slip of paper picked out of a hat at the start of each round.

Admittedly, compared to England's Six Nations rugby squad and a popular boy band from the 90s, leading figures in the government had provided few options for the 'snog' and 'marry' categories. But after a cursory search on the internet for an image of the Cabinet, Ollie had gone for a bit of French kissing with Dashing Dom and decided to say 'I do' to Dishy Rishi.

At least I'd have no money worries! He'd joked at the time.

Pushing these thoughts to the back of his mind, Ollie tuned back into the TV just in time to hear that until further notice, people would only be allowed to leave their homes to shop for basic necessities and one 'form' of exercise each day – alone or with members of their own household.

Given that he and Drew had been stockpiling booze and groceries all week, the former wasn't something which overly concerned him for the immediate future.

The new rules on exercise, though, were a different matter entirely.

As a personal trainer, helping people keep fit was his bread and butter, so there would be little of either if the only people he was allowed to train were his boyfriend, a wheelchair-using fortune-teller, and a 73-year-old man whose idea of exercise was a stroll to the seafront for fish and chips. With Plato's Gymnasium closed, Ollie had hoped that he would at least have been able to meet his clients in nearby Queen's Park – or on the beach. But what he was now hearing put paid to that idea! Faced with the prospect of going hungry, he suddenly remembered one of his colleagues mentioning something about doing classes online.

Confident he could make it work, Ollie returned his attention to the TV.

'If your friends ask to meet, you should say No! You should not be meeting family members who do not live in your home...' continued Mr Johnson.

Followed by the news that the police had been given the power to issue fines and disperse gatherings – *whatever that meant* – the next restriction was even more chilling: a list of all the places which were now off limits. Though which would cause the greatest concern amongst the populous; the closure of churches, synagogues, temples and mosques – or those other places of worship such as pubs and cut-price clothing stores, Ollie couldn't decide!

What did become clear, though, was that a *gathering* meant more than two people, which kind of put the kibosh on any weddings that had been booked to take place over the next few weeks.

'To be fair, that's one *gathering* which needs three people as a bare minimum!' scoffed Drew on hearing about the ban.

'Ha! Turns out 'three' *is* a crowd!' added George.

In fact, it seemed that the only religious ceremonies still allowed were funerals, a stark reminder of the gravity of the situation they were all facing. Something which was not lost on the prime minister, who, after promising a huge and unprecedented programme of support for workers, businesses and the NHS, started talking about how 'the people of this country' would rise to the challenge and come through stronger than ever.

'We will beat the coronavirus and we will beat it together,' he said confidently. *'And therefore, I urge you at this moment of national emergency to stay at home, protect our NHS – and save lives.'*

It was rousing stuff.

In fact, had a seagull not chosen that very moment to deliver an aerial bombardment of crap against the lounge window, so heavy and loud that the shock of it caused Ollie to slip off the edge of his seat, the finale might have had the effect which Mr Johnson had no doubt intended.

'Bastards!' cried George. Not, as it turned out, directed at the TV, but at the perpetrator of the whitish splat which was now the focus of everyone's attention. 'I only cleaned them last week. Shame it's not bird flu. That'd teach the feathery little fuckers.'

The prime minister's Churchillian call to arms somewhat ruined by the avian air-raid, Drew grabbed the remote and turned off the TV.

'That's that then,' he said, sinking back into the sofa. 'Three weeks with you lot. Hope you've got some playing cards.'

'Probably been a run on them, too,' suggested Ollie with a sigh.

'Pah! I can do better than playing cards, cherub!' announced Pete, reaching into the pannier attached to the side of his wheelchair. 'I've got these!'

Though Ollie had never set eyes on them before, he knew immediately that the deck of cards, held together by a thick elastic band, could only be one thing. The famous Sarsenic Sigil Cards with which the old man plied his trade beneath the i360.

'Pete!' exclaimed George, with a tut.

'Oh, go on. I'm crap at pontoon anyway. I'd much prefer to have my fortune told instead. I haven't got any silver, but I can cross your palm with toilet roll and Sauvignon Blanc if you like,' joked Drew, demonstrating quite a gift for gallows humour.

Ollie, on the other hand, wasn't quite ready to dabble in the dark arts just yet.

'OK. Though I think you should tell us a little bit more about them first, before we part with any of our loo roll!' he suggested, looking over to George for a bit of moral support.

But where was he?

In the time it had taken Pete to lay out his deck of dog-eared cards, it seemed that the old man had made a sharp exit.

Ollie was about to ask if they should wait for him to return when their in-house fortune-teller loudly cleared his throat.

'So...' began Pete, pointing at the faded illustrations spread out before them. 'The Sarsenic Sigil Cards – representing the 25 symbols carved into stone by Anglo-Saxon Pagans, before they converted to Christianity in the 7th-century. Sigils because the signs are imbued with magic. And Sarsenic from the name of the stones into which they were carved. Basically, just large sandstones dumped here after the last ice age.

'Sarsen is from the word Saracen, what Christians used to call Muslims, so it became shorthand for anything considered non-Christian. And because Stonehenge – the most famous Pagan place of worship in Britain – was built with them, they became known as sarsen stones. Sadly, there's no evidence of any circles in Sussex, but there are lots of stones still around. Like the one in Hove Park.'

'Hove Park?' queried Ollie.

'Yes. Called 'Gieldstan' or 'Godstone' by the Saxons because of the strange face they saw in its surface, 'gield' is also Saxon for gold, which is why several street names in the area close to where it was found bear the name Goldstone,' explained Pete. 'But it was known about way before the Saxons arrived on the scene. In fact, myth has it that the rock was hurled into its original place by the Devil himself when he was making his famous dyke!'

'Oh wow!' exclaimed Drew.

'Became a bit of a tourist attraction after it was moved to Hove Park. But to the Saxons, these stones were much more than follies. They were important landmarks. That's why so many Sussex placenames have the Saxon word for stone in them. Stanmer, for instance, means 'stoney pond'. And Steyning is translated as 'people of the stone'.'

Pete paused for a moment.

It was clear from his next comment that he'd told this story many times before.

'But we don't have to leave Brighton to get in touch with our Saxon past. There's somewhere just around the corner. A *stone's* throw away, in fact.'

Ever the eager student, Drew was first to solve the riddle.

'Oh my God. The Old Steine. I wondered why it was sometimes spelled with a 'y',' interjected the Welshman.

'That's right,' confirmed Pete. 'Steine – or Steyne – is Saxon for stoney ground. In fact, there are still some sarsen stones at the base of the dolphin fountain.'

'No way!' gasped Drew.

'Yes, but there aren't any sigils on them, I'm afraid,' added Pete.

'Worn away by rain and seagull shit, I expect!' suggested Ollie, smirking.

Just then, as if on cue, the lesson was interrupted by the ha-ha-ha cry of the aforementioned bird and the dull thud of another poo bomb hitting the windowpane.

Once was not unusual. But twice in an hour! Now that *was* spooky.

And judging by the look on his face, Pete thought so, too.

Thankfully, Drew had a question which returned their attention back to the cards.

'But if they're so easily worn away, how do we even know about them?'

'Oddly enough, we have the monks to thank for that,' replied Pete. 'With their vellum manuscripts and Latin, they had the wherewithal to write stuff down. Of course, once the Church decided that it was the work of the Devil, anything they'd recorded about the Sarsenic Sigils was either destroyed or locked away. But over the last couple of hundred years, several manuscripts have come to light. And there are quite a few books about them now, as well. Including one by a certain Peter Sissinghurst!' added the old man with a knowing smile.

Only just getting used to being acquainted with someone who answered to the name Pagan Pete, it took Ollie a few seconds to get the old man's meaning.

'Oh God. You mean you've written a book on all of this?'

'I have indeed. *Sarsenic Sigil Cards: Unlocking the Magic Code of the Anglo-Saxons* it's called… in fact…' began Pete, looking over towards George's favourite armchair.

'Loo, I think,' suggested Ollie, guessing from the look on the old man's face that this was the first time he'd noticed that his friend had gone AWOL.

'Oh, well, never mind. There's plenty on the web about them these days, too, of course,' said Pete, causing the boys to reach for their mobiles.

'Bloody hell!' cried Ollie, presented with a page of links to websites and articles about the magical symbols.

Whatever the reason behind George's disappearing act, it was clear that Pete was far from alone in his passion.

And noting Drew's enthusiastic interest in the subject, Ollie was certain that the *Cult of the Sarsenic Sigils* had just recruited another disciple.

A suspicion confirmed by his boyfriend's next question.

'But what do they all mean?' asked Drew, putting his phone to one side.

'Well, dear boy… how long have you got?' replied Pete, tapping the Welshman's knee.

Mmmm… looks like the Cult of Drew has just recruited a new follower, too!

'Oh, about three weeks!' replied his boyfriend, making a play at looking at his watch.

'Well, it won't take that long, cherub,' assured Pete. 'Though I might need a G&T to loosen my tongue a little!'

Chapter Fourteen

When life gives you artisanal chocolate-coated candied kumquats...

Monday 23rd March 2020 – Cameron & Alex's house – Wyndham Street, Brighton

A few streets away in the more gentrified end of Kemptown, another lockdown household was also digesting the prime minister's announcement. Though after a short analysis of the main points, a question from Cameron was providing more food for thought.

'SOUR DOUG?' he squirmed, spotting a jar of something bubbling away in the airing cupboard.

'Ha ha, very funny. I ran out of space on the label,' replied Alex. 'It's the sourdough starter I made this morning.'

'Och, is that what it is?' queried Cameron, pulling a face. 'Though tae be fair, there's only one other thing it remotely looks like!'

'Porridge?' suggested Alex, his facetious tone making it clear that he knew exactly to what Cameron was alluding.

Adam, on the other hand, having been downstairs throughout the boys' discussion about the contents of the jar, wasn't quite as up to speed with their banter.

'Jaysus, it's bad enough *doing* porridge for the next three weeks; I hope you don't expect us to eat it, too!' growled the Irishman, joining them on the landing.

Reminded by the appearance of his friend as to why he'd been digging around in the airing cupboard, Cameron put the offending goo back on its shelf and grabbed an armful of clean bedding for their temporary lodger.

As the owner of a café-deli in Queen's Park, like everyone else employed in 'non-essential' work, Adam would also be on enforced holiday leave. And with the clubs and pubs that were his usual stomping ground also closed, Alex and Cameron had taken pity on their singleton friend and invited him to move into Wyndham Street with his fellow Velociraptors; the collective name they knew Izzy called them behind their backs, on account of the sharpness of their tongues and the fear they instilled in others whenever they were together. Transparently meant as an insult, Adam had actually been rather impressed with the fierce reputation suggested by the nickname.

The forced closure of his 'non-essential' business, however…

'Feckin' gobshites! Anyone who considers oat milk cappuccinos and gluten-free croissants as 'non-essential' has clearly never had to serve a posse of yummy mummies after the school run!' the Irishman had grumbled earlier.

Just one of numerous criticisms of the government's response to the pandemic which he'd shared with the boys that morning when he'd swung by theirs to drop off boxes of groceries from his deli which would probably not survive the lockdown.

Though less perishable, the delivery had also included several bags of flour and quite a few rolls of toilet paper. Stories of panic-buying were on the increase, and he didn't want to leave anything quite so 'valuable' in the shop; at one point even considering making up a bed in the basement.

But after being invited to stay with the boys in Wyndham Street, he'd decided a sign on the door saying *'No cash, flour or loo roll kept on premises overnight!'* would suffice.

The same could not have been said about Alex and Cameron's coal bunker, which now resembled a regional outpost of the British Red Cross, albeit a rather fancy one, with trays of quail eggs and bottles of pomegranate juice rather than rice and powdered milk.

Whether access to the deli's larder had been a factor in Alex suggesting their friend move in with them, Cameron wasn't sure. But Adam had clearly decided that the offer, like the sourdough starter, was not to be sniffed at.

'Here you go, hen,' said Cameron, lifting the pile of sheets and pillowslips over the jar of bubbling yeast and flour. 'We've put you on the front with the view of the pier.'

'On a clear day, with Cameron's opera glasses,' added Alex wryly.

Despite the remark, the boys' five-storey townhouse, in a terraced street just off the seafront, was utterly charming. And though tall and narrow, it was positively Tardis-like, somehow managing to squeeze eight rooms into its slender frame.

On the first floor, Cameron and Alex's bedroom was basically two rooms knocked into one, with an en-suite. Up a flight of narrow stairs, Adam's temporary accommodation was the bigger of two guest rooms on the second floor, with a separate bathroom at the end of the corridor. The smaller bedroom adjacent to his had already been commandeered as the home office, and the attic space above turned into a makeshift gymnasium. Complete with open plan lounge on the ground floor, kitchen and dining room in the basement, and a shady patio on the back, there was no denying that there were worse places in Brighton – or indeed the world – to be locked down.

'Cheers, fellas, I'll get settled in and be down in five. Help yourself to the beers I've left on the patio,' offered Adam, disappearing upstairs with the linen under one arm and a sports bag thrown over his shoulder.

True to his word, five minutes later, all three 'inmates' were sat around the dining-room table sampling the spoils of Adam's swag and chewing the cud about the impending doom.

'Well, at least all those meetings about Disaster Recovery I've had to endure over the years have come in useful at last,' said Cameron, taking a swig of organic pale ale and reaching for a packet of oven-baked lentil crisps.

Just because he was going tae be a 'prisoner' for the next three weeks, there was nae reason why he had tae eat and drink like one, too!

'God yeah! I remember those. Snoooooooze-city,' added the Irishman, who before opening his café-deli, had been an internet-whiz kid in London. 'Though back then, we thought it'd be a dirty bomb or a flood that'd feck us in the arse. Our agency kept a place on an industrial estate near Potters Bar just in case. If we'd known the solution was to get everyone to work from home, we could have saved a fortune!'

'Aye, best-laid plans and all that,' sighed Cameron, opening a tin of dark chocolate-covered candied kumquats, another upmarket delicacy unlikely to survive the lockdown.

Or, in all probability, the evening!

'Ha! It'll take more than getting staff to work from home to keep the airlines going!' barked Alex.

As a travel agent for a company which specialised in booking flights for high-flying business executives, he had good reason to be concerned, for it was clear that the closure of borders was going to be particularly disastrous for his industry.

'Aye, well, I think they should've grounded the planes weeks ago. We're an island, for feck's sake,' snarled Adam, chomping down on a chocolate-coated kumquat.

'I'm just glad we were able tae di the Rakewell's relaunch before all this kicked off. Though I think we can put the Singapore gig on the back-burner for noo,' acquiesced Cameron, cutting a slice of truffle-infused Brie and spreading it on a sour-cherry and spelt cracker. 'At least the next stage of the campaign is all online. And thank fuck we decided to do a big push in the supermarkets. Much better margins than pubs, anyways.'

Whoops! thought Cameron to himself. The harsh reminder that – unlike Adam's café-deli – and virtually every other type of business selling food and booze – supermarkets *had* been allowed to remain open, was not, perhaps, the most sensitive of comments given the circumstances.

Noting the frosty look he was getting from the other side of the table, Cameron quickly changed the subject.

'Anyone fancy a gin? Rakewell's sent me a crate as a thank you.'

'Oh, go on then, it's not like I need to be anywhere tomorrow,' said Adam, with a yawn.

But if Cameron and Adam were happy to drown their sorrows, it seemed that Alex wasn't quite ready to move on just yet.

'It's like 9/11 all over again!' he exclaimed, drawing his fellow prisoners back to worries about the effect the lockdown would have on the airlines.

'It's worse than that, mate,' disagreed Adam. 'All those spacemen outfits and masks. People crossing the road to avoid getting too close to yous. I reckon it's more like AIDS!'

'Well, I think that's a bit—' began Cameron, reaching for a bottle of tonic water.

'Aye, but you weren't there, mate,' protested Adam, cutting his friend off mid-sentence. 'Not in the beginning anyways.'

It was true. Being a few years older than Cameron, when AIDS had first raised its ugly head, the Irishman would have been a teenager.

'Triggering is what one of the old fellas on my shift at The Sussex Beacon called it,' said Adam, referring to the local charity that cared for people living with HIV, for which he volunteered. Though given the heavy footfall of gay and bisexual men who came through the doors of its shops, Cameron suspected that his friend's motivation was driven as much by his reputation as a philanderer as it was by philanthropy.

Hadn't he given enough of himself to the community, already? mused Cameron, before tuning back into why Adam thought this new pandemic had echoes of the one in the 80s and 90s.

'There was one customer this week who wouldn't take his change from my hand!' continued the Irishman. 'Told me to put it in the collection tin. But I could tell from the way he hesitated what he was really thinking. Just like people were scared to touch AIDS patients or anyone they thought might be a risk. It got me and the other volunteer on my shift talking about those ads with the feckin' icebergs and shit.'

Even though Cameron had still been at school when they were first aired, he was familiar with the controversial public health campaign to which Adam was referring.

As it seemed, so was his husband.

'Fuck yeah, and the one with the grave and the white lilies,' said Alex, knocking over the empty box of sour-cherry and spelt crackers, like the tombstone from the aforementioned advert. 'Don't die of ignorance or something, wasn't it?'

'Don't die of ignorance! Right. It wasn't feckin' ignorance that was gonna be the death of me back then. It was the skinheads on the bus who used to tell people not to sit next to me 'cos I had AIDS. I remember one of 'em got right in my face once and ordered me to get off!' growled Adam.

'Nae way!' fumed Cameron.

'Aye, and not one single person stuck up for me!' continued the Irishman before taking a big gulp of his G&T and reaching for the tin of chocolate-coated dried fruit.

'Well, at least this time around we're not the ones most at risk,' interjected Alex. 'From what I've been reading, it's more dangerous for older people.'

'Or anyone carrying a few extra pounds,' added Cameron, reminded of his dead colleague, Yang.

'Well, no more choccie treats for you then, Grandad!' teased Alex, prising the tin of candied kumquats out of Adam's paws.

Doubtless meant as a friendly jibe, Alex's little dig at the age difference between them only served to drag up further memories of the decade that had been so horrific for the LGBTQ+ community as a whole – and especially for gay and bisexual men.

'Ha! Elderly and overweight! Definitely not two words you'd associate with AIDS!' snapped Adam. "Skin and bone' was the phrase they used to use. And so young. Most of the ones I knew were in their 20s and 30s. Feckin' tragic.'

Without the usual hum of traffic on Marine Parade, the silence which greeted the end of the Irishman's sentence seemed to last an eternity until…

'Sorry, Adam, I didn't…' began Alex.

'Oh, ignore me. I just get so angry when I think about how differently everyone's responding to this pandemic compared to the last one. Like, I know the government's getting a lot of stick for not shutting the borders quicker. But thinking back to how their predecessors dealt with AIDS. *Or rather, how they didn't!* There's no comparison. The amount of money that's being spent on trying to find a vaccine for coronavirus – and the urgency – is incredible. I just wish they'd been half as concerned the last time around,' huffed Adam before taking another swig of his G&T.

'Aye, well, they could hardly have done a worse job, that's for sure! Especially earlier on,' agreed Cameron, touched by the Irishman's candour. And, he had to admit, a little thrown, too. In all the years they'd known each other, he couldn't recall Adam ever talking about the friends he'd lost to AIDS.

Intrigued by this little-discussed chapter of the Irishman's life, Cameron urged him to continue.

'So, what was it like? Y'ken, being queer in the 80s, I mean?' he asked.

'Well, when I came out, it was illegal for a start!' replied Adam before polishing off his drink. 'It was years before we had an equal age of consent. In fact, I turned 16 just a couple of months after the world found out about Rock Hudson. That's when it really kicked off.

'Though to be honest, even without the headlines about AIDS, 'coming out' would still have been pretty challenging in 1985. Especially for a little gay boy with a funny accent living in a Yorkshire mining village! Of course, I'd heard about the 'gay plague', as they used to call it, before I 'came out'. There'd been a couple of documentaries about it. But there was no internet. No mobile phones. So, other than what I'd managed to pick up from the occasional mention of it on the telly, I was pretty much in the dark about it all.

'What I did know, though, was that if you got infected… there was a very, *very* good chance you'd die! Simple as that. For the vast majority of people back then, it really was a death sentence!'

'Fuck!' exclaimed Alex.

'Yeah, well, it certainly made you think twice about who you slept with,' continued Adam. 'Not that sex was really an issue till I got to university. And even then, it was usually with someone my own age. *Sometimes not even gay!* Though I suppose, in retrospect, some of 'em were probably bi. I think I thought it was safer somehow. In any case, the lads I got off with never wanted to do much. Hand-shandies mostly. Occasional blow job.'

'What! No anal?' cried Alex.

'Well, I'm sure it still went on. But knowing it was one of the riskiest things you could do, loads of my gay friends were terrified of it,' replied Adam, reaching for a bottle of beer and giving Cameron the chance to ask a question which had occurred to him while his friend had been in full flow.

'But surely yous had protection back then?'

'So. Much. Rubber,' replied Adam, stressing each word individually. 'By the late 80s, there were bowls of free condoms in every gay bar you went to. Even had them for blow jobs! Flavoured condoms. Cherry was my fave. Tasted less like sucking a tyre!

'And once the community got its act together, there was more information around too. You know, about safe sex and that. Posters in the bars and ads in gay magazines and newspapers. I remember I had one stuck to the back of my bedroom door, to remind me to be careful when I went on a night out. A bit like the sign you've put up, telling us to wash our hands as soon as we come in.'

It was a chilling comparison, for within hours of the lockdown, Alex had scrawled, *'Clean your hands, you filthy bitches!'* on a sheet of paper and stuck it up in their entrance hall.

'Fuck! It really is like corona,' conceded Cameron. 'And did it work? The safe sex campaign, I mean?'

'Apparently. In fact, I read somewhere that cases of all STDs fell massively amongst gay and bisexual men in the late 80s, so I guess I wasn't the only one wrapping myself up in rubber,' replied Adam. 'And for the ladies, there were these little squares of latex called dental dams.'

'Ew!' squealed Alex, his usual response to any mention of female genitalia.

Unperturbed by his husband's squeamishness, Cameron tentatively broached another question that had been swirling around his head since Adam's comment about his fears around anal sex.

'So, when did you first… y'ken…'

'Bum sex?' queried Adam. 'Well, I know you won't believe it, but I honestly don't think it was until I was in my mid-20s!'

'Nooooo!' exclaimed Alex.

'Seriously, mate, you've no idea what it was like,' continued the Irishman. 'Don't forget, there wasn't anything approaching treatment until the early 90s. So up until then, there was always that nagging fear. Every time you got a cold. Every time you got a rash. Every time you couldn't sleep 'cos you were too hot. You always thought the worst. Especially if you'd recently been with someone. No matter how safe you thought you'd been. *No matter how much rubber you'd used!'*

Reminded of how worried he himself had been after receiving the terrible news about his colleague, Cameron felt he understood a little bit of what Adam was saying. But for him, it'd been for just a couple of days. He couldn't imagine what it must have been like harbouring those worries after every single sexual encounter. It certainly went some way to explain why the Irishman had spent the last three decades making up for lost time!

That is to say, becoming the town bike.

Cameron made a mental note to be less critical of his friend's regular trips to Duke's Mound, the notorious cruising ground which ran behind the nudist beach up the road, and tuned back into Adam's recollections of the 80s.

'At least they're not blaming the unlucky sods that get ill this time!' he said, pausing to open his bottle of beer. 'You know, like they did with AIDS. When it wasn't enough that people had to deal with the prospect of a horrible death, there was the nastiness which went with it, as well. Stories of people coming back from hospital to find their homes ransacked and their belongings thrown out onto the street. People telling us we deserved it. That we had it coming to us. The homophobia was off the scale. Especially in the newspapers. Articles about how we were all lepers and should be forced to end our days on a desert island somewhere. I remember one story about a vicar who said that if any of his kids got AIDS, he'd shoot them. Even posed for a picture, holding a shotgun to his son's head! There really were no depths to which they wouldn't sink. In fact, you got the sense the journos actually enjoyed it. Like it was some kind of sick game.'

Ending this last sentence with a deep sigh, it was clear from the way Adam was staring into space that memories of those dark times haunted him still.

Faced with the prospect of another uncomfortable silence, Cameron tried desperately to think of some way to change the subject. Suddenly it came to him. An exhibition at Brighton Museum about queer history. Recalling one particular cabinet which was focused on the 1980s, after a few seconds, he attempted to steer the Irishman in a new direction.

'It was how the Tories got away with Section 28, wasn't it,' he said, referring to the notorious anti-gay legislation that had been introduced in the late 80s.

'Feck yeah,' agreed Adam, taking a swig of beer.

And the detour.

Of course, the protest rallies weren't just the subject of a museum exhibit for Adam. He'd actually been on them. Gripped by this first-hand account of the fight against Section 28, Cameron took a sip of his drink and readied himself for more of the Irishman's reminiscences of being a teenager in the 80s.

'I can still remember the day I first heard about it,' continued Adam. 'I was walking through the Peace Gardens in Sheffield when some guy with a tash handed me a leaflet. Cloney type. Well, anyways, on one side, they'd printed that famous poem about how it was silence which enabled the Nazis to rise to power...'

'Oh yeah, the one that starts... First they came for the socialists...' interrupted Alex, reaching for his tablet. 'Hang on a minute!' he added, halting the proceedings while he tapped something into the keyboard. 'Here it is. Martin *Niemöller*. Protestant pastor and critic of Adolf Hitler. It goes through a list of groups the Nazis picked off until there was no one left to object.'

'Yeah, that's it,' confirmed Adam before returning to his memories of Section 28. 'Well, on the back of the poem was information about some new legislation the government was trying to bring in. An amendment to an existing law, which is why it was called Clause 28 at the time.

'Anyway, according to the blurb, the changes they wanted to introduce would make it illegal for teachers to protect pupils from homophobic bullying or for libraries to stock books with homos and lesbians in them. To be honest, I'm not sure how many kids would have asked their teachers for help in those days. And I don't remember borrowing any library books which had queers in them, either. But to actually make it illegal! *I mean, what the feck!* And then there was all this crap about 'pretended family relationships' too.'

Adam paused for a moment to make bunny ears with two fingers of each hand.

'Total bullshit. But you can see why my lesbian friends were terrified they'd lose their kids,' he said, taking another gulp from his bottle.

'Oh God, remember that newsreader and those protesters?' interjected Alex.

'Fuck yeah,' replied Cameron. 'Sue Lawley, wasn't it?'

In fact, the moment a group of lesbian activists stormed a live news broadcast had become the stuff of legend. And not just in Queer World, either. In the pantheon of the greatest moments in TV history, it was up there with Richard Whitely being attacked by a razor-toothed ferret and some bloke in *Only Fools and Horses* falling through a bar-hatch.

'Yeah… well, reading that flyer was like being punched in the stomach,' continued Adam. 'I could hardly believe what I was reading. In Britain! In my own lifetime. I was in a complete daze. In the space of three or four years, I'd come to terms with being gay, got my head around this feckin' awful virus, and then, just when I thought it couldn't get any worse, I discovered that they were trying to outlaw my very existence.

'The next thing I knew, I was sitting on a bench, bawling my eyes out. I remember some bloke coming over and asking me if I was alright. I didn't let on, though. Just said I'd had some really bad news.'

'Well, it wasnae a lie!' said Cameron, reassuringly, a heartbeat away from jumping up and giving his friend a hug, so moved was he by this sensitive new side to him.

In fact, who was this person they'd invited into their home?

And what had they done with the real Adam?

'I can still picture him now,' continued the Irishman. 'Great arse!'

Phew, it was the real Adam after all, thought Cameron to himself. No hugs required. Relieved that the conversation had been pulled back from the emotional cliff edge, he polished off the last of his G&T, reached for a bottle of beer and returned to the earlier discussion about coronavirus.

'So, what's the latest thinking on who's to blame this time around?'

'Well…' began Alex, still on his tablet. 'Seems it's a toss-up between bats or pangolins.'

'Pangolins? Really?' asked Adam, snatching back the tin of chocolate-coated kumquats.

'Aye, I read somewhere that their scales are used in medicine… it's why they reckon it started in Wuhan… something tae di wi the animal markets there,' added Cameron, looking suspiciously at the packet of Szechuan pepper corn chips he'd just opened.

'Just like AIDS!' blurted out the Irishman, before tapping on his mobile. 'They reckon HIV crossed to humans from monkeys and chimpanzees. In Africa somewhere. Back in the

1920s. Look! Here it is. Simian Immunodeficiency Virus. Closely related to HIV.'

Clearly Adam's volunteering for The Sussex Beacon had involved more than sorting through Judy Garland CDs and answering the telephone. Swap his beaten leather jacket and army ID chain for blue scrubs and a stethoscope, and he might have been mistaken for a handsome doctor from a popular medical drama. *Albeit more SCRUFF than scrubs!*

In truth, it wasn't the first time Cameron had had impure thoughts about his friend; compared to the fey campery of his husband, Adam's bearlike demeanour had always been a little bit arousing to Cameron. But the flashes of intellect and sensitivity he was showing today made him even more alluring than usual.

'Oh yeah. I'd totally forgotten about that,' said Cameron, focusing back on what Adam was saying about the link between chimps and HIV.

Until a new thought entered his head.

'Fuck!' he exclaimed. 'Pagan Pete's reading! The one he had in the 80s, around the time that folk started tae get worried aboot AIDS. The same one he had in January this year, which he thinks predicted coronavirus. Perhaps there's something in it after all!'

'You think? What did it say exactly?' asked Adam, putting down his mobile and reaching for the corn chips.

'Dunno,' replied Cameron. 'Ollie was rather fuzzy on the details. But now that the old fella's moved in with George, it shouldn't be too difficult tae find out. Three weeks locked down with a fortune-teller. It's bound to come up at some point, surely.'

What did come up just then was a message on Adam's phone.

'Lock-down – cock-down?' squealed Alex, reading the text before their temporary lodger could grab his mobile off the table.

That proved it. The Irishman in their home was definitively no imposter. And if the pings coming from his friend's phone were anything to go by, he was still very much in demand, even with the closure of bars and clubs.

'OK, I think I'll hit the sack. I've got business to attend to!' said Adam, followed by one of his trademark dirty laughs.

'Mmmmm… no need to consult Pagan Pete to know how his evening's gonna end!' sighed Alex, pulling a face like the smell of gas.

'Ah well, as long as he's only doing it on his phone,' added Cameron, jealously wishing he could follow the Irishman's behind up the stairs.

Chapter Fifteen

Witches, dragons, and jokers!

Monday 23rd March 2020 – George's flat – St. James's Street, Brighton

While Adam was swapping dick pics in Cameron and Alex's guest room, a few hundred yards down the road, George was also enjoying a bit of 'alone' time.

Or rather, he'd decided that instead of listening to Pete divulge the secrets of the Sarsenic Sigils, yet again, it would be a good opportunity to give the toilet a bit of a seeing to.

So, after powdering his nose, he dug out the cleaning things from the cupboard underneath the bathroom sink, slowly lowered himself into a crouching position next to the loo and set about attacking the limescale which had worked its evil on the bowl and rim. *Heavens above! If this is a taste of what it's going to be like being stuck with Pete for the next few weeks, I'll be climbing the walls by the time we're allowed out again,* thought George to himself.

Oh well, at least they'll be super clean. And perhaps even repapered!

Satisfied he'd removed most of the chalky deposit from the ceramic surface, George looked around the bathroom for other tasks to tackle while he was down there. Truth to tell, it wasn't an area that often received much of his attention. In fact, anything below skirting-board level adhered to the old adage 'out of sight, out of mind' – making it a safe haven for any number of creepy-crawlies which had probably set up home in the vicinity.

Assessing that there wasn't anything particularly threatening lurking in the shadows, George sat back on his heels and rested for a moment against the toilet bowl. As he did so, a distant memory floated into his head. From the 1960s, in fact. A brief encounter in a public lavatory. Though, of course, on that occasion, cleaning the toilet wasn't the reason why he'd been kneeling on the floor!

From what he could remember, his cubicle companion worked at a grocery store he often frequented. It was all very cloak and dagger. Or raincoat and brolly, as he recalled that the chap was rather conservatively dressed and most likely straight. It was over in a few minutes, and by the time he'd got up off the floor, the man had already scarpered. *Back to his wife and kids, I expect.* Never saw him in the bogs again. *Probably convinced his missus to go on the pill.* No need to have sex in public lavvies when you could get it at home. *Reckon that's what killed the cottages in the end.* Well, that and the police raids.

Certainly, the threat of arrest was enough to keep George away, after his fumble with the grocer.

But worst of all, he'd also had to shop elsewhere for his ham-on-the-bone!

'Ham-on-the-bone!' he said out loud. How quaint and old-fashioned it sounded.

Hearing the phrase echoing around the toilet bowl, George was suddenly transported back to the present, where, noting an aching in his *own* bones, he decided that he'd done enough cleaning for one day and eased himself up off the floor.

Once he was upright, he turned his good ear towards the bathroom door.

Assuming from the silence which greeted him that Pete's lesson was over, and it was safe to come out at last, George reached for the chain and flushed away the acrid odour of bleach.

But was it over? As the gurgling sound of the refilling cistern subsided, he thought he heard the clinking of glass and someone saying 'Cheers'.

Sadly, his suspicions had been correct, for when he reached the entrance to the lounge it transpired that, far from being over, it was just the intermission.

Grabbing a feather duster from a vase in the hallway, he toyed with the idea of returning to the bathroom. *Perhaps it was time to evict those spiders after all!* But feeling the soreness in his knees, he decided that listening to Pete talk about the Sarsenic Sigils was slightly more preferable.

'Ah, Georgie Boy, just in time for *part deux*,' said Pete, raising his glass. 'What's with the tickling stick? Been brushing up on your Ken Dodd impressions?' he added, nodding towards the feather duster.

'Not quite,' replied George. 'I was going to wage war on the insect colony along the bathroom skirting, but my legs aren't quite what they used to be.'

'No! Mine neither,' howled Pete.

Reminded of his friend's more compromised mobility, George felt a little guilty about being so sniffy about Pete's passion for Paganism. Hilarious circumstances aside, the injuries he'd sustained from the accident were no laughing matter. Whatever he himself thought about Pete's line of work, he knew that his old friend genuinely believed in it. And if he'd found two eager students to enthral with his knowledge, then who was George to snipe from the sidelines. Besides which, his knees really were beginning to swell. That being the case, he put down his tickling stick, poured himself a G&T, and made his way over to his favourite armchair opposite the sofa, where Drew and Ollie were already waiting for the show to resume.

Which, after a theatrical sigh from Pete, it did.

'So, my cherubic students…' he said, glancing flirtatiously at Ollie and Drew. 'Make yourselves comfortable because I'm about to transport you 1500 years back in time.'

Crikey! I'd be happy with 20, thought George to himself, still suffering from the throbbing pain in his joints.

'The Romans are gone, and the people of Britain have returned to their old ways. Old gods. Old beliefs…' began Pete, in a hushed voice, '…for over 50 years, all seems well… until sometime after AD 470… when the red and white striped sails of Saxon warships are spotted in the English Channel.'

Scene set; Pete began to pick up the pace.

'At the helm is a fearsome warrior called Ælle. Behind him, his three sons, Cissa, Cymen and Wlencing. Hell-bent on seizing this land for themselves, the local tribes are no match for these terrifying invaders, and after several raids, those that aren't slain are driven into the thick forests which still cover much of the area.'

Pausing for a moment to wet his whistle, Pete adopted a more 'matter of fact' tone.

'Signalling the end for the Romano-Britons, by the beginning of the 6th-century, the whole area – from the Isle of Wight to Pevensey – became known as the Kingdom of the South Saxons. A stretch of coastline which roughly sits inside the borders of modern-day Sussex.'

'So, are they the ones who came up with the magic symbols?' asked Drew.

'Not exactly. But they are connected. The four suits of the sigils are named after them,' replied Pete. 'They were probably given the names many years later, but they do seem quite fitting given the family's significance to Sussex.

'The important thing is that there were four distinct groups of symbols – each representing one of the four key elements of the ancient world. Mineral, animal, arboreal – relating to trees – and spiritual. 1500 years ago, people were much more in touch with their surroundings, including the very ground upon which they walked. And, of course, there was the supernatural world too. The gods who controlled the weather, the outcome of battles, and the success or failure of crops.'

'Oh yes, I see it now,' said Ollie.

Laid out in four rows of six, aided by Pete's explanation, it was clear from the comment that the images on the cards had begun to reveal themselves.

'This row is Ælle's Six,' continued Pete, waving his hand over the line of cards furthest away from him.

'As the Founding Father of Sussex, he gets the most important group: the suit of cards featuring gods and mystical characters from Norse and Anglo-Saxon folklore.'

After a short pause, Pete tapped the first two cards in the row.

'*Woden* and *Thunar*, the Saxon versions of Viking gods, Odin and Thor, you will probably have heard of,' he said, looking up at his students. 'But the other four will be less familiar, I think.'

Hearing no protests to the contrary, Pete turned his attention to the remaining cards.

'*The Wyrds*, the three witches of fate. *Fenrir,* a savage wolf who was so strong that not even the gods could control him. And *Nicor*, a shape-shifting river-spirit who would lure people to their watery graves.'

'And what about this honey?' asked Ollie, pointing to the final card in the row.

'That's *Bedwig*… the Saxon god of fertility,' replied Pete.

'Phwoar!' woofed Drew. 'Total DILF!'

'Or *Druid* I'd like to fuck!' suggested Ollie with a smirk.

'Only he's a Saxon not a Druid. But as you will see in a moment, the new rulers of Sussex were just as happy borrowing from the Celts as they were from the Norsemen when it came to the sigils,' clarified Pete.

'Ah well, I think I prefer *Thunar*, anyway!' added Ollie, reaching for the second card, which George knew depicted another Hairy Mary, this time brandishing a hammer.

'Looks a bit like that real-life Norse god you used to know. Odi wasn't he called?' asked Drew, in the direction of the armchair by the window.

'God, yeah, total dreamboat,' agreed Ollie.

George knew that the allusion to his old crush was just Drew's little tease. But with all this talk of a new pandemic, being reminded of the friend he'd lost to the last one had him reaching for his comfort blanket.

In other words, his drag queen persona.

'Yes, and we knew quite a few witches back then, too, didn't we, Pete!' he replied, in Bette's sardonic best.

'And one or two of these, for that matter,' added his lockdown lodger, picking up a card which was laid to one side of the others.

For this reason alone, George got the reference.

'Known as *The Scop*, this sigil is the equivalent of the Joker in a traditional pack of cards. He belongs to no particular suit and represents pleasure, entertainment and sociability,' continued Pete.

Phew! thought George to himself, relieved that the focus had returned to the cards.

Confident he was off the hook, he readied himself for the next line of sigils.

'The second row, named after Ælle's son, Cymen, honours the magic which was attributed to trees. As I said earlier, after the Romans left Britain, many of the locals returned to their old belief systems. And one of the most revered was the ogham, a Celtic alphabet used by the Druids which consisted of simple lines and mostly represented trees. Given its popularity when the Saxons first arrived here, it's likely that Cymen's sigils were 'borrowed' from these magical symbols,' explained Pete before tapping the first two cards in the row. 'Like *Honeysuckle*, instilled with the power to help you find inner knowledge. And *Blackthorn*, known as the keeper of dark secrets, its prickly branch suggesting a journey with many challenges.'

Moving onto the next one in the line, the boys sat quietly while Pete explained how *The Ash Tree* was prized by ancient Druids for its ability to heal and transform, making it a popular choice for magic wands.

Yet it was the tree's importance to Norse mythology that the old man was especially keen to impart.

'Sometimes called the *Tree of Life*, it is the one from which Odin – or Woden to the Saxons – hung himself in order to learn the secrets of the runes,' said Pete before tapping the fourth card in the row.

'Next up. *The Yew Tree.*'

Even though George was too far from the coffee table to see the illustration under Pete's finger, the mention of this particular sigil brought to mind the yew that he'd seen on a recent trip to St. Wulfran's in Ovingdean, which, according to the vicar, was almost a thousand years old!

But that wasn't all he'd had to say on the subject. Apparently quite common in graveyards up and down the country, the reason for their popularity amongst Medieval Monty Dons was because of the tree's sprawling roots. In essence, the way they wrapped themselves around recently interred corpses enabled mourners to still feel connected with their departed loved ones.

That was the idea, anyway. For George, the thought of dead bodies entwined in the yew's subterranean entrails was reminiscent of a horror movie he'd watched with Grace back in the 80s. Just the thought of it made him shudder and caused him to reach for the Welsh blanket he always kept on the back of his armchair.

Thankfully, the penultimate card in the row, *The Apple Tree*, was far less ominous. Associated with the mythological Isle of Avalon where, according to legend, apples once grew in abundance, and King Arthur was nursed back to health after some battle or other, he was well aware that this card was usually interpreted as something to do with medicine.

Reminded suddenly of the pills he had to take each evening, George instinctively glanced at his wristwatch. Thrown somewhat by the deathly quiet which had fallen upon the street outside, he was surprised to note that it wasn't quite as late as he'd thought. Panic over, he refocused his attention on the huddle in front of him, where it seemed that Pete had arrived at the last card in Cymen's suit of sigils: the venerable *Oak Tree*.

'Boasting great branches and deep roots, drawing this card means you will be secure and strong in your pursuits…' said Pete studiously before adopting a more mysterious tone. 'But it wasn't only the tree itself that was sacred to the Druids...'

Stopping mid-sentence, he scanned the room from left to right until his gaze fell upon his lockdown landlord in the corner. Or rather, the thing which was leaning against his armchair.

'Chuck us my stick, will you, Georgie Boy?' he requested.

Walking aid handed over, Pete placed the roughly hewn branch between his knees and returned his attention to his pupils.

'The acorn was imbued with great meaning, too,' he said, stroking the bulbous head of the stick before passing it over to Drew.

'Oh Em Gee!' squealed Ollie, the first to notice the significance of Pete's aide-memoire. 'It's a bell-end!'

'Fuck! It is!' added Drew.

Of course, George needed no explanation for the verbal ejaculations of the two boys. Made out of the branch of an oak tree, it had been his friend's constant companion for well over 30 years.

'That's right,' continued the old man, returning to the stick's crowning glory, a later addition crafted by Pete himself. 'To the Druids, the acorn was a powerful symbol of fertility because of the nut's resemblance to the head of a penis – or *bell-end,* as you so eloquently put it! And so sacred were they to our Celtic ancestors, some people believe that Druid priests ate them to aid their powers of divination!'

'Divination?' enquired Drew, handing back the stick.

'As in being able to tell the future,' replied Pete.

'Oh wow! Have you ever… you know…?' asked Ollie.

Suddenly fearful about where this new line of chatter might lead, George coughed loudly and shot his old friend a look which he hoped would read 'Don't you dare!'

Thankfully, it did the trick.

'Oh yes, but let's leave that for another day,' said Pete, taking the hint and moving on to the third row of cards.

Satisfied he'd saved them all from having to listen to Pete talk about his attempt to contact the spirit world while under the supposed influence of Mother Nature's penal-crowned hallucinogens, George unfolded the blanket over his legs and made himself comfortable for the next instalment.

'And this row… Cissa's Six… represents the rocks that made up the very ground upon which our Pagan ancestors walked, for as well as the sarsen stones into which the sigils were carved, the Saxon invaders soon found their new lands to be rich in a multitude of valuable minerals,' began Pete, moving onto the first card in the line-up.

'One found to be in plentiful supply all over Sussex was flint – or *Fyrstone* – as the Saxons called it. And there were few aspects of daily life more important than fire. Heating, eating, metalworking. They all depended on it. No surprise then that the stone which made it all possible was suffused with so much magic.'

'Of course, that's why there are so many flint walls around town,' said Drew.

'And bungaroosh!' added George, referring to the mixture of rocks and stones – almost unique to Brighton – which formed the structure of many of the city's oldest houses.

'Bunga-what?' asked Ollie.

'You might well ask, dear,' replied George. 'Horrible stuff. Flint, rubble, sand – even pebbles. All my walls are made of it. Crumbles as soon as you look at it. One strategically aimed hosepipe and you could wash half of Brighton off the map in an afternoon!'

Choosing to ignore the unruly student in the corner, Pete continued with his lesson.

'And next we have *Ironstone* – from which came the ore needed to make the deadliest weapons of the day. As a consequence, the card bearing the *Ironstone* suggests an upcoming fight.'

Directed towards George, it was clear that Pete had chosen his words specifically to discourage any further interruptions from over by the window.

He needn't have worried.

The remaining cards did not inspire any more comedic outbursts, and over the next few minutes, Pete quickly rattled through the healing qualities of *Crystal*, the purity of *Chalk*, and the longevity of *Mudstone*.

The last card in the row, however, saw a return to a more theatrical Pete as he explained the meaning behind *Salt*: how it owed its importance to the fact that it came from the sea, the thing which had delivered the Saxons to their promised land in the first place.

As captivating as all this might have been to Ollie and Drew, having heard it umpteen times before, George was more than a little relieved when Pete downed the last of his G&T and moved onto the final row.

'Named after Ælle's son, Wlencing, these sigils represent animals which were considered sacred to the Saxons,' said Pete before explaining the meanings behind the *Horse, Boar, Stag, Eagle* and *Bear Sigils.* And though each had its own colourful story, it was clear from the menacing introduction to the last card in the row that Pete was saving the best – or worst – for last.

'And this one here is one of the most feared sigils of all.'

George knew only too well to which card Pete was referring. It was the one from his infamous reading: the tower besieged by a ferocious wolf and a terrifying raven.

But as blood-curdling as Pete's description of *The Wolf Sigil* card was, it seemed that Ollie was more interested in another aspect of the illustration.

'What's with the dome?' he asked. 'Looks a bit like the Pavilion!'

Pete looked over at George.

Returning his stare for a moment too long, it soon became apparent that their conspiratorial glance had not gone unnoticed.

'Oh Em Gee! Is that one of the cards from 'the reading'?' cried Ollie.

'It is, isn't it?' added Drew. 'Oh, come on. You can't leave us hanging after all that. Especially if you think it's got something to do with this shit-fest we've all just entered.'

Adopting the facial expressions of hungry urchins looking through the window of a pie shop, the boys waited expectantly for their answer.

George glanced at his watch.

'Oh, go on then,' he said after a moment or two.

'As you wish,' replied his friend, with an air of playful reluctance.

And while Drew and Ollie made themselves useful refilling everyone's drinks, Pete selected the seven cards which made up 'the reading' and laid them face down on the table.

Joined seconds later by his students with the promised drinks, after a few deep breaths, he reached for the first card in the row...

Chapter Sixteen

We'll meet again

Monday 6th April 2020 – Cameron & Alex's house – Wyndham Street, Brighton

After two weeks of lockdown, the novelty of being creative in the kitchen with whatever was left on the supermarket shelves or seeing what new cocktail you could concoct with the liqueurs gathering dust at the back of your drinks cabinet was beginning to lose its sparkle, and the boys at Wyndham Street had moved onto more innovative ways to kill time.

The most imaginative of these was a board game they'd devised as an antidote to being stuck indoors for most of the day.

True, the location of the house meant they could enjoy their permitted one hour of daily exercise on the beach or in Queen's Park. But the once-bustling gay quarter, clustered around St. James's Street, was now a shadow of its former self: a ghost town of boarded-up pubs and almost deserted streets.

Not so in a game of *'Out!'* – which enabled them to enjoy the former delights of their once buzzy neighbourhood without actually leaving their front room.

Representing the limits of their confinement, the board itself focused upon the district between Upper and Lower Rock Gardens and the Old Steine, edged on either side by Edward Street and Marine Parade. Inside this oblong shape, Cameron had drawn the grid-like network of streets that joined the two main thoroughfares and inserted the names of the area's queer meccas, including Legends hotel and discotheque, the Queens Arms drag bar, and traditional boozers like the Camelford Arms and the Marine Tavern.

In the real world, closed for the foreseeable – in a game of *Out!* still very much alive and kicking.

But it wasn't just the pubs and clubs that had thrown open their doors in this two-dimensional village; there were the businesses which served the community, too.

Popular 'adult' shops, Prowler and Nice 'n' Naughty, were still doing a roaring trade in underwear, sex toys and poppers. And Hunter Florist flower shop and Bone Idol pet emporium continued to tempt patrons inside with their fabulous window displays.

Yet the fun didn't even stop there, for dotted around the main street plan were a series of satellite attractions as well.

To the east, there was the cruising area known as Duke's Mound. And also in that trajectory was the city's sexual health service – the Claude Nicol Centre.

To the west, there was an arrow pointing to places of interest, such as the *Queer the Pier* exhibition at Brighton Museum, LGBTQ+ pubs outside the main quarter, and a popular sauna and massage parlour just a short walk from the Old Steine.

And completing the constellation of satellites, to the north of the village, you had Adam's café-deli, and to the south, an arrow pointed to Plato's Gym, where both he and

Cameron used to pick up weights – and gossip – while training with Ollie.

So, having recreated their pre-pandemic world on a bit of cardboard, the outburst which greeted the Scot on his return from the loo wasn't quite as strange as one might otherwise have thought. Even coming from a 43-year-old man.

'There's a twerking competition at the Charles Street Tap!' shrieked Alex. 'I have to go there immediately to take part!'

'Jeez, I bet Miley's crapping herself!' chuckled Adam, reaching for the dice as Alex moved his counter to the venue that had requested the presence of his ass. According to the card he'd just picked up anyway, which in the game of *Out!* was known as an *Opulence Card* and usually meant some kind of reward.

Also on the board was a pile of *Shade Cards*, which, as the name suggested, was usually some kind of forfeit.

A nod to catchphrases from the famous documentary about New York drag balls, *Paris is Burning*, at one point in the game's incarnation, the boys had flirted with calling it *Brighton is Burning*. But after a short debate, *Brighton is Burning* was out. And *Out!* was in.

Not that it was of any consequence since the route to victory would still have been the same: to visit the locations on the six *Destination Cards* you'd been dealt at the beginning of each game.

Of course, the real joy of *Out!* – and its appeal to the boys – wasn't so much the race to be first past the winning post, but how much mayhem they could cause with the *Shade* and *Opulence Cards*, written anew at the start of each game by the wittiest bitches in the village; the Velociraptors themselves!

All things considered then, taking part in a twerking competition at the Charles Street Tap was pretty tame compared to some of the things they'd come up with to screw each other over.

For example, so far that evening, the *Shade Cards* had sent Alex to the police station to get cautioned for relieving himself in public, decided that Cameron should spend three consecutive goes in Legends for losing his cloakroom ticket, and required Adam to take a detour to the launderette after being shat on by a seagull. A mishap followed moments later by a further delay involving an altercation with a hen party and an inflatable phallus!

In short, the slings and arrows of outrageous misfortune which, before lockdown, occurred almost daily in their particular corner of Brighton.

But it wasn't all bad news.

By virtue of the *Opulence Cards*, Alex had been invited to enjoy shots of Tuaca in the Saint James Tavern – the pub famed for popularising the Italian liqueur in the city. Followed swiftly by a trip to Adam's deli for a 'turmeric-and-cinnamon-baby-woke-a-chino'. Visits which enabled him to get rid of two of his *Destination Cards*. Adam himself had had the pleasure of sending his fellow players on a private tour of the queer exhibition at the museum with Bottomless Pitt, taking them out of *Out!* for two whole rounds. And most fabulous of all, Cameron had received a *Slut Pass*, giving him the opportunity to visit three infamous copping-off hotspots, enabling him to offload half his *Destination Cards* in the bargain!

The fact that you were as likely as your fellow players to pick up one of your own forfeits or rewards only added to the chaos. Indeed, so dramatic were the twists and turns that an hour and a half into play, the boys were level-pegging, with each of them needing to visit just one more venue in order to win.

Next to throw was Adam.

'Five! Yes! Queens Arms, here I come!' shouted the Irishman, moving his yellow plastic counter one square short of entering Brighton's oldest drag bar and prompting him to start a new topic of conversation. 'Ooh, talking of queens, did you watch it?'

'Aye, we did,' replied Cameron, humming the tune to 'We'll Meet Again', guessing that the 'it' to which Adam was referring was the Queen's address to the nation that had been broadcast the night before. A heartfelt pep-talk about the hardships facing the country in which she'd referenced the wartime hit by Forces Sweetheart, Dame Vera Lynn.

Peppered with the same Churchillian language adopted by the prime minister for *his* announcement on the eve of the National Lockdown, HRH's speech had been especially poignant given that she'd actually been alive during the Blitz. Albeit squirrelled away at Windsor Castle for her safety, while her folks had stuck it out at Buckingham Palace.

In point of fact, she'd even compared the address on Sunday evening to the one she and Princess Margaret had made from the same location in 1939. On that occasion for child evacuees, who, like the young royals, had also been separated from their parents by the war.

'Where were yous last night, anyways?' asked Cameron, his homage to Dame Vera's famous tune having come to an end.

But rather than answer, Adam simply tapped the arrow on the board which pointed towards Duke's Mound.

'Seriously, Adam!' exclaimed Alex. 'Do you really think you should be doing that?'

'Don't worry, Mary. I followed the two-metre rule. No physical contact,' replied Adam.

'Ha! Sounds more like the *six-inch rule* to me,' added Cameron with a grin.

'Nah, mate. The chap I was watching was closer to ten!' cackled Adam before realising that his throw meant he had to pick up a *Shade Card.* 'Feck!'

'Go on. What's it say?' jeered Cameron, girding his loins for the expected reversal of fortune which was about to befall the Irishman.

'You have gonorrhoea. Make your way to the clap clinic to get it sorted!' moaned Adam, reading the forfeit.

'Ha! One of mine. Serves you right, y'filthy who-oar! Nae drag for yous tonight,' snorted Cameron, picking up Adam's yellow counter and plonking it on the satellite square denoting the Claude Nicol Centre on the other side of the board.

'Aaaargh, yer feckin' gobshite!' growled the Irishman, taking a swig of beer. 'But I caught it online!'

Still savouring the sweet elixir of scuppering Adam's immediate chances of winning, it took Cameron a moment to realise that his friend wasn't referring to the dose of knob rot he'd just been dealt but to the Queen's promise that we'd 'all meet again'.

'Really moving, I thought,' continued Adam, as Alex grabbed the dice and rolled it on the board. 'You've got to hand it to the old dear. She knows how to work a crowd!'

'Aye, and I bet Dame Vera's greatest hits are racing up the charts faster than y'can say White Cliffs of Dover!' howled Cameron, exposing his Jacobite tendencies.

Though even an ardent supporter of Scottish Independence, like himself, had conceded that Her Majesty's words would have provided some much-needed comfort and reassurance for people. Especially after the recent announcement from the Church of England that all places of worship would remain closed until further notice.

A move which had resulted in clergy up and down the country being dragged kicking and screaming into the 21st century as they worked out how to harness the World Wide Web to stay connected with their flock.

Christ almighty! Y'ken things have got bad when the Father, the Son and the Holy Ghost have tae move their business online! Cameron had joked sacrilegiously on hearing the news.

Not that he was entirely without faith. As a student, he'd flirted with Buddhism. And now there was the new creed on the block: the Sarsenic Sigils. A subject with which he'd become so fascinated since the beginning of lockdown that he'd had Pagan Pete read his fortune no less than three times in the last fortnight.

Starting out as a bit of a giggle, they'd quickly become one of the highlights of his week. And not just for Cameron, either. All the boys had had their fortunes read by George's in-house Oracle. In fact, whether in person – as was the case with Ollie and Drew – or by video call for the Wyndham Street boys, Pete's readings had been a welcome distraction from the distressing situation that was unfolding all around them.

A state of affairs which, if anything, was getting worse by the day.

So much so that even as the Queen gave her broadcast, Prince Charles was self-isolating after being struck down with the virus. And over the past week or so, an increasing number of MPs had also tested positive – including several members of the government.

But perhaps most shocking of all was the news that Prime Minister Johnson had been taken into intensive care, such was the seriousness of his condition.

'Yes!' cried Alex suddenly. 'Revenge!'

Thoughts elsewhere, Cameron had failed to see his husband throw a four, the exact number of steps he needed to get to his final destination, the Revenge nightclub.

'Buggeration,' cursed Cameron, acknowledging the end of the game. 'Good laugh, though. I loved the one about Adam's 'woke-a-chinos'. Alex, you shady bitch!'

'Aye, well, you try running a café on the Queen's Park-Hanover border,' protested Adam defensively. 'And you have to admit, I do make a mean cappuccino.'

'Yeah, in fact, it's a shame you weren't able to bring your fancy espresso machine with you when you moved in here,' said Alex, referring to the deli's 1960s coffeemaker which Adam had rescued from an Italian café in the East End, and lovingly restored to its former glory.

'Aye, but at least you won't want for lentil crisps and organic biscuits. I'll get another load when I pop into the café this week,' promised Adam, talking about the boxes of perishables from the deli that would be approaching their sell-by-dates.

'Gawd yeah. Thank fuck for Ollie's exercise classes,' said Cameron, referring to the online gym their friend had set up in his flat.

'Aye, it's the only thing keeping my bugger grips in check!' laughed Adam. A comment that was somewhat at odds with the Irishman's profiles on the sex apps, which definitely stated that he was a top! But not wanting to admit to having seen them or any of the accompanying photos, Cameron happily went along with the fib and quickly changed the subject.

'Such a shame we cannae introduce Ollie and Drew tae oor wee game here,' he said as he was gathering up the cards.

'Actually, thinking about it, perhaps we can,' suggested Adam. 'Especially now he's set up that overhead camera in his lounge for his online gym classes. Maybe their house could have the board, and we could have the cards. You know, to even things out. We just need some way to distribute the *Destination Cards*, and there's probably some plug-in I can hack for that.'

Yet whilst the thought of harnessing Adam's technical nous to enable the boys to join them in a game of *Out!* was rather appealing – another idea suddenly popped into Cameron's head.

'Or what if… rather than using your skills tae enable us tae create an online version of oor wee game here…'

'Oh feck. You mean the Sarsenic Sigils?' asked Adam.

'Yeah, why not?' quizzed Cameron. 'I mean, I know *Out!* is hilarious. But once we're actually allowed *out*, there's nae way I'm gonna be staying *in*. And how many readings did Pete say he did on the seafront each day? Two or three at the most. Sometimes, none at aw.'

'Aye, something like that,' agreed the Irishman.

'But if yous could build him a website wi a chatroom in which tae di his readings, a bit like the way he's been doing 'em for us, I reckon he'd get loads of interest. From aw over the world,' suggested Cameron.

'And no need for yer man to freeze his bollocks off in that rusty circle down there on the promenade anymore, either!' continued Adam, enthusiastically getting on board Cameron's train of thought.

'Blimey! I think you could be onto something,' interjected Alex, who, for much of the discussion, had been scrolling through his phone. 'Look!' he added, passing it to his husband. 'Tarot-reading sites. There are loads of 'em! Sarsenic Sigils could be the next big craze.'

Alex was right. It was clear that even before lockdown, there'd been a huge market for this kind of thing.

And considering how the pandemic had thrown into question many of life's certainties, it was likely that interest in the old ways of looking at the world would be greater than ever.

'Wow!' said Cameron, his mind already fizzing with ways to rebrand Pagan Pete as some kind of digital Druid.

Fired up by the chance to flex his advertising muscles, he boxed up the bits and pieces which went with their board game and reached for his laptop. Opening up a new document, he looked around the room for inspiration.

'Yes! Cracked it!' he exclaimed, after spotting the gold embossed spines of his volumes of J R R Tolkien's *Lord of the Rings* trilogy in the bookcase at the far end of the lounge…

THE FELLOWSHIP OF THE SARSENIC SIGILS

Chapter Seventeen

House of cards

Wednesday 15th April 2020 –
Izzy's house – Bear Road, Brighton

<u>Lockdown – To-Do List – Week Three</u>

Learn how to make banana bread. *Tick.*
Get bike from shed. *Tick.*
Clear out broom cupboard. *Tick.*
Tidy attic. *Tick.*
Learn how to use sewing machine. *Tick.*
Put photos in albums. *Tick.*
Do a reading with Sarsenic Sigil Cards.

'Mmmm…' pondered Izzy, as her pen hovered over the last item on that week's 'to-do' list.

Jobs she thought she'd never get around to tackling. Crafts she assumed she'd never have time to master. The latest batch of tasks, which, thanks to the lockdown, had now been successfully ticked off.

Truth be told, the house had never been more spick and span. The oven rarely cold. And thanks to her newly acquired sewing skills, the dining room table now boasted a neatly hemmed cover!

Fortunate really, since breakfast, lunch and supper had become key highlights of the day. No longer rushed, picked at, or simply ignored. But focal points at which she, Ken, Josh and Kwan would gather to discuss the zeitgeist.

Over sourdough pancakes, they trawled through the grim statistics of deaths and hospitalisations caused by the virus. While munching sourdough sandwiches, they shared human interest stories and conspiracy theories they'd found on the web. And after gorging on sourdough pizzas, they retired to the lounge to binge-watch whichever boxset they'd chosen that evening.

In fact, with so many of their meals containing this 'miraculous' ingredient, it was hard to imagine just how they'd managed to survive without it for so long.

Yet at that precise moment on Day 24 of the National Lockdown, this was not the question which occupied Izzy's thoughts, for there was still one task on her 'to-do' list that remained unticked.

'Where could they be?' she wondered out loud, realising that it was over three weeks since she'd ordered Pete's book and a set of Sarsenic Sigil fortune-telling cards.

But no sooner had she asked the question than she got her answer.

Not by way of a vision or a mystical sign, which would, perhaps, have been more appropriate, but from the sound of something heavy landing on the welcome mat in the hall. She put down her pen and rushed to the front door. A few moments later, box and book pushed to one side, Izzy was staring at a full set of brightly coloured Sarsenic Sigil Cards.

'Que interesante,' she said, falling into her native Spanish, which she did very occasionally when she was alone. Indeed, the delivery couldn't have happened at a more convenient moment as Ken, Josh and Kwan had gone for a walk up Whitehawk Hill, allowing her to immerse herself in her new obsession without interruption.

To call it an obsession was no exaggeration either. In the first days of lockdown, Izzy had combed the internet for information about the magical symbols of the Saxons. As illuminating as George's account of the reading had been, it covered only seven of the 25 cards, so she was eager to discover what she could about the remaining 18. And even more exciting was the thought that she might have stumbled upon Brighton's newest fad. The lockdown wouldn't last forever. She could use the time to memorise their meanings, and when allowed out again, she would organise a series of fortune-telling parties with herself as Mistress of Ceremonies.

In fact, so driven had she been by her hunger for both knowledge and popularity that in the time which had passed since ordering the book and cards, Izzy had already unearthed quite a lot about the strange signs which seemed peculiar to Sussex.

Of course, there was nothing quite like being in the presence of the real thing. So, for almost half an hour, her eyes darted from image to image until, satisfied that she'd familiarised herself with them all, she reached for the accompanying book.

'Sarsenic Sigil Cards. Unlocking the Magic Code of the Anglo-Saxons by Peter Sissinghurst,' she whispered deferentially under her breath before adopting a more flippant tone. 'Or Pagan Pete to friends!'

Although, she soon realised that *his* wasn't the only name she recognised.

As she turned to the dedication page, her eyes fell upon another with whom she'd recently become acquainted.

I dedicate this edition to my dear friend Odi Olafson and all the other beautiful souls I knew whose lives were cut short by AIDS.

Intrigued by this glimpse into the past, Izzy scanned the opposite page for a publication date. 1992. *How long after Odi's death was that? Didn't George say he'd died in early 1987?* She was certain it had been quite a few years before doctors had begun using combinations of antiretroviral drugs to fight the onset of the disease.

Just how many thousands of lives had been cut short before then was impossible to say.

Let's hope they're a bit quicker this time around!

At least with coronavirus, the world's governments did seem to be on the case, pumping billions into research and healthcare.

Reassured that the response to *this* pandemic was far more robust than it had been to the *last* one, Izzy turned to the Contents page.

'OK, Mr Sissinghurst, let the unlocking begin!' she said as she scrutinised the list.

Chapter One – The history of Paganism.
Chapter Two – Decoding symbols and cyphers.
Chapter Three – The continuing allure of divination.

A cursory glance at the titles of the first three chapters promised nothing she hadn't already discovered for herself on the internet. Indeed, given the book's publication date, she suspected that her own research was probably more comprehensive!

Buoyed up by this self-belief, Izzy skipped to the chapter on how to do an actual reading.

Information absorbed, she gathered up the cards, shuffled them and laid the top seven face down in a row on the table.

Satisfied she'd done it correctly, she turned over the first one in the formation, which, according to the diagram in the book meant 'the past'.

Placing her spectacles on the end of her nose, she studied the illustration of three robed women beneath a twisted and knobbly tree. Known as *The Wyrds*, she knew from her research that they were supposedly blessed with the power to control fate. In fact, she'd read somewhere that they were the inspiration for Shakespeare's three witches in the Scottish play.

Pleased with the idea that her past was somehow connected with these three mysterious women, Izzy smiled at the drawing and moved on to the next card in the row, which represented 'the present'.

Depicting a large pig, *The Boar Sigil* wasn't quite as appealing. Though after reading that the card alluded to friends or family coming to your aid during a difficult time, she felt that it was a fair summation of her current situation. Perhaps there's more to this than meets the eye. Piggy or otherwise.

Representing 'the future', the next card she turned over featured a wolf climbing an onion-dome-topped tower. The same as the third one in Pete's now infamous reading from the mid-80s. Izzy felt a shudder down her spine. But hearing the cat flap rattling away at the end of the hall, she attributed it to the gust of wind their tabby had let in rather than someone walking over her grave. Warmed by this thought, Izzy moved on to card number four, that according to the blurb in the book, was the most important in the formation, signifying the thing which must be overcome. That being so, considering the weight attached to it, coming face-to-face with *The Mudstone Sigil* fell somewhat short of her expectations.

After three witches, two fearsome-looking beasts and an exotic tower, the image of an ammonite was a little underwhelming. Perhaps the book would provide more sizzle, she mused as she studied the relevant page.

Shoving her glasses further up her nose, she read the short paragraph out loud.

'*Mudstone* – meaning stability and longevity. Ideal for preserving flora and fauna, mudstones are associated with fossils. As such, *The Mudstone Sigil* suggests the return of some event, thing or person connected with the distant past.'

Ooh, that's more like it, thought Izzy to herself. And on closer inspection, the image on the card was rather similar to a framed drawing she'd ummed and ahhed over in a gift shop on the promenade at Lyme Regis, the pretty seaside resort which she and her husband, Ken, had visited the previous year.

Reminded of the current restrictions they were all living under, Izzy's thoughts drifted back to that wonderful weekend. And to the reason why she'd decided not to buy the print.

What would Mary have thought? she recalled tutting to Ken while they'd been perusing the establishment's display of ammonite fossils; her academically snobbish inner saboteur, offended by the touristy repackaging of the town's history, which owed much to the 19th-century palaeontologist, Mary Anning.

Yet whilst Izzy often said that regrets ought to be reserved for dinner invitations alone, looking at the image on the card before her, she couldn't help wishing she'd bought that framed illustration. And picked up a souvenir fossil too.

'Ha-Ha-Ha!'

Still thinking about her and Ken's trip to the Dorset coast, at first, the cry of a seagull somewhere nearby didn't seem particularly out of place. But remembering, after a few seconds, that their house was quite some distance from the seafront, she was struck by how common the sound had become in her neck of the woods recently. Perhaps the sudden loss of tourists to the city was depriving the birds of their main source of food, that is to say, chips, and they'd been forced to look further afield for their supper.

And also to broaden their culinary repertoire.

So much so that there'd even been sightings of gulls diving for fish in the sea itself.

What was the world coming to!

The one she'd heard in the street had no doubt decided that pecking through the mountains of takeaway pizza boxes overflowing from every recycling bin in the neighbourhood was easier than venturing into the thing after which it was named.

Putting thoughts of Lyme Regis to the back of her mind, Izzy returned her attention to the card bearing the image of an ammonite. *But what could it mean?* The book said that it foretold the return of some event or person connected with the distant past. Given that most countries had closed their borders and travel was restricted even within counties, a visitor was highly unlikely. No. It had to mean the return of an event.

For the second time that morning, she felt a chill.

Not a gust of wind entering through the cat flap this time, but a shiver caused by the memory of what George had said Pete feared was foretold by his recent reading.

Was coronavirus going to be as devastating as AIDS?

Her heart pounding a little faster, she reached for the fifth card in the series with a little more caution. But before she could get back to the task of unlocking the magic code of the Saxons, the sound of something more prosaic being opened entered her ears.

Ken, Josh and Kwan had returned from their hike.

Hearing the kerfuffle in the entrance hall, Izzy unceremoniously gathered up the cards on the table and shoved them into the small tote bag they'd come with.

'Appearing' to be blessed with the gift of divination would take a little bit more practice!

To that end, by the time her husband had made his way into the kitchen, everything was safely packed away, and for all intents and purposes, Izzy was 'absorbed' in an article about Georgian snuffboxes in the latest issue of *History Now*.

'Well, you'll never guess who we bumped into on Whitehawk Hill,' announced Ken, plonking himself down in the chair opposite Izzy.

Not particularly interested in tobacco-related silverware and knowing that the area where they'd been walking was near a Neolithic camp, she decided to humour him.

'Oh, I don't know, darlink. Neil Oliver? Tony Robinson? Mary Anning?'

'Ha! Oddly enough, you're not too far off the mark,' he replied. 'How about if I said dinosaurs…'

Immediately getting the reference, she dropped the pretence of reading and placed the magazine down on the table.

'Cameron? What was Chief Velociraptor doing up there?' she asked as casually as she could manage.

'Looking for some ancient tree. Pagan apparently,' replied Ken.

'Pagan?' repeated Izzy, alerted to the word that seemed to be on everyone's lips these days. Second only to coronavirus, in fact!

'Yes, according to the old fella who's staying with George,' added her husband.

'Pagan Pete?' asked Izzy, somewhat confirming her previous point but also a little concerned that Cameron and the fortune-teller were acquainted.

Just like him to annex the source of the ominous reading before she'd even had the chance to get a look in.

'Yes, of course. That's his name. To be honest, between the face mask and social distancing, it was hard to make out what he was saying, but now you come to mention it, I think that's what he said he was called,' replied Ken, pulling off one of his socks.

'Pagan Pete was there? On Whitehawk Hill? Doesn't he use a wheelchair?' queried Izzy, still trying to sound less intrigued than she actually was.

'Yes. But I doubt he wheeled himself up there, dear! I imagine they all went together in Cameron's people carrier,' suggested Ken, with more than a smattering of sarcasm.

'All?' exclaimed Izzy, finding it increasingly difficult to feign a *lack* of interest in what her husband was telling her.

'Yes, dear. Adam was with them too. He's staying at Cameron and Alex's at the moment.'

'Good Lord! How many were there at this super-spreader event?' she cried.

Ken stopped removing his other sock and smiled benignly at his wife.

'Just the three, my sweet. No need to call the corona police! Rather decent of them really, don't you think? Taking the old man up there for a bit of fresh air.'

Izzy was fully aware that Adam had moved in with his fellow Velociraptors for the duration. But she also knew there was more to this than 'care in the community'. Maybe George might know something. Or Meena, even. She and Adam were besties from way back and were still as thick as thieves. Perhaps she should take a trip out to Rottingdean to see if her sister-in-law knew what the Witches of East Cliff were up to.

Racking her brains as to why the boys were so interested in an old tree, suddenly it came to her. The image of *The Wyrds* – the three witches of fate. Weren't they seated beneath a tree that was supposed to be hugely significant in Norse mythology? If only she could get a sneak at her new book.

She was about to make her excuses and retreat upstairs when...

'An old oak tree!' exclaimed Ken, referring back to what Cameron had said they were looking for. 'Apparently, the name Whitehawk is nothing to do with hawks at all. It's a Saxon word meaning 'holy oak'. To be honest, I didn't fancy hanging around. I know we were outside and everything, but until they know how this thing spreads, I didn't want to get too close. And besides, I wanted to get back to mow the lawn.'

Izzy could hardly believe what she was hearing.

Not Ken's concerns about the virus or cutting the grass, but rather the sudden interest that Cameron and Adam were showing in Paganism – and the sound of her dreams of becoming Brighton's High Priestess of Anglo-Saxon Magic crashing around her ears.

She had to find out what they were up to.

There was only one thing for it. A trip to Rottingdean to see if Meena knew anything.

But that wasn't the only thing driving her decision to break the law.

Her mind still awash with images from the cards she'd just cleared away, a new thought came into view.

The Wolf Sigil card.

In the fateful reading from the 1980s, the dome-topped tower had been interpreted as representing the Royal Pavilion and, by association, Brighton itself. But in her own reading, it could just as easily have been the ruined tower which the girls had recently renovated and made into their home.

Remove the cupola, and the similarity was uncanny.

The cards had spoken. Lockdown rules or not, first chance she had tomorrow, she would call on Meena and Maria.

Chapter Eighteen

Knot in my backyard!

Wednesday 15th April 2020 – Ollie's flat – St. James's Street, Brighton

By the time Ken had inadvertently alerted Izzy to Cameron and Adam's 'kidnapping' of the old fortune-teller, Pete had been safely returned to George's flat, and the boys were ready to report back to the other members of the *Fellowship of the Sarsenic Sigils* team.

'Yer on mute!' cried Ollie, doing an impression of what could best be described as a fish singing into a microphone.

Thankfully, Cameron understood what his friend was trying to communicate and turned on his mic.

'Can ye hear me noo, laddie?' asked Cameron in his familiar Scottish brogue.

But was it familiar? Although the two friends lived just a few hundred metres from each other in Kemptown, under lockdown rules, they may as well have been on different planets. Of course, they'd had the odd catch-up through Ollie's kitchen window whenever Cameron had popped down to the supermarket at the bottom of St. James's Street. But doorstep chats were a bit too public for their usual topics of discussion, so these laptop hook-ups had become a regular feature of their week.

'I'm dying to hear about your trip up Baker's Bottom,' said Ollie, using the name which locals called the area of woodland where Cameron, Adam and Pete had been earlier that day.

'Aye, shame y'couldnae join us. I heard they're fining people for sitting on the beach, so I thought it best to keep numbers tae a minimum. Especially as we'd already got one person from a different household. Best no push oor luck too much. But I think you'll be happy wi the wee snaps we took,' assured Cameron.

The 'wee snaps' to which the Scot was referring were needed for *The Fellowship of the Sarsenic Sigils* website, that had progressed at speed since Pete had agreed to get on board. Driven in part, no doubt, by the desire to take his life's work to the four corners of the globe without having to brave the seagulls and gale-force winds on the seafront. But also, perhaps, by the prospect of making a bit of cash. Whatever his motivation, Pete had given the project his full blessing, and Adam had begun building the website that was at the heart of the enterprise.

In fact, with not much else to occupy him, by mid-April he'd got to the stage where he needed a few images. So, when Pete mentioned an oak tree up on Whitehawk Hill which was deemed holy by local Pagans, a photoshoot had been arranged under the pretext of helping an old man get a bit of exercise.

At least that is what they'd agreed to say had they been challenged by any lockdown law enforcers.

'As it happened, we didnae need t'have worried. There were loads of people up there. Bumped into Ken and Josh, in fact. Kwan, too. And no a single community police officer in sight,' said Cameron.

'Crikey. Though it's unlikely they'd have come down heavily on a couple of fellas out walking with a bloke using a wheelchair,' suggested Ollie. 'Not when they saw who it was. Be terrified he'd turn 'em into frogs or something.'

'Aye, if only his mastery of the occult stretched that far. I could think of a few candidates I'd like tae put forward,' sniggered Cameron as Adam appeared on the screen.

'Hello, ladies,' growled the Irishman from the desk which Ollie recognised as the one in Cameron and Alex's guest room. 'Did Pete enjoy his little outing?'

'Dunno, went straight to bed when he got in,' replied Ollie. 'According to George, he looked proper done in.'

'Jaysus, I don't know why,' began Adam. 'Just sat on his hole, barking orders at us both. It's me and Cameron who should be knackered.'

'And who knew there was a mini forest up there?' said Cameron, returning to the conversation about Baker's Bottom.

'Aye, if they ever get rid of Duke's Mound, it'd make a great replacement,' chuckled Adam.

But despite the mirth that accompanied this last comment, Ollie suspected he wasn't entirely joking about it being a potential location to meet strangers for casual sex.

'Ha! If it wasnae for the sheep,' added Cameron.

'God yeah, wouldn't want to get into a tussle with one of them woolly aul hoors,' agreed Adam.

'Y'say that. But if this lockdown goes on much longer, you might be glad of the attention!' laughed Cameron.

'Will I, yeah?! Don't you believe it. Phone's never been busier,' replied Adam, referring to the 'dating' apps he was on. 'All this working from home seems to be making everyone even more horny than usual.'

'So, anyway…' said Ollie abruptly, in an attempt to shift the chatter away from Adam's favourite subject. *Definitely one thing he hadn't missed as a result of the temporary embargo on their weekly training sessions at Plato's Gym.* 'Did you manage to find out anything more about Pete's oak tree?'

'Aye, loads,' confirmed Adam. 'More than you can shake a stick at, ha ha. It even has its own social media profile!'

'Nae shit, that's priceless,' said Cameron. 'Better no have more followers than me. What's the handle?'

'It's Vied underscore ac,' replied Adam.

'Eh?' queried Cameron.

'Upper case V lower case i e d underscore a c – both in lower case,' clarified Adam. 'You know, Saxon for 'holy oak'. Where Pete said Whitehawk gets its name from. In fact, it's got a photo of a Dara Knot next to it.'

'A *what* knot?' asked Ollie.

'This!' replied Adam, rising out of his seat and pushing down his jeans and underpants just far enough to reveal a tattoo of an intertwining rope design at the top of his groin.

Slightly distracted by the silvery grey pubic hair peeping over the band of the Irishman's Y-fronts, Ollie realised from the stirring in his own groin area that there was at least one thing he did miss about their weekly sessions. And the money, of course. Although, thanks to the recent handout from Dishy Rishi, he was safe from Adam's incessant tirade of dad jokes for a little while yet.

And from the wolf at his door!

'Oh, I see!' said Ollie, fidgeting in his seat as Alex appeared behind Cameron's head.

'So, what are you boys up to?' asked the new arrival as he budged up next to his husband. 'I see Adam hasn't quite grasped the rudiments of *face*-timing yet.'

'Very amusing,' said the Irishman, tucking his shirt back into his jeans. 'I was just showing them my Dara Knot.'

'*Dora who?* Sounds like a drag queen,' quipped Alex, 'Oh, your tattoo. Why, pray tell, were you showing them your tramp stamp?'

'Feck yous. I'm helping Cameron look for the social media profile of that old oak up Baker's Bottom,' replied Adam, back in his seat. The potential for innuendo offered by this last comment was not lost on Ollie, but before the Irishman had a chance to capitalise on it, Cameron found what he was looking for.

'Wow! Over 2,000 followers! No bahd for a bit of auld wood,' he said, notably impressed. 'And what's the significance of this Dara Knot?'

'Well,' began Adam. 'Celtic. Obvs. The design is based on the roots of an oak; to the Druids, the most sacred of all the trees.'

'Ahhh, like Pete's walking stick. It's made from the branch of an old oak!' interjected Ollie.

'Oh aye, the one he had with him today… with the bell-end,' contributed Adam, predictably.

'Fuck, yeah. What's that all aboot?' asked Cameron.

'Well, it's not a bell-end exactly…' replied Ollie. 'It's supposed to be an acorn. But the similarity is no accident. Apparently, the medical term for the head of a penis is glans. From the Latin word for acorn. Because of the shape.'

'Eh?' asked Alex.

'Like your bell-end. You *bell-end!*' snorted Adam.

His thoughts returning to the evening when Pete had explained to him and Drew about the significance of the oak, Ollie suddenly remembered another tantalising fact.

'Yeah, in fact, according to Pete, some people believe that the Druids ate acorns to help them with their divination.'

Since this wasn't a word which passed often from Ollie's lips, he happily let it hang in the air for a second or two so he could enjoy the bemused looks on the faces in the tiny screens in front of him. Moment cherished, he continued.

'You know, predicting the future.'

'Feck!' exclaimed Adam suddenly. 'That's what he was doing with his stick this afternoon. Remember I said I thought he was drawing sigils. It wasn't that at all. He was raking the soil for acorns.'

'What? In April?' asked Cameron incredulously.

In truth, it did seem pretty unlikely, and the focus returned to the shoot, until…

'Look!' demanded Adam, sharing his screen to show them all a website he'd found while Cameron had been talking Alex and Ollie through the photos he'd taken. 'It says here that you might be able to find good acorns even in late spring. As long as the flesh is white and free from mould.'

'Aye, well, it *has* been pretty mild these last few months, I suppose,' said Cameron.

'Sneaky bastard. I wonder what yer man's planning,' mused Adam.

'Maybe he'll go into a trance and start speaking in tongues?' squealed Ollie.

'Oooh yes. Praps he'll try and get in touch with that Danish bloke from the 80s. Odi wasn't he called?' asked Alex.

George's photos of the parties at Hazelpits had been the subject of one of their video calls, so the Viking god to whom he was referring was familiar to them all.

'That blond chap with the tash?' piped in Adam. 'God yeah, I'd let him *tongue* me anytime. He was feckin' gorgeous.'

'Aye. I wouldnae mind 'channelling' him myself,' added Cameron.

'No way, mate, he was definitely a top,' guffawed Adam. 'Written all over his face.'

'What about his mustard hanky?' interjected Alex. 'Left pocket, wasn't it? That means you *want* 8 inches, not that you've *got* 8 inches.'

'Aye, trust yous to remember that,' said Cameron, with a sideways glance.

'Well, I'd be happy to park my long boat in his harbour any day,' roared Adam.

Sensing from the hilarity caused by the talk of hot Vikings and the size of their longboats that it would only be a matter of time before the Irishman began regaling them all with tales of his latest pillaging on Duke's Mound, Ollie promised to see what he could find out from Pete and ended the call.

As he did so, he suddenly became aware of unusually loud footsteps on the floor above. And music, too. Intrigued by what might be the cause, he changed out of the onesie he'd had on since breakfast and made his way upstairs.

Living as one household since the beginning of lockdown, George rarely closed the door to his flat anymore, and a polite 'helloooo' had replaced the need to knock. But since the noise coming from inside would have drowned out both, on this occasion, Ollie made his way to the commotion without announcement to find George crisscrossing the room to a song whose principal lyrics seemed to be 'Boom boom… boom boom!"

'Oliver Simpson!' cried George, more than a little out of breath. 'Trying to steal my moves, are we, you naughty boy! How long have you been standing there?'

'I just got here…' began Ollie.

'Sorry, dear?' asked George, lurching towards the gramophone to turn down the crackly old record.

'I said, I just got here…' repeated Ollie, a little louder.

'Mmmm… I believe you… thousands wouldn't!' said George.

Not entirely sure what his neighbour meant, Ollie smiled and looked around the room for some way of changing the subject. Noticing the discarded sleeve on top of the record player, he saw his opportunity and picked it up to see if he recognised the singer whose dulcet tones George had just been dancing along to.

He didn't.

'Who is she, anyway?' he asked, nodding at the photo of a woman with long curly hair. 'Bit different from your usual…'

Unsure how best to describe the hotch-potch of show tunes and ballads that was George's usual playlist, Ollie decided to let his sentence fade away like the song had just done.

'*Who is she?* Not the cat's mother, dear!' shrieked George, pursing his lips.

Another phrase, which, like his neighbour's music collection, belonged to a bygone age!

'*She*, my dear, is Scotland's premier disco diva, Kelly Marie, with her number one smash-hit, 'Feels Like I'm In Love'.'

'Boom boom, boom boom!' added Pete with a reprisal of what Ollie had heard earlier.

'I haven't listened to it in years. But back in the early 80s, it was everywhere. And when they played it at Hazelpits, the crowd went nuts. Had its own dance routine, too,' continued George.

'Yes, so I saw…' began Ollie before realising this slightly contradicted his earlier claim to have missed the floorshow.

George glowered at him playfully from across the room.

'Oh, don't worry, I only saw a few seconds. Your moves are safe,' Ollie assured his neighbour. 'At least until Legends opens up again. Though actually it was Pete I wanted to steal.'

'Not for my moves, I hope!' scoffed George's temporary lodger.

'Don't worry, *your* moves are safe, too,' replied Ollie. 'It's about your walking stick.'

'My walking stick? What about it?' asked Pete, reaching for the item in question.

'Mmmmm… sounds a bit daft now that I'm stood in front of you, but on the shoot this afternoon…' began Ollie.

'Yes, cherub, spit it out,' encouraged the old man.

'The thing is… Adam seems to think you were raking through the soil for something… you know, beneath that old oak tree…' continued Ollie before being interrupted mid-sentence.

'Well, he'd know all about that, wouldn't he! From what you've told me, Adam's no stranger to poking around in the undergrowth himself,' said Pete mischievously.

'Ha! You're not wrong there,' agreed Ollie, happy to share a joke at his friend's expense before returning to the matter at hand. 'It's just that… well, at first he thought you were drawing something. But then I mentioned what you'd said about the Druids eating acorns as part of their magic rituals. How it made them extra sensitive to the spirit world or something… and so we thought perhaps you were looking for… well… you know…'

Feeling increasingly like he was barking up the wrong tree. Or more accurately, underneath it! Ollie was about to drop the whole subject when…

'Oh Pete! You old fool!' cried George. 'Do you really want a repeat of what happened in Copenhagen? You know how well that ended. Besides which. Foraging for acorns at this time of year! Don't you think the NHS have got enough on their plate at the minute!'

Oh Em Gee. Adam was right. Pete had been looking for acorns. But what did George mean by 'last time'? There was only one way to find out.

'Copenhagen? Why, what happened in Copenhagen?' asked Ollie, hoping that there was more to this story than a bit of food poisoning.

George and Pete exchanged one of their conspiratorial glances.

'Oh, go on then. You already know half the story. You may as well know the rest,' replied George, eventually.

'Ooh, that sounds intriguing!' said a new voice. 'Looks like I've turned up just in time!'

Caught up in the discussion about acorns, the appearance of Drew in his motorcycle gear took them all by surprise. Especially George, whose startled look was that of someone who'd just seen a ghost.

'Sorry, I didn't mean to make you jump. I did knock,' apologised the Welshman.

'Oh, don't worry about me, dear. It's just that…' began George, putting on his glasses. 'I haven't seen you in your leathers before. You reminded me of...'

'Fuck yes,' interrupted Pete. 'He's the image of him.'

Like lots of men during lockdown, the closure of barber shops had forced Drew to rethink his usual hairstyle, and in place of the closely cropped buzz-cut that he'd had since his army days, he now sported a medium-length short back and sides with a matching moustache in a hue which was somewhere between ginger and light brown. So light, in fact, that caught in the shaft of late evening sunshine which pierced the lounge at that moment, it had an iridescent strawberry blond glow about it.

Ollie knew immediately to which particular ghost they were referring: their friend Odi!

'A proper Sussex Lancer!' exclaimed George.

'Quite a coincidence, too, don't you think?' added Pete.

'I'll say,' agreed George, as the beam of light disappeared, and the golden-haired Viking from Valhalla returned to being just a brown-haired mechanic from the Valleys.

It was more than Ollie could bear.

'Coincidence?' he shouted at both of them. 'What is?'

'Calm down, dear, anyone would think you'd just seen a ghost!' chided George.

Copenhagen. Acorns. Drew's leathers. Finally, the pieces of the jigsaw fell into place.

'Oh fuck. The last time you did a reading on acorns. You were with your friend Odi, weren't you?' cried Ollie.

'Acorns?' chipped in Drew, taking a moment to catch up. 'Oh right, yeah. Druid drugs! What they took to help with their divination.'

'And did they? Help, I mean?' asked Ollie.

'Well, the jury's still out on that one, dear,' replied George. 'But if you'd be kind enough to make me a G&T, I'll tell you my version of what happened.'

And after a few moments, that's exactly what he did.

Chapter Nineteen

Something is rotten in the state of Denmark

Friday 9th August 1985 – Frederiksberg Gardens – Copenhagen, Denmark

In the weeks following Pete's reading at Whispers in August 1984, his gloomy premonition started to come true.

The first person from Brighton known to have died from AIDS was recorded soon afterwards, and by the end of that year, there were at least 20 people registered with the Brighton & Hove HIV Clinic.

Indeed, such was the speed at which the virus had taken hold, 12 months after Pete's reading, the number of people known to be infected in the town was already at least double that.

But with little assistance from elsewhere, it soon became apparent that any help beyond medical care would have to come from the community itself. So, following a public meeting, where it was decided that the most pressing need was to provide advice for people who'd tested positive, a new organisation was formed called the Sussex AIDS Helpline.

Joining shortly after the service was set up, George and Grace had been spending more and more of their evenings at the Helpline, which had quickly become the first port of call for any questions relating to the virus.

What were the symptoms? How did you go about getting tested? What kind of sex was most risky?

With so few places offering information, it was as much a lifeline as a helpline.

And during opening hours, the phones hardly ever stopped ringing.

So much so that Grace and George had been in two minds about whether they should go ahead with their plans to visit Odi in Copenhagen.

But reassured by the other volunteers that they could manage without them for a few days, the pair had stuck to their guns, and together with Pete, they were now enjoying a well-earned break in the stunning capital of Denmark.

Just a short plane ride from the UK, Copenhagen in August was a world away from the horrors which were unfolding in Brighton. Not that AIDS hadn't hit Denmark yet. It was just that the unfamiliarity of the city left little room for them to think about anything but the sights, sounds and smells which greeted their eyes, ears and noses.

The ornately decorated townhouses. The tranquil canals. The sweet smell of pancakes. And the snatched conversations in a strange language.

A welcome change from the haunted faces in the bars, the sound of people sobbing at the other end of the Helpline phone, and the smell of disinfectant, which seemed to have gradually replaced fish and chips as the prevailing odour of Brighton over the last few months.

In fact, since arriving in the city, George's senses had been working overtime. After settling them in at his gorgeous townhouse, Odi had arranged supper aboard a canal boat. A marvellous treat in itself, it had also been the perfect way for them to get a feel for the city without running the risk of being mowed down by one of the many cyclists who, it appeared, had commandeered every spare bit of pavement, footpath and bridge.

But as well as being practical, it was magical, too!

From his viewing spot beneath the road, the unfeasibly tall houses had looked more like drawings from the pages of a Hans Christian Anderson book of fairy tales than bricks, wood and mortar. And as if to land the point, the excursion had also taken in the famous statue of the Little Mermaid, one of the storyteller's most adored creations.

On day two, George and Pete had spent the morning in the city's main museum and the afternoon sampling the delights of Tivoli – Copenhagen's popular fairground park – while Grace and Odi had driven over to the clinic where more than a decade earlier she'd been a patient, and he, a young surgeon.

In fact, after 48 hours of sightseeing, the picnic that Odi had laid on for them in the stunning Frederiksberg Gardens was just what the doctor ordered.

Especially for George and his aching feet.

And judging by the gentle snoring which he could hear amongst the chatter of the birds, it seemed that he wasn't the only one who'd been in need of a rest; a state of relaxed calm owed in no small part to the generous lunch that Odi had served up and the several glasses of sparkling wine with which they'd washed it down. But that wasn't all. Their host had also packed a bottle of Copenhagen's famous cherry liqueur, a favourite of the locals for years and, as it turned out, a tipple for which Gracie had an especial fondness.

George observed the scene before him for a few moments and gave a contented sigh. After the trauma of the last few months, the sight of his friends enjoying a little peace and quiet with their own thoughts under the branches of a large oak tree a few hundred yards from the impressive Frederiksberg Palace was truly a sight for sore eyes.

Feeling a sudden urge to capture it for posterity, he propped himself up on his elbows and reached for Pete's camera.

Making sure all his friends were in shot, George pressed the button and took the photo.

Just in the nick of time as it turned out, for the second he did so, one of the figures in the tableau of serenity before him suddenly sprang to life.

'Hill of a fool,' announced Odi, getting up from his horizontal position.

Alerted by the notion that he'd just been insulted, George put down the camera and focused in on his friend.

"Tulehøj'. It's what Frederiksberg used to be called before the Palace was built,' continued Odi, pointing towards the immense building in the near distance. *"Høj'* is Danish for high. And *'tule'* or *'thyle'* refers to a member of the ancient royal household whose job it was to entertain everyone with stories and such like. A bit like your court jester or fool. So, a rough translation could be 'hill of a fool.'

Ah, *hill*. Not *hell!* thought George to himself.

Satisfied he'd not been slandered after all, he was just about to say how beautiful he thought it all was when Pete beat him to it with a contribution of his own.

'Like the Saxon word 'scop',' he said from his wheelchair, that was parked halfway between the picnic blanket on which Odi and George were camped and the oak tree.

'I guess so,' agreed their host. 'In fact, the word for storyteller is one of the oldest in the Danish language. Etched on the *Snoldelev Runestone*, even.'

'The *what* runestone?' asked George.

'Snol-del-ev,' repeated Odi, spelling it out one syllable at a time.

George wasn't sure whether it was the wine or his friend's accent, but the sound and sight of the Dane talking in his native tongue reawakened the attraction he'd felt for him on the evening of their first meeting at Hazelpits years before. From behind his sunglasses, George studied the way Odi's moustache – turned golden in the sunlight – bunched up in the middle as he said 'snol'. The way that 'del' forced his mouth into a wide smile, creating sexy little dimples in his cheeks. And how pronouncing the 'ev' sound emphasised the gap in his front teeth which used to cause George to swoon.

Was he still in love with his Viking god? Surely that ship had sailed long ago.

Deciding it was just the effect of the booze, he took a sip from his glass and tuned back in to Odi's lesson.

'The Snoldelev Runestone is one of the biggest ever found. As tall as a man and decorated with painted etchings depicting three drinking horns.'

As his attention drifted back to the present, it was clear that their host was still talking about the famous runestone. *Perhaps it was one of those which he and Pete had come across in the National Museum the day before.*

Initially a little resistant to the idea of spending the morning peering into case after case of Viking antiquities, the masterful craftsmanship of Odi's ancestors had soon won George over. Though it was Pete who'd been the most bewitched. Especially with the carvings on the large runestones that were remarkably similar to the Sarsenic Sigils on which he'd become quite the expert since his tumble.

Or rather, since he'd crashed down onto the floor of the hayloft at Hazelpits, broken several bones and permanently injured his spine.

Of course, it was Pete's legendary status as a lover that had suffered the most damage. For whilst he assured anyone who asked – *and many more who didn't* – that his manhood was still in working order, his reputation in the trouser department wasn't quite what it had been.

Perhaps not so surprising then that since the accident, his lust for leather-clad gods on the dance floor had gradually been replaced with a passion for the deities of the Saxons instead.

A transformation so dramatic that everyone now called him Pagan Pete, the nickname 'Python' eventually dropping out of use altogether.

'No shit! That's how we know about *The Scop*,' enthused Pete, stepping up to his soapbox. 'From an inscription on a stone. It's one of the Sarsenic Sigils. The first card in the reading I showed you at Whispers. Remember?'

'Oh yes, your premonition about AIDS. Well, perhaps your Saxon 'runes' were right all along!' suggested Odi.

Now that was interesting. Thinking back to his friend's barely disguised cynicism about Pete's fortune-telling at the motorcycle fetish club in the basement of the aforementioned gay pub, George couldn't help but wonder what was behind this apparent change of heart.

Odi certainly seemed to be more in touch with his Danish heritage than he used to be.

Despite looking like a Norse god – albeit a Tom of Finland version with clipped clone tash and tight leathers whatever the weather – in the five years that he and George had been friends, the Dane had rarely talked about Vikings. Or even Denmark, for that matter. As such, George had assumed that the mention of *runes* and *thyles* was simply part of the tour-guide patter.

Hearing this last comment, he couldn't help thinking there was more to it than that.

But rather than picking up on Pete's reference to the Sarsenic Sigils, Odi's attention shifted to the hamper instead. Perhaps he was just humouring his guest after all. Satisfied he'd misread the signs, George's eyes fell upon the basket from which his friend had just lifted a slice of something he now knew to be called rugbrød.

Just one of several new words that George had picked up in the last couple of days, this one easy to remember since the dense rye bread had the same taste and texture he imaged an old rug would have.

'*Not that I've munched on many of those!*' he'd joked to Pete.

And smørrebrød, the open sandwich which Odi was assembling from various cartons of cold meats and cheeses, that was just as memorable since it sounded a lot like 'smörgåsbord', a platter which had even reached Brighton!

Though at the party where George remembered a smörgåsbord had made an appearance; on that occasion, it had been a plate of crackers, haphazardly arranged around a foil-covered grapefruit, pierced with cocktail sticks skewered with cheese cubes, pickled onions and pineapple chunks. *And hadn't one of the Sussex Lancers used the word to describe the contents of his dungeon?* In truth, George wasn't very keen on the former and found the idea of the latter just as unappetising.

In fact, as he watched Odi create his smørrebrød, he couldn't help but yearn for a plate of good old-fashioned fish and chips.

Recalling a recent stroll he'd taken on the Palace Pier, George was happily lost in memories of the vinegar-drenched battered cod he'd enjoyed that day when…

'Olives anyone?' asked the Dane. Another favourite of the Continentals which had made it onto the tables of every posh restaurant in Brighton in recent months.

What was wrong with breadsticks, for Christ's sake!

'No thanks, I'm stuffed,' lied George. 'Couldn't eat another thing!'

'Oh, Georgie Boy. Not even an olive?' enquired Pete, goading him from his wheelchair, fully aware that his friend's views on the little green Devil's spawn – as George called them – were on a par with those he held on rugbrød.

'No! Not even one of these!' replied George, spying an acorn in the grass and hurling it at his adversary.

That had been the plan, at least.

Unfortunately, throwing not being one of George's strong suits, the nut flew past Pete and landed at the foot of the tree where Grace had found a comfortable spot to rest. So comfortable, in fact, that judging by her reaction, she'd been enjoying a little snooze.

'Oi! Cos'è quello? Smettila ora!' she yelled in her native tongue.

Despite it being her first language, having lived in England and the US for most of her life, Grace spoke Italian very rarely, and the shock of hearing it come out of her mouth caused them all to freeze for a moment.

'I think I've been shat on!' she added in English.

'Keep yer hair on Gracie. It was just an acorn falling from the tree. Your kaftan is safe from squirrel crap,' George reassured her before throwing Odi a wink; his gesture hitting its target with considerably more success than the acorn had done!

Merriment over, a peaceful calm fell upon the group once again, until…

'The oak tree is one of the sigils, too,' said Pete, picking up the thread of an earlier discussion.

'Sorry, dear?' asked Grace, confirming that she *had* been napping.

'You know, the cards I do my readings with. It's one of the symbols borrowed from the ogham, the Celtic tree alphabet,' replied Pete, returning to his favourite subject. 'Though it wasn't just the tree that was sacred to the Celts. Acorns, too, were imbued with great power. Apparently, their priests used to eat them to aid their divination. Foretelling the future and getting in touch with the spirits. In fact, the word *Druid* literally means 'oak-knower'. It's why they used to practise their magic in oak groves.'

'Far out!' said Odi. 'Have you ever tried it yourself? Eating them, I mean.'

Once again, Odi was exhibiting a level of interest in ancient magic which seemed out of step with the way he'd poo-pooed it just a few months earlier. There was definitely something afoot. But before George could turn his attention to this little conundrum, the situation suddenly took a dramatic new twist.

'Well,' began Pete, popping a handful of the small green nuts into his mouth, 'not until…' he continued, while chewing them, '… now!' he said finally, washing the whole mush down with a slug of wine.

George could hardly believe his eyes.

'Pete! What the…? They might be poisonous!' he cried. 'Give you the shits at the very least!'

A sobering thought since he and Pete were sharing a bathroom at Odi's.

'For cooking, you're supposed to roast them. Gets rid of the tannins, the bitter taste. But I think you can eat them raw. Besides which, three or four's not gonna kill me,' reassured Pete before suggesting something that had the potential to be even messier than an upset tummy. 'Now all I need is a willing guinea pig. Fancy a reading, anyone?'

Said as soberly as when Odi had asked if anyone wanted an olive, George assumed he was joking and decided it was a good time to find the public loo. Until…

'I'm game,' announced the Dane suddenly. 'If you are!'

First, George thought his eyes were deceiving him. Now it appeared his ears were too!

Swapping stories of ancient symbols was one thing. Agreeing to have his fortune read was quite a different matter. Surely, not even Pete could have predicted that! But where would they do it? Time was getting on, and the effects of the acorns, should there be any, would soon be apparent.

He needn't have worried. It seemed that Pete had it all worked out.

'Oh goodie! How about over there?' he suggested, pointing at Grace with a branch he'd picked up earlier.

'Oh yes! Under an oak tree. Just like your Druids,' added Odi, getting up from the picnic blanket and reaching for the cooler box. 'Grab the hamper, Georgie Boy. We can use it as a table.'

'Great idea,' agreed Pete, wheeling himself a little closer to the place where, just a few minutes earlier, Grace had been enjoying 40 winks.

Basket in position, all four of them gathered beneath the old tree and prepared themselves for Odi's reading, which, judging by the crazed look in Pete's eyes, wasn't a moment too soon.

Of course, it could just have been part of the theatricals that often accompanied one of his readings. George couldn't say. But the heavy breathing and occasional giggle were definitely new additions.

Stage set: Pete placed a deck of cards on Odi's side of the makeshift table.

'As the reader, I am just a conduit between the sigils and your future. A mere messenger if you like,' began Pete in a hushed voice. 'So, first of all, you must commune with the cards. Let them peer into your subconscious.'

Met with a look of confusion from Odi and no further help forthcoming from the acorn-happy Druid, George interjected with a more direct approach.

'He wants you to shuffle them, dear!'

Meaning understood and request completed, Pete counted seven from the top of the deck and laid them face down in a row.

After another deep breath, he turned over the first card in the formation, which depicted a man resting his head on the lap of a golden-haired woman sitting beneath a tree.

'*The Apple Tree Sigil.* Perfect!' said Pete excitedly.

'How so?' asked Grace, giving voice to what George was also thinking.

'Because the card depicts Avalon, the Island of Apples. The mythical place where King Arthur was healed by his sister,' whispered Pete mysteriously. 'Associated with medicine and health. That's why it's the perfect card to represent your past.'

George had to admit, the 'doctor' sigil was weirdly apt.

Attention caught; he focused his eyes on the second card in the row.

'The brown one!' announced Pete before treating them to another of those slightly disturbing sniggers.

But once the strange chortle had left his lips, his attention returned to the animal which had presumably been its cause: a ferocious-looking bear.

'The name 'brown one' comes from an old folk tale dating back to a time before the Saxons came to Britain when the bear was the most feared animal in the forests of what is now Germany,' continued Pete. 'In essence, hunters believed that if they used the animal's real name, the bear would gain power over them, and they, in turn, would become the hunted. Which is why they referred to the most feared creature in their world as 'bruin' or 'brown one'; the actual name for 'bear' eventually being lost forever.'

But what did it mean? thought George to himself.

He was about to ask when his friend provided him with his answer.

'And because the word was taboo, *The Bear Sigil* refers to *something that dare not speak its name*.'

There was one thing which sprang to George's mind immediately.

But, like Grace and Odi, he remained silent.

'Mmmm… perhaps the 'future' card will add some clarity,' suggested Pete.

Like Las Vegas poker players captivated by the hands of the dealer, all eyes were fixed on the turn of the next card.

'Not you again!' announced their Celtic croupier, revealing the all-too-familiar image of a wolf climbing up the side of a dome-topped tower.

Remembering it as one of the cards that had appeared in the reading at Whispers, in which Pete had suggested that the tower represented Brighton, and the wolf, the disease which would bring disruption and the end of friendships, George began to feel a little faint.

At first, like Odi, he'd dismissed Pete's prophecy. But as more and more people started to get ill, he began to see the dome-topped tower everywhere he went. In the minarets of the Pavilion. The roof of the Bombay Bar in Kemptown. Even the helter-skelter on the Palace Pier.

And judging by the looks of dread which accompanied the card, it seemed to George that he wasn't the only one disturbed by the appearance of *The Wolf Sigil* card. Or the only one whose thoughts had turned to the 'thing' whose name people dared not speak!

'Is anyone thinking what I'm thinking?' asked Grace.

'Well, if what you're thinking is AIDS, then yes,' replied George. 'I mean, what could be more terrifying than that?'

Was AIDS the 'brown one' who'd turned the hunters into the hunted?

An eerie silence fell upon the group.

Even the cheerful birdsong that had been wafting down from the branches above had ceased, and a séance-like atmosphere enveloped them all. Until…

'Pop!'

'Aaaaargh!' shrieked George, almost jumping out of his skin.

Followed by the glug-glug sound of pouring liquid, it seemed that the Underworld hadn't contacted them just yet! No! In fact, rather than spirits from beyond the grave, the interruption turned out to be spirits from the cooler box. Or at least a bottle of sparkling wine that had been chilling in there. And which Odi was now emptying into their glasses.

Nerves steadied by more of the fizzy stuff, George made himself comfortable again, and Pete returned to the reading.

'OK. Next up, the thing we must overcome,' he advised, turning over the fourth card in the series.

'Ah, *the curing stone*,' said Pete.

After the terrifying wolf, the picture of a crystal was a welcome sight to George, for even if he had no idea what it actually meant, he knew that crystals had something to do with healing. *That had to be a good thing, right?*

He took a sip of his drink and waited to see.

'Finding a cure!' exclaimed Pete. 'Of course! The thing we have to overcome is this fucking virus! So, drawing *The Crystal Sigil* card is an excellent omen.'

But before George had the chance to digest this, the Oracle had already moved on.

'Ha! It's you!' said Pete, tapping the image of a bearded chap and locking eyes on Odi.

Since the fella looked more like Father Christmas than the Dane, George struggled to see what Pete was getting at until he saw the distinctive winged helmet of the sort associated with the Vikings.

The card was from the suit of sigils which included characters from Saxon mythology, that George had learnt were interchangeable with those of the Norsemen. And given Pete's exclamation, he guessed that the man on the card was Woden, the Saxon version of Odin. *But what did it foretell?* Accompanied by another ferocious wolf, which if the Sarsenic Sigils were to be believed, were absolutely everywhere in ancient Sussex, the scene didn't exactly shout, 'Ho ho ho! Come and sit on my knee, boys and girls!'

That being the case, George decided the beard was where Woden's similarity with Santa Claus ended.

And as for the description of him being *'The Lord of Frenzy. The Leader of the Possessed'*. That didn't sound very festive at all. Especially as Pete's eyes seemed to roll into the back of his head as he said it.

But like a passerby at a car crash, George leaned in closer to find out just how awful it might be. Which, as it turned out, wasn't quite as bad as he'd originally thought.

'Lord of Frenzy is simply the literal translation of his Saxon name *Wodanaz*,' explained Pete. 'But his card could also signify wisdom and healing. Or knowledge and sorcery.'

'So, which is it?' asked Grace, who'd seemed a little distant since the mention of AIDS, the thing from which they were all supposed to be taking a break.

'Well, you have to look at the bigger picture,' replied Pete. 'The other cards in the reading. And most importantly of all, where it appears in the formation.'

Casting his eyes along the row of pictures in front of him, George suddenly had an idea.

'Oh, my goodness,' he gasped. 'Maybe it means that Odi is going to help them find a cure for this fucking disease.'

'Well, yes, that could be one interpretation, Georgie Boy,' agreed Pete. 'In the modern vernacular, sorcery and wisdom could refer to medicine.'

'But I'm a surgeon, not a haematologist,' said Odi. 'Blood isn't really my field.'

'Field is right,' interrupted Grace. 'Bloody battlefield!'

Spoken with a ferocity which was unusual for their friend, the outburst caused them all to face her at once.

'Seriously. You should see the newspaper cuttings my friends in San Francisco and Los Angeles have sent me this month. The number of people known to be infected over there is off the scale. And that's on top of the thousands who have already died. The ones they know about anyway. There's a whole lot more who've just disappeared. Even amongst the people I've written to. Of the 50 or so I've contacted, almost half have yet to reply. I even had one letter returned to me last week in a plastic bag! But the craziest thing was what had been scrawled across the back of it.

NO LONGER AT THIS ADDRESS. FOR GOD'S SAKE. DO NOT CONTACT AGAIN!!!

'Why would anyone write that? It hadn't even been opened! Did they think they might get infected from dried saliva on the flap? Christ! People are so freakin' stupid. I bet all those right-wingers are loving it. Just when we thought we were getting somewhere. Just when we thought we'd won the argument. The basic human right to exist and love who we want. Then wham, out of the blue. AIDS. But rather than trying to find out how to treat or vaccinate against it, all the politicians do is use it to further their fucked-up agenda. Queers. Drug addicts. Prostitutes. Immigrants. Prisoners. Apart from haemophiliacs, it's like a Who's Who of folk those god-fearing fundamentalist fuckwits want to be rid of.

'But the ones they're especially pleased about are the queers. AIDS is like Manna from Heaven for the religious right. Jesus! Before you know it, we'll all be back in the closet, and it'll be like Stonewall and Harvey never happened. Our very existence ripped from the history books. And who knows what else after that!'

Punctuating this last sentence with a Nazi salute and finger moustache, no one was left in any doubt about where Grace thought we were heading.

'Yeah, it'd be a whole different ball game if it were *their* friends who were getting sick, wouldn't it?' suggested George.

'Would it, though?' replied Grace angrily. 'Reagan has lived most of his life in California. *He was an actor, for Christ's sake!* He must have known about Rock, before last week!' she added, referring to the announcement just a few days earlier that Hollywood legend, Rock Hudson, had been diagnosed with AIDS.

'Over 5,000 US citizens dead already, and Reagan *still* hasn't said 'AIDS' in public. How many more lives need to be cut short before…'

'Fuck!' exclaimed Pete suddenly, drawing their attention to the next card in the row, which depicted three women beneath a tree.

As if to prove an earlier point about AIDS being something that people didn't want to talk about, the opportunity to return to the reading was welcomed by George. But rather than a change in direction, it just seemed to lead them back to the very subject whose name they dared not speak.

'*...lives being cut short...*' said Pete, repeating the end of Grace's last sentence. 'But that's what they did. Known as *The Wyrd Sisters* or *The Three Fates*, in Norse mythology they were sometimes called the Norns – from the Nordic word meaning 'to twine' – because of the way they *twined* the thread of fate.'

Once again, the huddle around the picnic basket was struck dumb.

But unlike last time, the sound of birds could now be heard in the branches above, and not too far away from where they were sitting, George could hear human voices too.

It was starting to get dark, and it seemed that the park was beginning to empty.

If they were going to finish the reading, they ought to get a move on, so, in an effort to wrap things up, he plucked up the courage and broached the 'bear in the room'.

'So, you think it's to do with all those young lives being cut short by this horrible disease?' asked George.

But before Pete could answer, Grace picked up the baton.

'Well, I'm as sceptical as the next person about all this Sarsenic Sigil stuff, but I accept that not everything in this world can be explained by science. This fucking disease, maybe. But not without proper funding. Which, if the powers that be have anything to do with it, definitely won't happen anytime soon.

'So, I've been thinking. I'm not a scientist. I can't find a cure. But there is one thing I *can* do. And this has made up my mind. When I get back to Brighton, I'm going to offer rooms at Gracie's Palace to anyone with the virus who has nowhere else to go.'

In contrast to the growing cacophony of tourists packing away their picnics and rounding up their kids, the gathering under the oak tree became subdued once again until…

'You're being serious, aren't you?' asked George.

'Deadly!' she replied, gesticulating towards the six cards laid out in front of her. 'This might be total cockamamie, but it's certainly convinced me that opening up the hotel is the right thing to do.'

Yet despite the finality of her last comment, it soon became clear that for one person at least, this was not the end…

'Well, that's fantastic, Gracie. It really is. But we've not finished my reading yet!' said Odi, in a manner which was more petulant than indignant. 'If I'm going to be *The Leader of the Possessed*, I'd at least like to know where I'm taking them!'

'And so you shall!' announced Pete with another of those maniacal giggles which had become part and parcel of the reading.

But if anyone had been buoyed up by Pete's childlike enthusiasm, the last card put paid to that.

'Oh!' said Pete, staring at the new image, the sudden cessation of hubris reflected in the look on his face. *'The Ash Tree Sigil!'*

'Yes…' began Odi. '…but what does it mean?'

'Mmmm…' replied Pete, hunching his shoulders and cracking his neck. *Another side-effect of the acorns or a response to the card's meaning?* George wasn't sure. Which, it soon transpired, neither was Pete!

'Lots of things, actually…'

'Go on,' urged Odi.

'Well, in Norse mythology, the ash is sometimes called *The Tree of Life*, underneath which the gods held their court and meted out justice. A sort of bridge between Heaven and Earth,' explained Pete, pausing to take a sip of wine before continuing with his detour into Viking folklore.

'But in one of their most famous poems, *The Poetic Edda*, it's also known as the hanging tree. Or to be more precise, Odin's – or Woden's – hanging tree. Where he hung himself for nine days and nights in order to gain knowledge and understand the runes. For this reason, it also represents the circle of life, death and rebirth.'

Despite Pete's description, Odi seemed to be taking it all in his stride. A suspicion confirmed moments later with his own summary of the card's rather ominous meaning.

'So, in short, my future's not looking particularly bright?' he asked, half grinning.

George, on the other hand, unable to be quite so philosophical, decided he'd had enough of Pete's amateur dramatics for one day.

'Oh, come on. It's just a bit of fun. Don't read too much into it,' he said, trying to sound as reassuring as he could. 'Tell him you're pulling his leg.'

But before Pete had the chance to do as requested, a more alarming admission was delivered by Odi himself.

'It's alright, Georgie Boy. Fact is, if anyone's been pulling anyone's legs, it's me. I didn't need Pete to get in touch with his Saxon soothsayers to find out what my future holds. I've known for the last few hours. Much longer, if I'm totally honest.'

As the enormity of what Odi was telling them all began to sink in, George's eyes fell upon the piece of paper his friend had retrieved from one of the pockets in his leather waistcoat.

Gradually unfolding it as he was speaking, once it was fully open, he turned to Grace.

'Yesterday at the clinic. I didn't just want to show you around the old place. I was also picking up my test results. And…'

Stopping mid-sentence, he gently placed his hand on top of hers.

'Well… let's just say, if you go through with your plans for the hotel… you'll be seeing a whole lot more of me over the next few months. So, you better free up a room with a sea view!'

Chapter Twenty

Leave no sarsen stone unturned

Thursday 16th April 2020 –
East Sussex

With the family's groceries still delivered to her door each week, the only reason Izzy had ventured outside the house since the beginning of lockdown was for her daily exercise allowance. Which had usually meant a stroll around the cemetery across the road. Or, on one occasion, a cycle up to Woodingdean.

As a consequence, her SUV hadn't seen much action of late and sitting behind the steering wheel for the first time in four weeks felt quite alien to her. She hesitated for a moment. Would she even remember how to drive? *Of course she would!* But what if she got stopped en route? What would she say was the reason for her breaking lockdown rules? In fact, was driving over to her sister's place, on the off chance that Meena knew what Cameron and Adam were up to, really worth the risk of getting arrested? Perhaps it would be better to phone instead.

On the verge of changing her mind about driving over to Rottingdean, she was about to release her seatbelt when she was distracted by something in her rearview mirror: the bushy tail of a fox disappearing through the open gate of the cemetery across the road.

But that wasn't all she saw.

Turning her head to get a better view, it seemed he wasn't alone, for perched on the dome-topped stone gatepost was a seagull.

A canine and a large bird!

'¡Dios! *The Wolf Sigil* card!' she said out loud. 'It's a sign!'

Rallied by this apparent intervention from the divine, after one final look in the mirror, she was on her way to the old tower which Maria and Meena now called home.

Standing four storeys tall in the middle of a grassy field, Izzy could see their place as soon as she turned onto the pot-holed dirt track that led to the spot which had once been the location of Coleshill Abbey.

Falling into ruin shortly after the dissolution of the monasteries in the middle of the 16th-century, the tower, which was all that was left of the original abbey, had been repurposed several times in the intervening years, enjoying stints as a hunting lodge, a prison, and a cattle shed.

Decidedly more homely was its latest incarnation, remodelled by Izzy's sister into a love nest for Meena and herself.

Indeed, once out of the car, it became clear that Maria was up to her ears in some new building project at the base of the tower. Quite literally, in fact, since all Izzy could see of her sister was her green baseball cap.

Surely the girls weren't digging a moat!

There was only one way to find out.

'Yoo-hoo!' she cried, marching at speed towards the tower.

The owner of the baseball cap popped her head over the top of the trench.

'¡Que sorpresa!' shouted Maria before adding a few warnings about the sodden ground between them.

'¡Ten cuidado! Está muy mojado. Son los antiguos desagues. Medievales, creo.'

Aha, not a moat. Medieval drains, instead, understood Izzy rather less enviously. Especially when the stench hit her nostrils a moment later.

'¡Qué horror!' she said, holding her nose.

'¡Yo se! Lo siento!' apologised Maria in her native tongue before switching to her usual Spanglish. 'Go inside, cariño. Meena's indoors. En la cocina, I think.'

Hearing the squelch of muddy boots as Maria returned to her toil, Izzy was suddenly reminded of the card bearing the image of the ammonite, *The Mudstone Sigil*. Was it another sign? Perhaps the girls really would be able to shed some light on what Cameron had been up to over at Whitehawk Hill. She said a little prayer and hoped to god that they could. But whether this was the Catholic God of her youth or one of the Pagan gods with whom she was just getting acquainted, she didn't know. What was certain, though, was how desperately she wanted to get away from the god-awful smell wafting from the leaky drains. That being the case, she scuttled across the drawbridge – a couple of old floorboards – and into the kitchen beyond.

But instead of the warm welcome she'd expected from her sister-in-law, she was met with another of those words which had recently become commonplace.

'Maaaask!' shouted Meena as Izzy stepped through the doorway.

In point of fact, such was the ferocity of the demand, had the entrance boasted a portcullis befitting such a Medieval structure, it would surely have been lowered at that very moment.

Fortunately for Izzy, it didn't, and she made her way across the threshold with nothing more injurious than a bruised ego and shaken nerves.

'Oh God, yes, of course, daaaarlink!' she acquiesced, fishing around for the designer mask which she now kept in her handbag at all times.

In all fairness, she thought Meena's reaction was a little extreme. But given the unpleasant odour from the ditch that had followed her into the kitchen, she was more than happy to oblige.

'Sorry, love, I know we're in the countryside, but...' mumbled Meena from behind her hastily fixed muffler.

'Yes, better safe than sorry, darlink!' agreed Izzy.

'Fancy a cuppa?' enquired Meena.

Or at least that was what Izzy thought she'd said.

'Yes please. An orangey one, if you've got any?' she replied.

'Of course, love. Though I do hope you've stocked up on your fancy teas. This was the last box they had in our local supermarket. Looks like they're prioritising essentials at the mo,' continued Meena, raising her voice a little to compensate for the fabric over her mouth.

Her sister-in-law was right. And it wasn't just her fancy teas that seemed to be in short supply. Maple syrup, wholemeal pittas, halloumi cheese. Just three speciality items which Izzy had been unable to order from her online grocery service that week. Though how any kind of tea could ever be considered non-essential in the country famed for it was beyond her.

What would be next? No olive oil in Spain. A dearth of runny Brie in France!

'Gosh yes, darlink. Couldn't survive without my fancy tea,' she giggled, hoping her self-deprecation would make

Meena more amenable to divulging any intel she might have gleaned from Adam about what Cameron was up to.

But before she could begin, Meena took the lead once again.

'In fact, come to think of it, you're the first person we've set eyes on since our last shopping trip. Not seen a soul for weeks. But rules *is* rules. Until they find a vaccine, makes sense to keep out of each other's way, don't you think? Well, two metres, at least,' said Meena, pushing Izzy's mug of tea to the other end of the table.

Not quite two metres, but far enough.

Certainly, the statements, contradictions, questions and philosophical musings which had been fired at Izzy with machine gun rapidity in the few minutes since she'd entered the kitchen confirmed Meena's comment about her and Maria's isolation from the rest of the world.

Even if she hadn't succumbed to the virus yet, her babbling did suggest that she was showing symptoms of video-call-itis, a speech impediment brought on by the constant round of online chats which had quickly replaced real-world interactions.

'Sorry about the mess outside, love… bloody drains… awful pong… when it rains it pours, eh?' began Meena, resuming the verbal waterfall until…

'Yes!' interrupted Izzy, spotting an opportunity to stem her sister-in-law's stream of consciousness.

'Though we haven't had much of that recently, have we? Rain, I mean. So lovely to have been able to get outside and enjoy this wonderful part of the world we live in. In fact, when the boys returned from their little jaunt up to Whitehawk Hill yesterday, I thought… what's good for the goose and all that… why not pay Maria and Meena a visit?' said Izzy, pleased not only to have wrestled the talking stick from Meena but also to have referenced an English proverb.

'Especially as Ken said that there were quite a few people out and about up there. Even bumped into Adam and Cameron. With that fortune-teller who's moved in with George. Pagan Pete, I think he's called. Looking for some old tree, apparently!'

The occasional proverb was one thing. But where Izzy's command of the language really came into its own was when she used it to steer the conversation in the direction she wanted. Which, on this occasion, turned out to be even more direct than she'd expected.

'Ah yes, probably to do with that Druid stuff they're all ga-ga about at the minute,' revealed Meena. 'Load of old codswallop if you ask me!'

So, she'd been right all along. Yesterday's ramble wasn't about helping the old fella get a bit of fresh air. As she'd suspected, the Velociraptors had swooped in on Pagan Pete to exploit his knowledge of the occult.

Sensing blood, Izzy decided to go in for the kill.

'Codswallop, darlink?' she repeated, trying to sound dispassionate about the very thing she'd driven over to discuss.

'Oh, you know. Those cards which the Velociraptors are obsessing about,' explained Meena.

Perhaps it was time to do a little more steering.

'Ah! The Sarsenic Sigils, you mean? What Pagan Pete uses to tell fortunes on the seafront. George mentioned them over lunch a while back,' continued Izzy, keen to impress on Meena that she'd been acquainted with the mystical signs much longer than Cameron and Adam had.

'That's them. All made up, I reckon,' scoffed her sister-in-law dismissively.

'Ha! I know what you mean,' concurred Izzy. 'I thought so at first, but I've been doing a bit of digging, and there's plenty of historical evidence to suggest that they once formed the basis of a genuine belief system.'

'Oh really…' began Meena.

'Yes,' interrupted Izzy before her sister-in-law had a chance to snatch back the talking stick. 'According to my research, a 'sigil' is a symbol that is believed to possess magical powers. And 'sarsen' refers to the sandstones into which they were carved.'

'So, the cards were a later thing?' asked Meena, suddenly rather interested in the subject that only seconds ago she'd dismissed as a load of old codswallop. Perhaps a little too interested, thought Izzy, before returning to her history lesson.

'I believe so, yes,' she replied. 'From what I've been able to find out, they only really came into play around the time that tarot cards were being popularised in Europe. During the 15th-century. The pictures on the cards are an interpretation of the engravings.'

'Oh, how fascinating,' said Meena, as Izzy continued to fill her sister-in-law in on what she'd discovered, with special mention of Sussex towns and villages named after stones.

'So, you see, they're all around us,' concluded Izzy, after mentioning the sarsen stones which were rumoured to sit in the fountain on the Old Steine.

'Hiding in plain sight as it were,' suggested Meena, lowering her mask and blowing into her mug.

'Precisely!' agreed Izzy, following suit.

Assuming from the tea cooling that the discussion had reached its climax, Izzy was about to shift the conversation back to Adam and Cameron when Meena had another question.

'But no Stonehenge?' she asked before replacing her mask.

'None that anyone knows about,' replied Izzy, beginning to feel like she was the one being steered. 'Some think it's because Sussex was one of the first parts of England to be cultivated. Any circles which might have existed were probably dismantled by early farmers and used in the structure of other buildings. Especially religious ones. Like the old church at Alfriston, which apparently has sarsen stones incorporated into its walls. In fact, as the Saxons gradually converted to Christianity, churches were often built on top of Pagan holy places.'

'Like an abbey, for example,' suggested Meena, her eyes narrowing.

'That's right,' confirmed Izzy, seeing instantly what her sister-in-law was implying.

Of course, Coleshill may well have been built on a Pagan place of worship!

But before she could regain control of the talking stick, Meena was off again.

'So, if Coleshill was built using these old stones, we might be able to see them from the turret,' she cried, with the zeal of a new convert, the prospect of discovering a Sussex Stonehenge in her backyard clearly casting its spell. 'Perhaps it's not a load of old codswallop, after all!'

To have said that Izzy was surprised by Meena's volte-face on her earlier view would have been quite an understatement. But quickly deciding that the reason her sister-in-law had changed her tune was down to the insightful knowledge which she herself had provided on the subject, Izzy was about to give herself a mental pat on the back when…

'Adam certainly thinks there's something in it. When he came over the other day, I…' began Meena before stopping mid-sentence.

Prompted, no doubt, by the sudden realisation that she'd accidentally implicated the Irishman in a bout of lockdown rule-breaking, she lowered her mask again and started slurping her tea.

Not that Izzy was in any position to judge, given that she herself was at that very moment guilty of the same crime.

A case of 'let he without sin...' if ever there was one!

Sensing Meena's discomfort, Izzy decided that if she was going to get to the truth, this was her chance.

'Oh, go on, darlink, what did he say?' she urged.

It was all the encouragement her sister-in-law needed, and seconds later, her mask removed entirely, Meena excitedly divulged what she knew.

'Went on about some reading that had foretold the pandemic!'

'Yes, I know,' exclaimed Izzy, removing her muffler, too. 'George told me about it weeks ago. Remember that old hanky of his. The one the waitress gave me at the end of our lunch in the Pavilion Café? Well, when I returned it to him on the eve of lockdown, he talked me through the sigils which had appeared in the actual premonition! It's why I started researching them. Sent for my own pack the following day. And yesterday morning, I even did my first reading!'

'No way!' gushed Meena.

Gracious me! Interest in the Sarsenic Sigils was almost as infectious as coronavirus!

'Yes. In fact, it's partly why I'm here today,' continued Izzy. 'One of the cards in my reading was very much like your tower. Well, apart from the enormous wolf scaling the walls!'

'The one that everyone thinks means Brighton?' suggested Meena.

Izzy locked eyes with her sister-in-law. The academic authority her curatorial reputation had given the sigils went some way to explain Meena's apparent re-evaluation of them, but recognising *The Wolf Sigil* card did seem to point to a deeper knowledge than she was letting on! With mention of the ferocious canine still hanging in the air, Izzy decided to proceed with caution. Which, in her case, meant flattery.

'That's right, darlink. Here am I thinking I'm telling you something new, when you probably know more about it all than I do. Gosh. I'll be teaching you to suck eggs next!' cried Izzy, with one of her schoolgirl giggles which were almost as chilling as her famous glares.

'Oh, I don't know about that, love. Adam's the expert, not me,' said Meena, taking a sip of tea. 'And Cameron…'

'Cameron?' asked Izzy, trying her best to sound blasé about the mention of her arch-rival.

'Yes, he's roped Pete into some project he's working on,' replied Meena.

Now this was too much!

'Oh God. Which one of his clients is the old fortune-teller going to be working with, I wonder? For whom shall he be 'brand ambassador'?' she asked facetiously. 'Pensions… health care… life insurance? *Your future in our hands with Pagan Pete!*'

'Ha! I think you've missed your vocation, love!' exclaimed Meena, acknowledging Izzy's reference to George's involvement with Rakewell's Gin. 'But no. Nothing like that. In fact, it's Pete himself who Cameron's interested in. He wants to help him go digital.'

'Digital!' shrieked Izzy, blindsided by the audacity of Cameron's countermove.

'Yes, they're building a website so that the old man can read fortunes online. Adam's doing the technical side.

And they've asked me to design some new cards! It's a real team effort,' said Meena.

Aaaaargh! It was even worse than she'd feared. With each new piece of information, her dream of holding candlelit Sarsenic Sigil reading parties in her study was disappearing into thin air. And certainly, there'd be no need to dig out those musty old turbans from the dressing-up box in the attic.

Once again, the Velociraptors had joined forces and ripped her plans to shreds!

Bong… bong… bong…

Thankfully, her fall into despair was halted by the sound of Meena and Maria's grandfather clock striking three.

'Oh hell. Is that the time? There's that big announcement tonight, isn't there? We better get up to the turret,' she said, returning to the discussion about looking for evidence of a stone circle in the grounds where the abbey had once stood, which had now gained even more importance given what she'd just learnt from her sister-in-law about Cameron's intentions.

'You go up, love. I need to help Maria cover the drains. I'll join you in a sec,' promised Meena as she pulled on her wellies.

For a brief moment, Izzy considered lending a hand, but a quick glance at her suede boots put an end to that idea, and seconds later she was at the foot of the winding staircase which led to the top of the tower. About to take the first step, she noticed something that stopped her in her tracks. The spiral of stone steps she was about to climb. Wasn't it strangely reminiscent of the image of the ammonite on *The Mudstone Sigil* card?

Convinced it was yet another message from the gods, minutes later, she was turning the handle on the door to the turret.

Compared to the dimly lit stairwell, the bright afternoon sunshine on the other side came as quite a shock. *Though it wasn't the only surprise waiting for her up there.* Temporarily blinded by the light, she gradually became aware of a seagull perched on the parapet wall opposite her.

'Shooo, shooo!' she squawked before marching over to a gap in the crenelations and scanning the ground below.

Nothing.

She walked to the other side and did the same.

Nothing there either.

Noticing that the seagull from before was guarding the final wall, she faced her feathery interloper once again.

'Now will you just shoooooooo!' she screamed at the bird.

Mission accomplished, Izzy surveyed the grassy field for lumps or bumps, the tell-tale signs of buried sarsen stones.

Nothing.

Damn and blast!

She knew it had been a long shot, but Meena's theory did seem plausible. Coleshill would have been built around the same time as the church at Alfriston. It wasn't beyond the bounds of possibility that an important Christian building like an abbey had been constructed on the site of an old Pagan place of worship.

Crestfallen, she turned towards the door to begin her gloomy descent back down to the kitchen. Until…

'Maria Martinez. Maria Martinez!' announced her phone.

Ah, perhaps they needed some help with the drains, Izzy thought to herself.

'Hola. ¿qué pasa?' she asked, with a sigh.

'It's not Maria, love. It's Meena. You won't believe it. The foundations of the tower. They're sarsen stones!'

'Noooooo!' cried Izzy, disorientated by feelings of shock and excitement. '¿De verdad? ¡Eso es increíble!'

'Yes! I know. And what's more, they're covered in etchings!' added Meena.

Could it really be true? Had her sister-in-law's hunch been even closer to the truth than she could have hoped? There was only one way to find out. Reminded of the prayers she'd made earlier, Izzy skipped down the staircase, and suede boots or not, moments later, she was being helped into the ditch around the tower.

What she saw made her want to jump for joy. Whether it was Meena or the sigils that had led to the discovery, she couldn't say. *Her money was still on the sigils, obviously.* Though it did seem that those up-cycling Medieval stonemasons had used sarsen stones to construct Coleshill, after all. Not for the main building but as foundations for its tallest structure. More than that, it appeared they'd built the tower on a complete stone circle: 25 boulders with a different sigil engraved into each one.

Yet the magnitude of what Maria had unearthed didn't even stop there!

Underneath every sigil was something else.

'¡Mira Isabella!' cried Maria, feverishly scrubbing one of the stones. '¡También hay algo de escritura!'

Writing too! Her thoughts awash with images of the Rosetta Stone, the famous rock whose engravings in Greek and Egyptian had enabled scholars to decipher hieroglyphics for the first time, Izzy leaned in closer to see what her sister had found.

'¿Griego?' she asked tentatively.

'¡No! Es latino, creo! Sí, sí, tengo razón,' replied Maria.

Of course, Latin. The language of the Christian monks!

As exciting as this clearly was, the fall into Spanish was too much for Meena.

'Oh, for God's sake. Whaaaaat?' she screamed.

Izzy was more than happy to oblige.

'Not only have we found a complete Saxon stone circle, darlink. We've discovered the Rosetta Stone of Sigils!'

Just wait until Cameron hears about this!

Chapter Twenty-One

The last days of Rome

Thursday 16th April 2020 – Cameron & Alex's house – Wyndham Street, Brighton

While Izzy was happily engrossed in the removal of mud from sarsen stones buried in a ditch just outside Rottingdean, in somewhat more hospitable surroundings, the Velociraptors were gearing up for the daily update about how the government was tackling the virus.

Well, at least two of them were.

'Adaaaaaam! It's aboot to start!' shouted Cameron from the bottom of the stairs.

Hearing no signs of movement from the floors above, he tried another tack.

'It's the fit one who's standing in for Boris!'

'Comiiiiiiiing!' sang Adam as he thundered down the wooden staircase from the attic, where he'd been working out in their makeshift gym.

Still a little sweaty from his session, the Irishman laid his towel across the seat of the armchair which had become 'his' spot since the beginning of lockdown and made himself comfortable for the update.

'Dishy Rishi or Dashing Dom?' he asked, shamelessly adjusting the ample contents of his green nylon shorts.

'Raab,' replied Alex, already seated in *his* favoured lockdown chair opposite their lodger.

As he fumbled blindly for the TV control on the coffee table between them both, it was clear that his attention was somewhat distracted by Adam's manspread. *Och, so that's why Alex chose to sit there.* Though Cameron had to admit, living with the testosterone-pumped Irishman did have a certain locker-room charm to it. And at least the seating arrangement had left him with no other choice but to commandeer the sofa. Suddenly aware that he, too, was a wee bit aroused by his lodger's armchair gymnastics, he propped a cushion under his head, another over his groin, and made himself comfortable for the evening's main event.

'Welcome to the daily coronavirus press conference from Downing Street,' began the younger of the three men standing behind podiums on the screen.

Whether it was Dom's heartfelt gratitude for NHS workers and remorse for the lives lost – or his public-school boy accent and smouldering good looks – Cameron couldn't quite decide. But whatever the reason, he sat transfixed while Deputy Prime Minister Raab summarised the story so far. Until…

'Over 300,000 tested. Is that a lot?' asked Alex after a few minutes.

'Dunno. But did he no say that 100,000 of them were positive? One in three sounds pretty high to me,' replied Cameron.

'Yeah, and 13,000 dead, too!' added Adam before Dashing Dom moved on to talk about something called the R-value – which turned out to be the rate at which infected people were infecting the previously uninfected. And whilst this sounded scarily like one of the many zombie movies the boys had watched over the previous month, the fact that the

R-value was now below 'one' was apparently a cause for celebration since it meant that each infected person was infecting less than one other.

'Unless you're one of the ones getting infected!' scoffed Alex.

'But overall, we still don't have the infection rate down as far as we need to,' continued the deputy prime minister.

'Oh, here we go,' said Adam, pre-empting the expected news that the government had decided to extend the lockdown and that it would not be relaxed until five specific goals had been achieved.

Despite the leaks and rumours which had been circulating all day, hearing it from the horse's mouth – even a stallion like Dashing Dom – resulted in a collective sigh of resignation from all three of them.

'Perhaps this is what it feels like when you get your request for parole turned down,' sighed Cameron as the update reached its predictable Churchillian climax.

'It's been an incredible national team effort. Now is not the moment to give the coronavirus a second chance. Let's stick together. Let's see this through. And let's defeat the coronavirus for good.'

Notwithstanding his previous quip, Cameron couldn't help being rather moved by the deputy prime minister's call to arms. So much so, in fact, that he found himself almost looking forward to the weekly 'Clap for Carers' later that evening, which, after an enthusiastic start, had gone off the boil recently. Even with the recent addition of pan-bashing. An upgrade which had led Cameron to note that, whilst we were still *'all in this together'*, it was clear that some of us had much nicer kitchenware! By which he meant himself and Alex.

But before Cameron had a chance to run off and dig out his fanciest copper-bottom, Adam leapt forward, grabbed the controls and turned off the TV.

'Sorry, chaps! Looks like you've got me for a few more weeks. Not to mention another load of crisps and biscuits which are gonna need eating before the end of the month. In fact, I popped into the café this morning and picked up another box of those lentil snacks you like. Gin and nibbles, anyone?' he asked, just as his phone began to ring.

'Ooh, go on then,' replied Alex in the direction of Adam's posterior as it disappeared downstairs to the kitchen below.

'Och, it's like the last days of Rome around here. We've barely emptied the coal bunker from the last haul,' noted Cameron.

'God yeah. Another month of lockdown, and I know who'll be playing Nero!' laughed Alex.

Mmmmm... he wasn't wrong, thought Cameron to himself.

His husband had certainly been making the most of the artisanal goodies from Adam's café-deli, that simply had to be eaten before their sell-by-dates. Add to this the drinks trolley, which seemed to come out earlier each day, and the almost sedentary lifestyle that Alex had adopted as a result of the many streaming services to which they were now subscribed – and it struck Cameron that his husband was enjoying all the perks of executive travel which he normally arranged for his high-flying clientele.

A situation that, with most planes still grounded, was likely to continue for some time.

'Actually, make mine a Martini, will you?' shouted Alex.

As it seemed, would his husband's stay in business class!

Though it was clear from the shrieks of 'Jayzuz!' and 'For the love of God!' coming from the basement that the

Irishman was far too wrapped up in the news from whoever was at the other end of his mobile to have heard Alex's revised cocktail order.

Equally distracted was Cameron, who'd picked up the TV controls to check out the multitude of shows which were now on offer.

The truth was that lockdown hadn't been all bad. Apart from his colleague, Yang, no-one in his social circle or extended family had succumbed to the virus yet. *Thank goodness!*

And in addition to being able to catch up on films and TV shows he'd never previously had time to watch, working from home meant he no longer had to drag his sorry ass out of bed at the crack of dawn every day, either.

A situation made even more favourable by the fact that, despite rumblings from his agency about the savings people were making by not having to commute anymore, he still drew the same salary. And even managed to fiddle his expenses, too!

In fact, on balance, perhaps it was he who should play Nero!

What's more, another month of lockdown meant he'd have plenty of time to get this thing with Pete up and running.

Reminded of the project, Cameron reached for his laptop and clicked on the yet-to-be-published website.

THE FELLOWSHIP OF THE SARSENIC SIGILS read the headline in a Gaelic-style serif typeface, running in an arch over an image of Pete dressed in a cloak and brandishing the famous acorn-headed walking stick. And below this, in slightly smaller type, was written:

Looking for guidance in these uncertain times? Enlist the power of Anglo-Saxon magic with world-renowned fortune-teller Peter Sissinghurst.

Scrolling down, Cameron re-familiarised himself with the text.

Sign up today for just £200, and you will receive a pack of beautifully designed Sarsenic Sigil Cards and a copy of Peter's best-selling guide: Sarsenic Sigil Cards: Unlocking the Magic Code of the Anglo-Saxons. *And that's not all. Your first online reading – normally costing £100 – is included in your joining fee. For more information, complete our* Membership Form *today.*

Knowing that Pete had a stack of his 'best-selling' books at his flat – and that the new edition was available as print-on-demand – once Meena had completed the designs for the new set of Sarsenic Sigil Cards and Adam had finished the website, they'd be good to go.

And now he didn't have to leave Brighton for the next few weeks – he'd have no difficulty getting everything ready for their proposed launch date.

In fact, where were those drinks that Adam had promised?

He was about to shout down to the kitchen when his friend came bounding back up the stairs in a manner which suggested he *wasn't* carrying their cocktails. Either that or he was engaged in an *It's a Knock-Out!*-inspired challenge to see how much liquid he could get from kitchen to lounge at speed.

As Cameron suspected, it was the former.

'Feck! You're never gonna believe what Meena was phoning about!' announced the Irishman. 'They've only gone and found a complete circle of Sarsenic Sigil stones at Coleshill!'

'Nooooo!' cried Cameron, not sure whether he was thrilled or seething with envy.

'Aye, underneath the fecking tower!' explained Adam.

'How the…' began Cameron.

'Drains!' came the reply. 'And that's not all.'

'Don't tell me they've found the remains of Lord Lucan and Shergar in the cellar?' interjected Alex.

'Not quite. Though it would explain the stink!' guffawed Adam. 'But no. As well as sigils, Meena says the stones are covered in letters too!'

'Noooo! Like the Rosetta Stone?' enthused Cameron.

'Aye! Only Latin rather than Greek. But yes, that's what Izzy thinks…' confirmed Adam.

'Izzy?' asked Cameron, with a sinking feeling of dread. 'What the fuck's Bottomless Pitt got tae di wi it?'

'Seems she was there when Maria uncovered the stones,' replied Adam. 'Once the Latin inscriptions have been cleaned up, she's going to take photos and get them translated.'

'Fuuuuuuk!' yelled Cameron, slamming down the lid of his laptop.

Chapter Twenty-Two

Lost in translation

Friday 17th April 2020 –
Izzy's summer house – Bear Road, Brighton

In contrast to the bitterest of pills which Cameron was still having difficulty swallowing, the day after the unearthing of the Saxon Stonehenge at Coleshill, the only thing Izzy was chewing over was how quickly she could decipher the Latin inscriptions underneath the Sarsenic Sigils.

Well, that and whether she'd been spotted driving between Brighton and Rottingdean.

First of all, on the day of the discovery. And again, when she'd returned home after helping the girls scrub away centuries of mud from the symbols and letters carved into the foundations of the tower.

Her crime made all the more serious by the fact that, in order to complete the task, she'd stayed at their place overnight! *Not that she'd had much sleep; fears of being woken up by lockdown law enforcers never being too far from her thoughts.*

Especially after reading an article before going to bed which said there'd been a significant increase in accusations of rule-breaking recently. Many of which the police suspected were motivated by people wanting to settle old scores!

Best not to be *too* complacent, thought Izzy. After all, who knew what lengths Cameron might go to in his attempts to scotch her chances of gaining the upper hand in the thing which had captivated nearly all in their shared social circle.

No stranger to 'social distancing' – even before lockdown – Izzy was under no illusion whatsoever that the minor role he'd allowed her to play at the Rakewell's relaunch event was a case of 'keeping his friends close and his enemies closer still'.

Of course, now Meena had let Adam in on the discovery – and who knew what else – Izzy's biggest fear was that the Velociraptors might pay a visit to Rottingdean and ambush the girls themselves.

So, with dirt from the morning's exertions still in her nails and hair, shortly after three o'clock, Izzy made her way to the summer house at the bottom of her garden and readied herself for part two of the excavation, cracking the code of the Saxon Rosetta Stone.

Getting to this juncture had been painstaking work. But after several hours of scrubbing, the 25 stones had finally revealed themselves enough for Izzy to begin the task of decoding. Which, if the ache in her lower back was anything to go by, wouldn't be anywhere near as arduous.

Certainly not for someone with Izzy's intellect and powers of detection.

Of course, it helped that aside from a few worn-away letters, the symbols and Latin inscriptions were largely intact. Remarkable considering they'd spent over half a millennium submerged in mud next to the abbey's drains. Especially the Saxon sigils, which had already endured 800 years exposed to the elements before the stones had been recycled by Medieval builders around the 14th-century.

In fact, it seemed that the most significant damage had been caused not by Mother Nature but by a Victorian plumber, who'd dug down to install that most civilising of inventions: a flushing loo.

Fortunately, the lead piping had been rather shallowly laid, missing all but one of the symbols and also ensuring the preservation of a line of Latin text which ran in a band around the base of the entire ring of stones.

What secrets that might reveal, Izzy couldn't wait to find out.

Ordinarily, she could have called upon any number of language and history specialists from her curatorial network. But with the world's museums mothballed and most colleagues furloughed – the human equivalent of being wrapped in naphthalene-infused cloth and put into storage – the usual channels were closed to her.

Thankfully, as with so many other things during lockdown, the internet came to her rescue once again, presenting her with several Latin translation websites.

Add to this the fact that her native tongue had its roots in the language of Ancient Rome, she'd decided that the best course of action was a DIY approach.

Or *fac te ipsum* – as they might have said back in Julius Caesar's day.

So, two thousand years later, plus the time it took Izzy to check the translation of one or two Latin phrases for which she already knew the meanings – such as *fiat lux* (let there be light) and *tempus fugit* (time flies) – and she was ready to start.

'OK, Mary Beard. Let's *carpe* the bloody *diem* out of this!' she said, clicking on the first photograph in the file containing pictures of the 25 engravings.

'Aha, I know you!' said Izzy, under her breath, staring at a diamond shape with a line drawn through it.

Glancing over at the pile of books she'd amassed on Viking runes, Sarsenic Sigils and other magical hieroglyphs – a hotchpotch of literature that ranged from the seminal work by Pagan Pete to the less academic *Runes for Goons* – Izzy reached for the one in which she'd placed a bookmark. Turning to that particular chapter, she reacquainted herself with the list of Germanic rune signs next to their Anglo-Saxon names and meanings.

'Yes, there you are!' she exclaimed, spotting the symbol, that was very similar to the one which had been crudely carved into the sarsen stone pictured in the photograph.

Reading the text afresh, she noted that it was known in Saxon as *Ger* and represented the spear and shield which was carried into battle by their warriors. For this reason, Izzy was pretty certain that the marking represented *The Ironstone Sigil*.

Obviously, there was only one way to find out.

After copying the letters etched underneath the symbol onto her notepad, she pulled up the translation engine and typed in LAPIS FERREUS.

'Huzzah!' cried Izzy victoriously. She'd been correct.

IRON STONE

Although to be fair, she knew *lapis* from the blue-coloured semi-precious stone, *lapis lazuli*, and *ferreus* was just one letter away from the word *ferrous*, which she was pretty sure meant 'metal containing iron'.

Maybe the next one would provide more of a challenge.

Opening the second photograph in the file, she was faced with another line. But rather than being etched across a diamond, this time it was crossed by four shorter diagonal grooves.

'Ah, the ogham,' she sighed, recognising the design as being rather like one of the symbols from the Celtic tree alphabet. But which tree was it depicting? Instead of turning to her book on the subject, she glanced down at the Latin script engraved below it.

'SPIN_NI_RA… mmmm…' she mused.

Noting how close the words were to ESPINA NEGRA, Spanish for *Blackthorn,* she quickly guessed the missing letters to be A and G and typed SPINA NIGRA into the translator.

Right again!

Perhaps she knew more Latin than she'd given herself credit for. Or was it just beginner's luck?

In fact, it turned out to be a bit of both.

The sigils representing the Saxon god of fertility and the three witches of fate, for instance, were a doddle to decipher since the word *BEDVIG* appeared quite clearly beneath an engraving of what looked like an ear of barley. And underneath the carving of a triangle was etched *TRIA FATA*, Latin for Three Fates.

Almost as easy were the sigils that appeared above the letters *_AL* and *S_REN,* the former being quickly deduced by Izzy as *Sal* for *Salt*, and the latter as *Syren*, which she decided was most likely the mermaid-like, *Nicor.*

But it wasn't all plain sailing, and after a run of quick wins, Izzy was thrilled when, at last, she was presented with a few sigils that required her to draw upon her extensive knowledge of the subject.

The first of these was the splayed hand which appeared above the Latin letters *C___SA_LO.* Recognising it as being similar to the symbol that early Germanic settlers called *Eloh*, which like *The Crystal Sigil* was imbued with the power to ward off evil, she was able to fill in the missing letters to form CRYSTALLO, the Latin word for the rock associated with healing.

And most fascinating of all was the marking which was very much like the Viking rune that represented a forest demon, which Izzy decided had to be *The Bear Sigil*, even though the only Latin letter from 'ursa' that had survived the mud was 'R'.

Gut feel, guesswork, an online translator and a pile of reference books. Like a *porcus* in *cacas*, Izzy spent a thoroughly enjoyable couple of hours matching the Saxon carvings with the Latin words written beneath each one.

Indeed, so immersed was she in her academic quagmire that by late afternoon she'd decrypted the symbols and inscriptions on all but three of the stones. A trio which included two with markings that were unlike any she'd come across in her research. And the stone which was missing its sigil altogether so damaged had it been by the Victorian drainpipe.

Something that she suspected would be far easier to decode was the line of text running around the entire circle of stones, the fragments of which she'd copied down onto slips of paper as she'd gone along.

As a result of this foresight, all she needed to do now was piece them together in the correct order.

With that in mind, she reached for her phone, clicked on the video she'd made of the inscription as it appeared on the stones at the bottom of the ditch, and replicated it with the slips of paper on the table.

Ut anulus symbolum est aeternitatis, sit hic sepultus circulus symbolum lux Domini Nostri Jesu Christi, qui regnabit super paganum Diabolum in aeternum. De mandato Clemetis Papae VI. Anno Domini. MCCCXLIII

That done, she carefully typed each word into her trusty translator and watched excitedly as the sentence gradually revealed itself.

As a ring is a symbol of eternity, let the circle buried here be a symbol of the light of Our Lord Jesus Christ, who will reign over the pagan Devil forever.
By order of Pope Clement VI AD 1343

'Eureka!' she cried.

As she'd suspected, the builders had known exactly what they were using to build the foundations of their new abbey.

But more exciting than this even, the inscription being unbroken meant that the foundations formed a complete Sarsenic Sigil stone circle.

Jolted suddenly by the sound of a large bird landing on the roof above her head, Izzy looked across the lawn towards the kitchen, where the movement she could see intimated that the rest of her lockdown household had returned from their hike up Devil's Dyke.

Noting from the clock in the corner of her laptop screen that it was gone six o'clock already, she sighed deeply. *Tempus fugit indeed!*

Determined to complete the task before supper, she clicked on the photos of the three remaining stones and positioned them side by side on her computer screen. By a process of elimination, she knew that two of them had to be the Saxon gods, *Woden* and *Thunar*, and the other, the fearsome wolf, *Fenrir*.

One by one she focused upon the Latin words on the stones, which despite being closest to the Victorian plumbing, had survived without any noticeable harm.

Not that it was particularly helpful since none of them bore the slightest resemblance to the names of either of the two gods or the wayward beast. In actual fact, rather than Norse or Saxon in origin, they were the names of the Roman deities, Mercury, Jupiter and Venus.

Returning to the first in the row, a vague thought entered her head.

Hadn't she read somewhere that the Christians often compared Mercury to Odin - or Woden - on account of his impressive ability to flit between the realms of the Dead and the Living? Convinced the passage was in Pete's magnum opus, Izzy reached for it and turned to the index.

'Yes! Page 56. I knew it,' she said under her breath as she flicked to the chapter containing the bit about the interplay between Woden, Odin and Mercury.

Satisfied that Mercury was Woden, she crossed him off her list and removed the photo of that sigil from her screen.

And then there were two!

On the left, the photo of the stone bearing a Z-shaped symbol above the word *JUPITER*.

On the right, the stone that was missing its sigil entirely, but on which was written the word *VENUS*.

As she stared at the Z-shaped symbol, its meaning came to her in a flash.

Rather than writing *Thunar*, the Saxon god of thunder and lightning, the scribes had plumped instead for the Roman god of inclement weather, Jupiter.

Annoyingly for Izzy, this flash of inspiration wasn't followed by any thunderbolts that helped her to work out the identity of the final sigil, for which only the Latin word had survived.

Of course, it had to be *Fenrir*. Yet though it was likely the engravers had used the Roman names for *Woden* and

Thunar, Izzy had to admit that it was quite a stretch of the imagination to suggest they'd choose Venus, the Roman goddess of love, to represent the terrifying wolf of Norse mythology.

'Bloody hell!' she cursed loudly, causing the bird which was still padding around on the roof to reveal itself with the familiar ha-ha-ha cackle of a seagull.

If only the final sigil would be so kind as to do the same!

Glancing back at the time in the corner of her screen, she was about to call it a day when her eyes fell upon the date which sat alongside it.

Friday 17 April.

Though a good deal longer than the usual seven seconds between a lightning flash and its thunderclap, the answer finally came to her.

It was all to do with days of the week.

In Spanish, the word for Friday was *viernes*. Named after Venus. But in Old English, the word was derived from the Pagan goddess of marriage, Frig.

To Saxons, Friday literally meant Frig's Day!

Izzy's brain spun into action once again.

In Old English, Tuesday, Wednesday, Thursday and Friday were named after Tiw, Woden, Thunar and Frig. But in countries where the language was derived from Latin, those particular days of the week took their names from the Roman deities: Mars, Mercury, Jupiter and Venus. In her own native tongue, for instance, these days of the week were martes, miércoles, jueves and viernes.

Finally, she'd cracked it.

The word *VENUS* was monk code for *Frig.*

She'd come, she'd seen, she'd conquered.

But wait…

There was just one problem.

Frig wasn't one of the 25 sigils!

Once again, her grey cells began to race.

'¡Increíble!' she said out loud. 'I've uncovered an entirely new sigil!'

She was about to rush off and inform her husband of her latest discovery when a less appealing thought occurred to her.

But where was *Fenrir the Wolf*?

Her heart beating audibly in her chest, she counted the photos in the file on her laptop.

There were only 25.

Perhaps, in her excitement, one had escaped being photographed?

She grabbed her phone and clicked on the video she'd taken of the entire circle.

No. There were definitely only 25 stones.

And then it dawned on her.

The reason why there was no *Fenrir Sigil*.

There had never been one.

Ever!

It had been *Frig* all along.

Its meaning lost in translation at some point and misinterpreted for over half a millennium. As would have been any of the readings in which the sigil attributed to *Fenrir* had appeared.

Faced with this information, a troubling new thought came to mind.

'¡Mierda!' she cried, causing the seagull to finally take flight.

Chapter Twenty-Three

Whose signs are they anyway?

Sunday 19th April 2020 –
Ollie's flat – St. James's Street, Brighton

In a locked-down world where one day was much the same as the next, Sundays had lost some of their sparkle of late.

That being the case, Ollie welcomed the fluttery sensation he felt in his stomach as he clicked on the link for the video call he'd arranged to talk about the Fellowship website.

Not least because it would include an update from Izzy about the discovery at Coleshill.

Being the lynchpin which held together the hopes of so many in his social circle, however, was something he approached with far less enthusiasm.

Of all Pete's disciples, he was the least knowledgeable about the magic of the Saxons.

Especially, compared to Izzy, who, since being invited to join the Fellowship team, had begun acting as if she was a Pagan Priestess!

So much so that had Pete suggested starting the meeting with a blood sacrifice, she would probably have obliged.

Thankfully for her lounge carpet, all the old man had requested was to be formally introduced to the two women who'd unearthed Sussex's only known stone circle.

Noting that everyone was in the waiting room, Ollie checked his microphone and let them all in.

'Hi everyone. Perhaps we should get the ball rolling with a few introductions…' he began before being interrupted by Pete's number one fan.

'Good afternoon, Mr Sissinghurst, I'm Isobel. But everyone calls me Izzy!'

Whilst everyone on the call knew that this wasn't strictly true, since the Velociraptors had their microphone on mute, Izzy was spared the sniggers which Ollie guessed would have been coming from Wyndham Street at that precise moment.

'So pleased to finally make your acquaintance. Always good to meet a fellow historian. Especially one as distinguished as yourself,' gushed Izzy, fangirling like a teenage autograph hunter camped outside the stage door at a boy-band concert.

Ollie had already given Pete the lowdown on Izzy. *Including the name the boys actually called her!* Nevertheless, he smiled appreciatively and was about to reply when...

'And I'm Meena. The owner of the building under which the circle was discovered!' blurted in Izzy's fellow 'uncoverer of the stones'. 'I'm also the one who's been designing your new set of Sarsenic Sigil Cards.'

'Ah, yes. They're gorgeous,' said Pete, seizing his chance to get a word in. 'It's so lovely to finally 'meet' you both. Of course, I'd always suspected we had our own Stonehenge somewhere in Sussex. I just never expected it to turn up in my lifetime. You've made an old man very happy.'

In truth, the person the old man should have been thanking was Maria, who it seemed had been written out of the story by both her sister and her wife! Not that Ollie thought she'd be too bothered; her absence on the call suggested she had more zest for cesspits than she did for sarsen stones.

Yet whilst there was no agreement on who should take most credit for the discovery, one thing was clear from the fractious introductions: the reason Ollie had been handed the job of chairing the video call.

In short, he was the only one they all trusted to play nice.

Indeed, given the antipathy the Velociraptors felt towards Izzy, he was pretty certain that the decision to involve her in the project had been made through razor-sharp gritted teeth. But he also knew that even her most ardent detractor – that is to say, Cameron – would have seen immediately how the expected media interest in the stone circle could benefit their website.

So, she'd been invited to join the party.

How long the truce would last, Ollie couldn't say, but given the potential for rancour amongst the players, the fact that he resided in the relatively neutral House Pagan made him the obvious choice for the job of referee. There was, of course, George. But since his grasp of technology didn't get much more advanced than sending texts and changing the channel on the TV, he wasn't best placed to handle the warring Houses of Pitt, Coleshill and Velociraptor across an internet chat room.

In fact, having been set up on Drew's tablet, all anyone had seen of his neighbour so far was his nasal hair.

Quite a contrast to the more technologically advanced House of Velociraptor, who had hooked a laptop up to a wide-angle camera so that all three of them could be seen together in their terrifying glory.

Introductions over, the meat of the meeting got underway.

First up was Adam with an update on the website. Next came Meena, who whizzed them through the latest versions of her illustrations for the new set of cards, prompting Cameron to suggest that she should order a small run of 50 packs as soon as possible. And after this, Ollie explained how he'd adapted the camera set-up which he used for his online personal training sessions to create a card reading area at George's kitchen table.

So, on the face of it, it seemed that they were all set to unleash the magic of the Sarsenic Sigils onto the world.

The big question was when?

Certainly, in order to get the media coverage the stones deserved, they'd have to wait until there had been a further relaxation in the rules surrounding mixing.

And then there were the circumstances in which the circle had first come to light!

Of special concern was that the 'discoverers' were from different households, and popping over for a cup of tea would probably not have been considered 'essential work' or 'an emergency' by the corona police.

This being so, some *alternative facts* would be required!

Once the reimagined chain of events leading to the discovery had been agreed, it was time to move on to the most anticipated item on the agenda: the Latin words that Izzy had photographed and translated.

As suspected, these *were* the names of the 25 sigils. Though the inscription which ran along the base of the stones was an unexpected addition to her update. And also the reason why she kept comparing the circle to the Rosetta Stone.

Aware that this would come up during the meeting, Ollie had done some research of his own and was now fully briefed on the famous rock.

What he hadn't been prepared for was the bombshell which Izzy had held back: the tantalising discovery of an entirely new sigil!

'But are you sure, Izzy? A new sigil. If you're right, that would be seismic,' said Pete, excitedly banging his walking stick on the floor.

'Well, not a new one *exactly*. Not in addition *to*... but rather instead *of*,' corrected Izzy.

'Oh!' gasped Pete. 'You mean…'

'Yes, according to the Latin translation, the symbol which has for centuries been interpreted as representing *Fenrir* is, in fact, *Frig*, the goddess of marriage…' began Izzy before filling them in on her reasoning about Venus and the days of the week.

'Oh my God, but if you're right, that changes everything… in the reading, I mean,' cried Pete. 'The one I had in the early 80s. And the one I had when we started to hear about the coronavirus.'

Given the importance of Izzy's latest discovery, the question from the House of Velociraptor came as no surprise.

'So, how would it have changed the meaning?' asked Cameron.

'Well…' began Pete, gripping the bulbous end of his walking stick. 'As you may recall, *Fenrir* represents savagery that ultimately cannot be controlled, not even by the gods. So, obviously, this sigil has always signified something bad. But *Frig*, on the other hand, representing motherhood and marriage, would mean something much more hopeful. In fact, in the context of the other cards in the reading, because it is the one that determines the outcome, *Frig*'s *Sigil* card would most likely be interpreted as meaning that a vaccine would be found, and the pandemics ended.'

Oh Em Gee! thought Ollie to himself as he looked at the gallery of silent faces on the screen in front of him.

All, in fact, except one.

A mute observer for the last hour or so, on hearing Pete's explanation, George suddenly found his voice.

'Well, for all our sakes, I hope they do it quicker for coronavirus than they did for AIDS!' he wailed, wiping a tear from each eye with Odi's mustard-coloured hanky before disappearing from the screen.

'Oh fuck, I better go and see if he's OK,' said Ollie, acutely aware of the reason for the old man's sudden departure.

That being the case, he ended the call and headed upstairs, where, as he had suspected, George was already lost in memories of the handkerchief's original owner.

Chapter Twenty-Four

Seaside rendezvous

Wednesday 7th May 1986 –
Gracie's Palace – New Steine, Brighton

'Oh God, here we go…' said Grace from behind her newspaper.

'Mmmmm?' murmured George, crunching down on a slice of toast as he watched a couple of seagulls fighting over a crisp packet on the New Steine, the rectangle of grass located between the seafront and St. James's Street, onto which Gracie's Palace looked.

His mind elsewhere, he wasn't quite ready to face the world just yet, until…

'AIDS-by-the-SEA!' exclaimed Grace, folding back the paper to show George the headline.

Wrested from his daydream by the mention of the all-too-familiar four-letter acronym, he dragged himself away from the view outside the window and focused on the article staring back at him from across the breakfast table.

'Gay plague comes to Brighton!' announced George, reading the sub-head. 'Ugh! Go on. Let me have it!'

Turning the newspaper back to face her, Grace did as she was requested.

'Forget 'kiss-me-quick' hats, saucy postcards and sticks of rock. Mention Brighton to any day-tripper these days and

the words you're most likely to hear are gays, plague and AIDS.'

Pausing for a moment, Grace lowered the paper.

'Gays, plague and AIDS. Oh my!' she sang to her breakfast companion before continuing.

'A magnet for homosexuals since the 1950s, members of the town's large gay community are dropping like coins in a penny arcade machine.'

Once again, Grace stopped reading and peered over the top of the newspaper.

'Oh, very clever! I wonder how long it took them to come up with that one,' she said, rolling her eyes before returning to the article. 'And get a load of this. A quote from some woman who the reporter says he interviewed. Down from the East End with her two toddlers.'

'Oh gawd!' sighed George, resignedly. 'What's she got to say for herself?'

'"It's really frightnin'",' began Grace, in a new voice which sounded like the tragic heroine from Brighton Rock; that is to say, cockney sparrow.

'"Brighton used to be sach a lavvly place. Now you daren't even sit down without worrying ya ganna catch samfink. I mean, I feel sorry for 'em. But from what I've read, they've brought it on 'emselves. I fink we'll go to Saarf-end next time."'

'Good riddance to her. Nasty-faced pig. *Saarf-end* can have her, as far as I'm concerned,' huffed George before taking a sip of tea.

'I wonder where she was taking the kids if she thought she could catch it off a seat? Duke's Mound? Surely, she'd be back on the train before those benches got busy!' said Grace with a smirk.

'Fuck knows. Probably all made up anyway,' added George.

'Of course, it is,' agreed Grace before returning to the article once more.

'According to figures obtained by this newspaper, at least 11 men in the once-popular seaside resort have already died of AIDS, and the number of infections could be as high as a thousand...'

For the third time in as many minutes, Grace stopped mid-sentence and crunched down the newspaper.

'Once popular! The cheek of it!'

'Once popular with nasty-faced pigs, don't forget!' snorted George before dipping his knife into a jar of marmalade and spreading a lump of it onto another slice of toast. 'But made up or not, the really scary thing is that we've no idea how many people are *actually* infected. I know loads who are just too frightened to get tested. Truth to tell, had I not been enjoying the sex life of a Trappist monk for the last 10 years, I'm not sure I'd have gone myself.'

'Hardly surprising really when you read rubbish like this,' agreed Grace, putting the paper to one side. 'As if the night sweats, pneumonia and diarrhoea weren't bad enough. Being constantly told you've only got yourself to blame. It's no wonder people are reluctant to find out.'

The fact was that since getting back from Denmark, there'd been more and more articles in the newspapers about the 'gay plague'. At best, they were ill-informed and scaremongering, like the one Grace had been reading. But mostly the stories were just an opportunity to indulge in a bit of queer bashing.

And some days, it seemed like there was no other news at all!

So much so that in the space of just a few months, AIDS had gone from the thing that dared not speak its name to the topic on everyone's lips.

The uninvited guest, to the one holding court at the head of the table.

The conversation they were having over breakfast being one such example.

Though, of course, it was Odi's announcement that had really brought it home to them. Not just because George was still a little bit in love with him, but because he was 'family'.

Sadly, in the nine months that had passed since their trip to Copenhagen, more and more people whom George counted as close friends had tested positive. After Odi there'd been Bill and Grant, who owned the florists, barmen Steve and Yuli, and several of the Sussex Lancers. Then there were the ones he'd got to know after they'd moved into the hotel.

Like David, who worked at the chemist, or at least used to, before he was 'let go'. In fact, how he'd ended up at Gracie's Palace was typical, for not only had the virus robbed him of his health and his job, but after a colleague 'accidentally-on-purpose' told his landlady about his 'condition', he'd also lost the roof over his head. He came back from the hospital one day to find his entire belongings on the street and a couple of ne'er-do-wells on the doorstep, telling him how his landlady had had to bleach all her cups and throw out his towels and bedsheets. That he should consider himself lucky they hadn't tied him up in them and set fire to the lot. *Fucking animals.* Thank goodness he knew about Grace's hotel. Turned up at her front door, crying his eyes out. Just 30 years old. His entire life in two bin-bags. It was all Grace could do not to break down in tears herself. Said that if she'd had any doubts about her plans for the hotel, the sight of David had convinced her that she'd made the right decision.

As did hearing the stories of every other waif and stray she took in. Some of whom were still there. Too weak to make it downstairs to the dining room that morning, but as comfortable as possible, safe in the knowledge that they'd have a place to stay for as long as they needed one. Which in David's case wasn't long, as his sister drove down from Huddersfield to take him back to the family home, where he passed away soon afterwards. Quietly, without fuss or ceremony. Just days after his 31st birthday.

News of David's death had been communicated in a letter from his family thanking Grace for her kindness, which did at least give hope that for every nasty-faced pig, there were generous and caring people out there too.

Dragged from his thoughts by the sound of the seagulls on the lawn outside the window, George's gaze was drawn to a couple walking arm-in-arm towards one of the benches opposite the hotel. The chap with the crutches he recognised from the Sussex AIDS Centre & Helpline. He'd been one of the first people George and Grace had met when they'd joined the group, but in recent months he'd been there less and less, and it was clear from the way he was being helped along by his friend that he didn't have much time left. Tragically, since the trip to Denmark, he was just one of several frail young men they regularly saw picking their way along the path which bordered the grassy lawn in front of the hotel.

No surprise then that, like the tower being scaled by the ferocious wolf in Pete's reading, George increasingly felt that Brighton was under siege.

How many more would have to die before the government did something about it?

If the headlines on the papers strewn around him were anything to go by, it didn't look very promising!

Faced with this depressing prospect, George was about to ask Grace if she had the horoscope page when his attention was drawn to the phone in the hallway.

'Ah! That must be Odi calling from the station,' announced Grace before making her way to the ringing.

George's heart skipped a beat. Placing the newspaper to one side, he got up from his seat and joined her at the reception desk in the hall for further instructions. Rendezvous agreed; half an hour later, they pulled up alongside the kerb where their friend was waiting with a large suitcase and a bunch of flowers.

'Pour moi?' asked George, kissing Odi on the cheek.

'For Grace, actually. I've got you a bottle of cherry liqueur!' replied the Dane.

'Good choice. Flowers will definitely last longer. You know what Gracie's like with that stuff!' laughed George.

'I do, that's why I've got her a bottle as well!' replied Odi, opening the passenger door and handing the flowers to Grace.

'Oh, come here, you handsome devil,' she said, giving him as big a hug as the fastened seatbelt would allow. 'Now let's get out of here before I get arrested for soliciting…'

She paused a moment for the punchline they all knew was coming.

'… again!'

Chapter Twenty-Five

The (not so sweet) smell of success

Wednesday 20th May 2020 –
Coleshill Abbey – Rottingdean, East Sussex

A month after the discovery of the stone circle, the day that Izzy had been waiting for was finally upon them.

'Two minutes before we go live…' announced the bearded cameraman whom she thought had introduced himself as Giles.

With limits still on the number of people allowed to mix, he was part of the small team sent by the local TV network to cover the discovery at Coleshill Abbey.

Also in the reduced crew was roving reporter Briony Beardsley, who, on hearing the countdown, began checking her hair and make-up using the camera on her mobile.

'One minute,' shouted Giles, as Cindy Allsop, the chirpy blonde anchor-woman of *Sussex Today*, appeared on the TV screen which had been erected on the grass just a few feet away from the ditch that Maria had dug around the tower.

In the last remaining seconds, Izzy's gaze followed the tangle of extension leads which ran like the tentacles of a sea monster from the screen to a van parked at the entrance to the property.

From this short distance, she could just about hear the faint hum of the engine against the more familiar sound of birdsong, that today included the ha-ha-ha cry of a seagull.

As she turned her head to the source of the cackle, her eyes were drawn up to the crenelations of the turret. Nestled in the same spot as the one she'd had to shoo away on the day they'd unearthed the stones, she wondered if it was the same bird. It certainly seemed to be singling her out for its attention. But before she could decide, it launched itself into the sky and flew away. Reminding Izzy of the raven on *The Wolf Sigil* card, she couldn't help feeling a little spooked by its appearance, but hearing Cindy summarising the day's news, she put it out of her mind.

> *'And... on the hottest day of the year so far... police reminded the public that they can still only meet one person outside their household, in the open air and two metres apart. These are the headlines for 20th May 2020.'*

Seeing some movement from the cameraman, Izzy took a deep breath and readied herself for the spotlight.

> *'And finally... in non-COVID-19 news... the chance discovery of an Anglo-Saxon stone circle, complete with strange markings, has got historians and archaeologists lining up to visit one sleepy corner of Sussex... once lockdown rules allow it. Not an issue for* Sussex Today *journalist and local resident Briony Beardsley, though, who under current lockdown guidelines has secured an exclusive interview with the two people who uncovered this remarkable find. And also with an expert on the fascinating subject of Paganism. Briony. It's over to you...'*

Right on cue, Briony picked up the baton from her colleague in the studio and stared into the camera perched on Giles's shoulder.

'Thanks, Cindy. That's right. Stunning beaches to the south. The Downs National Park to the north. I've often said that there are worse places to be locked down than this beautiful part of Sussex. Well, now it seems we have an ancient stone circle, too.

'Buried for centuries under a Medieval tower which once formed part of Coleshill Abbey near Rottingdean, of particular interest are the symbols that are believed to have been carved into the stones by the Saxon settlers who first came ashore here 1500 years ago. And that's not all. Underneath each one is engraved its Latin translation, leading some to hail the circle as the Saxon Rosetta Stone.

'In a moment, I'll be discussing the significance of the find with fortune-teller and Saxon magic enthusiast, Peter Sissinghurst. But first, let me introduce our two modern-day Indiana Joneses. *Or should that be Indiana Janes!* Designer and owner of the tower, Meena Ghosh-Martinez, and Brighton Museum curator, Isobel Pitt,' said Briony, thrusting the mic in Izzy's face.

Finally, she was able to crow about the discovery.

It was annoying that she had to share the limelight with Meena, but it was still destined to be the highlight of her career so far. Perhaps even eclipsing her recent exposé of the clandestine gay film industry which had existed in the town during the 1960s.

Certainly, no one could accuse her of not being versatile!

'So, let's start with you, Isobel. How did it come about?' enquired Briony.

Much like two petty criminals, Meena and Izzy had spent several hours corroborating their stories so as not to accidentally implicate each other in their flagrant lockdown rule-breaking. But given Izzy's reputation for being economical with the truth, it had been decided that she should be first up to speak.

'Well, as a historian, I've always been fascinated by the Saxons. Especially since moving to Sussex. So, when Meena told me that she and Maria, my sister, were excavating the abbey's old drains, I began doing some digging around myself. On the internet, of course. We were still in lockdown, so there was no chance of seeing it up close,' lied Izzy.

'And you had a hunch that there might be something important buried down there?' asked Briony.

'That's right. Having an inquisitive mind is part of the job. An occupational hazard, if you like. In fact, we historians are all Indiana Janes at heart!' replied Izzy, off-script and wonderfully obsequious. 'But yes, I knew that the early Christians often built their churches on Pagan places of worship. In addition to being symbolic, it meant they could repurpose the materials, too.'

'The original upcyclers!' exclaimed Briony.

'Absolutely!' agreed Izzy. 'So, I had an inkling that the foundations of Coleshill Abbey might have been constructed using something from an earlier building.'

For a professional lily-guilder like herself, the fibs and half-truths were second nature to Izzy. Even so, doing it on TV, she felt more exposed than usual and was greatly relieved when the time came to hand over to Meena.

Just one more falsehood and she'd be out of the woods.

'But the discovery of the sigils – the magic symbols etched into the stones – that was entirely down to Meena,' she said, glancing over at her sister-in-law.

'Yes, well… as a graphic designer,' began her partner in crime nervously. 'I've always been interested in typography, and when my wife and I bought what was left of the old abbey a few years back, I started to research the illuminated manuscripts of the monks. And it was through these that I came across the Sarsenic Sigils.'

Since Meena was not especially skilled in the art of subterfuge, that is to say, she couldn't lie to save her life, it was fortunate that her part of the interview was relatively brief.

'But how significant *is* the discovery?' asked Briony, looking into the camera. 'To explain why historians are queuing up to take a look, I am absolutely thrilled to be able to talk to one of the world's leading authorities on Saxon magic, Peter Sissinghurst.'

Not entirely sure whether she was out of shot or not, Izzy adopted her mildly interested face as Briony moved on to Pete's bit of the segment.

'Hello, Peter,' said Briony, bending down a little to his level. 'I understand that you've been studying these strange symbols for many years now?'

'Yes. Most of my life,' replied the old man. 'In fact, I've even written a book on them,' he added, shamelessly holding a copy to the camera.

'So, why is this find so important?' asked Briony, almost kneeling at the feet of Sussex's newest shaman.

While Pete explained the geological and historical importance of sarsen stones, Izzy found her eyes wandering over to the young man operating the camera, whom she noticed was sweating rather profusely. It was most likely the weight of the apparatus in the intense heat, on what she'd been reliably informed by Cindy was the hottest day of the year so far. But since she'd also noticed him sneezing quite a lot during rehearsal, she made a mental note to give him an even wider berth than the suggested two metres and zoned back into the interview with Pete, who was talking through the revelation about *Frig*.

'So, it's as significant as if the meaning behind a tarot card had been misinterpreted for centuries – potentially changing the outcome of readings in which it had appeared?' enquired Briony, in a voice suggesting surprise, even though she'd rehearsed her interview with Pete at least twice before going on air.

'That's right!' replied the old man.

'But surely, compared to the tarot, the Sarsenic Sigils are quite niche?' asked Briony.

'Compared to the tarot, yes,' confirmed Pete. 'But in these uncertain times, people are looking for new ways to explain the world and seek guidance within it. In fact, fortune-tellers of all kinds have never been busier. Especially now we can do it online.'

'Online?' asked Briony.

'Oh yes,' began Pete, briefly looking down at the script which Giles had kindly printed off and taped to the back of the old man's magnum opus. 'It's not all crystal balls and *cross my palm with silver* anymore. It's video calls and online payments. In fact, I've just launched my new website, the *Fellowship of the Sarsenic Sigils* dot com. And commissioned a new set of cards, too!'

Despite Meena's initial protests, it had been decided that it would be best for all concerned to keep mum about *who* exactly had been asked to design the cards in order to remove any whiff of cronyism. Or worse still, a scam!

Something that was *very* whiffy, however, was the stench from the drains which had just wafted past Izzy on the back of a light breeze.

Noticing that both Meena and Briony were contorting their lower faces in the manner of guests at a cocktail party when someone nearby had inadvertently broken wind, it was clear that she wasn't the only one gasping for breath.

Thankfully, it seemed that the interview was drawing to a close.

'So, there we have it,' began Briony, wrapping up. 'History, mystery and a discovery. Thank you, Isobel, Meena and Peter, for sharing this incredible find with us. I look forward to hearing how it develops. As I'm sure our viewers will, too. But for now, it's back to the studio for the latest on this amazing weather we've been enjoying. Cindy…'

Hearing the bubbly reporter hand back to the aptly named doll-faced woman in the studio was Izzy's signal to put her designer mask over her nose and get away from the drains as fast as her long legs would carry her. Which was much quicker than the more diminutive Meena and Briony, who joined her moments later by the van, bent double in fits of laughter as they shared notes about how they'd struggled to keep their faces straight during the last few seconds of the segment.

In fact, such was the hilarity of it all, it took them a minute or two to notice that they'd left Pete next to the source of the offending odour.

Fortunately, the cameraman, relieved of his heavy equipment, had gone to the old man's rescue and wheeled him over the bumpy ground to where they'd all congregated.

'So sorry, Pete,' apologised Meena, finally recovered from her fit of giggles. 'I thought I was going to be sick!'

Giles glanced over at her with a look which suggested he hadn't understood her meaning.

'The drains. Did you not smell them?' she asked. 'You mustn't have been in the downstream. Anyway, we're safe now. Went rather well, I thought. Ooh, I better call Adam and tell him we're done…'

Yet despite the orgy of backslapping that was going on in front of her, Izzy's mind was suddenly elsewhere.

The young man's coughing and excessive sweating.

The apparent loss of his olfactory senses.

Could it be?

No! Yes! Oh God.

Chapter Twenty-Six

Dress rehearsal

Wednesday 27th May 2020 – Cameron & Alex's house – Wyndham Street, Brighton

Despite Izzy's worst fears, the cameraman didn't go on to join the grizzly statistics that, by the end of May, had Britain high on the European leaderboard of infections and deaths attributed to COVID-19; the name for the virus which, over the summer, had gradually replaced corona.

Good news not just for Giles but for Cameron, too, for when he and Adam drove over to Rottingdean to collect Pete, it transpired that the cameraman had been the Irishman's most recent shag!

For Alex, however, it was yet another black mark against their 'temporary' lodger.

Never particularly happy with Adam's unfettered sexual activity throughout lockdown, the false alarm with Giles was a salutary reminder of the risk the Irishman's 'dating' posed to them both. Something that not even the endless supply of artisanal crisps and the sight of him lolling about the house in his gym kit made up for. Indeed, added to the plates and underwear which Alex claimed he was constantly picking up, the novelty of having Adam around had, like the crotch in the Irishman's nylon shorts, worn dangerously thin.

Cameron, on the other hand, wasn't quite ready to give his friend his marching orders.

In addition to enjoying his company, Adam's technical wizardry had been invaluable in developing the more complex aspects of the Fellowship website. The most inventive being the online reading room that would enable Pete to tell the fortunes of people all over the globe.

The Irishman having completed the coding the previous day, Cameron was keen to give it a go with their digital Druid. Not least because the TV interview had generated lots of traffic to the site and recruited over 100 members eager to have their 'free' reading. So, when Ollie phoned to say that the postman had delivered a pack of the newly designed cards, it seemed everything was in place for a proper dress rehearsal.

'Can you see me?' asked Cameron, looking at the small screen on the website which Adam had designed to look like a firmament of twinkling Sarsenic Sigils.

'Woah! Far out!' replied Pete, suddenly appearing in front of the celestial backdrop.

'Cool, eh! It comes on automatically. As long as you stay relatively still, the viewer will only be able tae see you and the sigils. Rather than a sink full of *dirrrty* dishes,' explained Cameron, aware that the location of the actual reading room was George's kitchen!

'Oh yes, I see what you mean!' confirmed Pete, moving back and forth. 'So clever! What will they think of next?'

'Aye, a ken. And now for the *really* smart bit. In the orange bar running along the top of your entire screen. See the wee button that says SHUFFLE & SELECT? Move the mouse across your mat until the arrow on the screen is over the button and press click,' directed Cameron in a manner which he usually reserved for conversations with his four-year-old nephew. *Who, in all fairness, would probably have been more adept at navigating a website than himself or Pete!*

Instruction executed, a grid consisting of five rows of five card-shaped boxes appeared against a green backdrop that Adam had designed to look like the baize tablecloth on which Pete laid out his cards for the readings he did in the circle of rusty pilings at the foot of the i360.

In a face-to-face fortune-telling session, the old man usually began by asking his client to shuffle the pack in order to impart some of their 'energy' into the cards. However, since this wasn't going to be possible with the online version, it had been decided that Pete would lay the 25 cards face down in the grid and ask his client to direct him to pick up their chosen seven: similar to how he'd done it for the Wyndham Street boys on their video call readings.

But given that the purpose of the run-through was simply to get Pete familiar with the technology, Cameron skipped this stage of the set-up and instructed the old man to return his attention to the gallery view of them both in their respective square screens.

'OK. We're almost ready. Have you got the cards handy?' asked Cameron.

'Yes, I have them here,' replied Pete. 'They're magical, aren't they?'

Whilst Cameron had yet to receive his own deck, having only recently signed off the PDFs of Meena's final visuals, he was more than familiar with the designs, which followed a woodcut illustration style similar to that which often adorned the book jackets of children's stories about dragons, wizards and enchanted forests.

As such, it was perfectly suited to the Sarsenic Sigils!

'Seems a shame to shuffle 'em really,' added the old man, preparing to do exactly that.

'Well, before you di, we've one more screen to test. Your 'reading table'. It'll appear when you click on the button labelled 'TABLE',' explained Cameron.

'Coooool!' said Pete, as a row of seven card-shaped boxes appeared across the entire lower half of the screen.

Representing the layout which the old man most often used when telling fortunes, underneath each one was written what a card placed in that particular box represented in the reading – from PAST, PRESENT and FUTURE – all the way along to OUTCOME.

'Oh wow!' exclaimed Pete, with the same wide-eyed awe kittens exhibit when they realise a puddle of water isn't solid.

'OK, doll. Let's get the show on the road!' suggested Cameron. 'Shuffle away!'

This done, Pete laid the top one face down in Box No.1, the second in Box No.2, and so on until the row was complete.

'Ready?' asked Cameron.

'Ready!' replied Pete, before turning over the first card in the row, which featured a handsome youth underneath an apple tree.

'The Apple Tree Sigil!' announced the old man. 'Associated with medicine and well-being. Does that mean anything to you?'

Cameron thought about it for a moment, but other than him being rather partial to the occasional Granny Smith, nothing came to mind.

'Well, I've always been in the rudest of health,' he replied, trying to be helpful. 'No once taken a day off sick. Perhaps, that's it?'

'Oh, don't worry, I'm sure it'll become clearer as we continue,' predicted Pete confidently before moving on to card number two, which turned out to be *The Bear Sigil*.

In the image, the fearsome animal took centre stage while a huntsman skulked in the trees beyond. Aware that Cameron was, by now, familiar with the meanings behind the cards, Pete's comments were a sort of sigil shorthand.

'Mmmmm… something taboo,' said the old man.

The only thing which entered Cameron's head was his and Alex's sexual attraction to their lodger. *And there was no way he was going to own up to that!* But before he could think of anything else, Pete had already moved on.

'Not you again!' he exclaimed, turning over *The Wolf Sigil* card.

'Oh God!' gasped Cameron before blurting out the thing which was definitely taboo. 'Rule-breaking!'

Since the discovery of the stone circle at Coleshill, the tower on *The Wolf Sigil* card no longer represented Brighton to Cameron and his friends, but the remains of the abbey's tallest structure instead. And as for *The Bear Sigil*, the 'illegal' trips out to Maria and Meena's place were crimes they'd all agreed to keep quiet about. The meaning behind the card, however, had not changed. That still pointed to disruption, abandonment and the end of friendships. *Perhaps there was some truth in reports circulating on the web about a second wave of 'Rona'.*

Cameron was about to share his thoughts when he noticed that Pete's attention had moved on once again, and in the box labelled CHALLENGE – signifying the thing which had to be overcome – was laid a card bearing the illustration of a crystal.

'Mmmmm… *the curing stone*,' said Pete.

Of course, thought Cameron to himself. The thing they needed to overcome was the virus. And the biggest challenge since the beginning of the lockdown had always been to find a vaccine. In fact, wasn't there one being trialled in the UK which had been showing promising results? Surely, that must be it.

Yet despite what appeared to Cameron to be a series of positive omens, the frown on Pete's forehead suggested otherwise and by the turn of the fifth card, which advised the BEST COURSE OF ACTION, he was noticeably rattled.

'Woden!' cried Pete, tapping the image of a bearded chap sitting in a wooden chair, who Cameron thought looked a bit like Adam.

He was just about to mention this when…

'Lord of Frenzy. Leader of the Possessed,' announced the old man.

'Ha! Sounds about right,' whispered Cameron to himself, reminded of Alex's concerns about Adam's rampant promiscuity. Yet, despite the humorous comparison, it didn't seem quite as welcoming as the previous run of cards, so he decided to intervene.

'Slow down, old man, you're losing me. Is he a good card or a bad card?'

'Both!' replied Pete, rather unhelpfully. 'On the one hand, *Woden* is associated with death and war. But on the other, his card could signify wisdom and healing.'

'Well, I choose the latter. Something tae di wi this vaccine everyone's talking aboot?' suggested Cameron cheerily.

'Mmmmm… maybe,' mumbled Pete, his stage presence somewhat less engaging than Cameron would have liked. *We're gonna have to work on that before we schedule any proper readings, I think!* But just as he was about to make a note of it…

'Fuck!' exclaimed the old man suddenly.

'Och no!' said Cameron under his breath as he wrote 'swearing' down on his notepad. But what was it that had provoked Pete's outburst?

In the space labelled OBSTACLES was the card featuring *The Wyrds.*

Fuck! Indeed! thought Cameron to himself.

Not because of the meaning behind the card but because of the image of the witches themselves. Or rather their likenesses to Izzy, Meena and Maria. And yes, he was right about *Woden*, too! The beardy chap in the chair was a total dead-ringer for Adam! *In fact… hang on a minute.* Cameron returned to the first card in the reading and the illustration of King Arthur sat beneath an apple tree. Longish red hair. Slim frame. Figure-hugging jacket and tights! Fuck! *It's me!*

Meena had obviously made a few last-minute caricatures before sending the final proof off to the printers. *Och, yer wee scoundrel! I wonder if she's done anyone else…*

But before he could draw attention to the ruse and ask Pete to have a look through the other cards in the new deck, there was a disconcerting moan from the reading room.

'Odi's hanging tree!' cried the old man, tapping on the card in the box labelled OUTCOME.

'Sorry?' enquired Cameron. 'Whose tree?'

But instead of providing an answer, Pete suddenly disappeared.

'Hello!?!' asked Cameron, a little concerned about the unexpected exit of the star of the show. 'Are you still there?'

Then, as if by magic, the old man was back.

'Sorry, Cameron, I was feeling a little faint. Needed to grab some water,' replied Pete, his face returning to the reading room.

'Nay worries. I think that's enough for our first run-through anyways. At least we know the technology works. I've got a few suggestions on your presentation. Nothing major, just a few tips on video chat etiquette. But we can pick it up later,' said Cameron, aware that Pete was looking decidedly pale.

'Yes, I got a bit caught up in the reading, didn't I? I'm sure I'll get better at it with practice. Let's catch up tomorrow and have another go,' suggested Pete before vanishing once again.

Assuming that their digital Druid had gone for a lie-down, Cameron was about to end the session when…

'One more thing...' began Pete, suddenly reappearing against the backdrop of sigils.

'Aye?' enquired Cameron absentmindedly.

'Just … well… *stay safe!'* replied Pete.

'Thanks, you too,' said Cameron before ending the call and closing his laptop.

Satisfied that the technical side of the website was in working order, he sat back and looked out of the window. *If only he could have been quite so confident about his digital Druid!* It wasn't just that he looked a little pasty, there was something odd about his behaviour too. Especially his sign-off at the end. Certainly, the old man's delivery of the hackneyed phrase seemed to carry more poignancy than was usually the case. And what had he meant by *Odi's* hanging tree? Shouldn't he stick to the Saxon names of the gods which are written on the cards rather than their Viking equivalents? It could get quite confusing for people otherwise.

After writing 'Saxon names of gods' on his pad, Cameron put down his pen and got up from his desk.

As he did so, he thought he heard the sound of something dropping through the letterbox.

'Ooh. Meena's new cards!' he said excitedly before making his way to the ground floor.

At least that's what he would have done had he not tripped over Adam's sports bag outside the bathroom door and gone hurtling headfirst down the stairs…

Chapter Twenty-Seven

Keeping it in the family

Wednesday 27th May 2020 – Kemptown, Brighton

Thanks to the introduction of new rules surrounding outdoor recreation, from the middle of May, Brightonians had at last been able to enjoy the unseasonably good weather with friends and relatives beyond their own lockdown household.

It was a shame then that by the end of the month, the more familiar summertime mix of sunshine and showers was being forecast. And whilst Brighton had so far been spared the promised downpour, from his vantage point on the walkway above the row of gift shops and cafés which ran along Madeira Drive, Ollie noticed fewer bathers on the beach than there had been of late.

Whether a seagull on the nearby wall was thinking the same, he couldn't say, but it certainly looked pretty depressed. Probably worried about the prospect of having to find an alternative source of food again should the steady flow of day-trippers begin to taper off, he thought to himself as a cloud fell across the sun and caused a noticeable drop in the temperature.

Feeling a slight chill, Ollie grabbed his tracksuit top and made his way to the arches cut into the cliffside. According to Adam, it was where the enormous chains that had once held up Brighton's first-ever pier used to be anchored. But with both chains and pier now long gone, the paved area between the arches and the wall provided an ideal space for Ollie to train his clients. At least while Plato's Gym remained closed. And as long as the weather stayed dry. Which was why he'd spent most of the afternoon there, trying to pack in as many sessions as he could before the expected change in the weather closed down his pop-up gym.

He looked at his watch. It was almost time to meet Drew and George for their communal shopping trip. Or weekly demonstration of 'Blitz spirit', as the old man often referred to it.

Though how hunting down extra rolls of toilet paper – one of the commodities still rationed by several supermarkets – was in any way comparable to sheltering from Nazi air raids, Ollie wasn't entirely sure.

It was, however, like the clapping and pan-banging, a reminder that they were still *'all in it together'*.

But for how long? Another reason for the group shop was to get everything they needed in time for that evening's update, which promised some big announcement about something called Test and Trace.

With that in mind, an hour or so later, all three of them were dragging their quarry upstairs to George's flat.

'Just in time,' said Ollie, noticing the clock above the sink as he entered the kitchen.

'No sign of Pete,' added Drew. 'Must be napping. Probably knackered after test-driving the website with Cameron.'

'Yeah, best leave him be,' advised George.

'Who is it tonight, anyway?' asked Ollie.

'Hancock, I think,' replied Drew, pouring beers for them all as George and Ollie unpacked the shopping.

Drinks and groceries sorted, they turned on the telly just in time to hear Health and Social Care Secretary, Matt Hancock, explain how Test and Trace would work.

At least that had probably been his intention.

Ollie actually found it all a bit confusing.

Was it an app or a website? How did you tell people you'd tested positive? And who were these 'contact tracers' whom the minister had mentioned?

Faced with so many questions, Ollie was rather relieved when Mr Hancock opened the floor to the assembled journos, which usually signalled the end of the update.

'So that's what they've spent millions on?' he asked, after switching off the TV. 'To be honest, I'm none the wiser.'

'Clear as mud, if you ask me,' added George.

Thankfully, at least one of them had managed to grasp some of the details.

'Well, from what I could make out…' began Drew, '… the gist of it is that if we feel ill, we must go and get tested as soon as we can. If we've got it, they'll notify us by text or email within 24 hours and tell us to self-isolate. At which point, they'll ask us to snitch on anyone we've been in contact with recently. And armed with this information, the tracers will then get in touch with everyone we've grassed on and ask them to self-isolate, too.'

'So, no app yet?' asked Ollie.

'Not unless you live on the Isle of Wight,' replied Drew.

'Really? What's so special about the Isle of Wight?' enquired Ollie.

'It's where they've been trialing it,' replied the Welshman.

'And don't forget Blackgang Chine!' added George. 'I went there with Pete once. What a day we had. Smugglers'

Cave. Crooked House. They even had a whale skeleton that had been washed up near The Needles.'

Smugglers' Cave. Crooked House. Whale bones. If the public announcement hadn't been baffling enough, the supposed delights of the Isle of Wight had Ollie's head spinning more than ever. Though The Needles seemed vaguely familiar for some reason.

Suddenly it came to him. Where he'd heard of them before.

'Chalk!' he announced.

'Chalk, dear? I don't remember an attraction about chalk,' said George.

'The Sarsenic Sigil Cards. The one that symbolises chalk. I'm sure it has a picture of The Needles on it,' clarified Ollie.

'Oh yes, you're right,' confirmed Drew. 'Something to do with purity.'

'It rings a bell, dear. You'll have to ask Pete when he gets up. Or look at the cards on the table where you've set up all those cameras,' suggested George, referring to the physical reading room which Ollie had created for the Fellowship website. 'I'm pretty sure they're the ones with Meena's new designs, too.'

'Oh wow, let's go and have a look. I'm dying to see them,' said Ollie, getting up from the sofa and making his way to the kitchen, where the cards were still laid out after Cameron and Pete's technical rehearsal.

Closely followed by Drew, that wasn't all they saw…

'Oh Em Gee!' cried Ollie, pointing at the card on which was illustrated the three witches of fate. 'Look! It's Izzy, Meena and Maria!'

'Fuck, you're right. And there's Adam,' added Drew, picking up the card bearing the name of *Woden*. 'And Cameron as King Arthur!'

'Yes! And is that Alex hiding behind the bush on the one with the bear? It is! It is!' squealed Ollie. 'She better have included us, too!'

Without disturbing the seven cards laid out in front of him, he picked up the remaining deck from the table.

Going through the cards one by one, it wasn't long before he came across his own likeness as *Bedwig*, the Saxon god of fertility, and Drew's face adorning the illustration of *Thunar* – the Saxon version of Thor.

'It's a wonder she didn't go the whole hog and have me carrying a dumbbell and you a monkey wrench!' said Ollie, barely able to contain his joy at being immortalised in print.

'And there's Pete!' announced Drew, pointing to *The Scop*. 'I suppose he is the Joker of the Pack, after all!'

As they came to the end of the remaining cards, there was still one person missing.

Ollie went back to the beginning and started again.

Looking through them with renewed concentration, he soon found who he was looking for.

'Aaaaaargh! That's hilarious!' laughed Ollie, showing *The Nicor Sigil* card to Drew.

But rather than George's face, Meena had drawn the visage of the old man's drag queen alter-ego, Bette y'Sweet Ass!

'Savage!' howled the Welshman to George, who'd joined them by the kitchen table.

'Oh God!' exclaimed the old man, visibly shaken.

A tad dramatic even for him, thought Ollie to himself until he realised that the outburst wasn't directed at the discovery that Bette had been depicted as a shape-shifting water spirit. No, that wasn't it. In fact, his neighbour's attention was focused not on the card in Ollie's hand but on the seven which were laid out in a row on the table.

'Oh God, oh God, oh God!' cried George repeatedly, the blood draining from his face as he fell backwards into them both.

'Steady on,' said Drew, putting his arm around the old man and sitting him down. 'What is it? What's wrong?'

'The reading Pete did for Cameron this afternoon. To test-drive the website. It's the same as the one he did for Odi in Copenhagen,' explained George.

'Fuck! So it is,' confirmed Ollie.

Was it possible that something terrible was about to happen to Cameron? It all seemed a bit far-fetched, but he reached for his phone nonetheless.

'Mmmmm,' said Ollie, after a few seconds. 'Voice mail!'

And whilst he felt this was hardly reason to send out a search party, it was clear that George was in no doubt what the next course of action should be.

'Go, go, go…' he cried.

'Are you sure? Do you not want one of us to stay with you?' asked Drew, releasing his hand from George's.

'No, I'll be OK!' replied the old man. 'I'll go and wake Pete.'

But was that really who'd be keeping him company?

From the look on his face – the faraway gaze he always seemed to have whenever he was about to take a trip down memory lane – Ollie guessed that George would soon be joined by some of the ghosts from his past instead.

Chapter Twenty-Eight

To Valhalla

Monday 12th January 1987 –
Gracie's Palace – New Steine, Brighton

By January 1987, a year and a half after Odi's diagnosis, AIDS had well and truly arrived in Brighton.

You didn't need statistics; you could see it all around you.

Especially on the New Steine, which, with so many people affected by the crisis living nearby, continued to be a popular spot for peaceful contemplation.

Looking onto it from the hotel dining room, where George and Grace often sat, the impact of the virus was literally staring them in the face.

But more heartbreaking than this even, in the months that had passed since Gracie's Palace had become a kind of hospice, they'd said their final goodbyes to several close friends in town and in London. Of course, the cause of death hadn't always been put down to AIDS. But for a community which was used to talking in secret code and euphemisms, cases of liver and stomach cancer were just part of a new lexicon that everyone was getting used to.

In the previous five months alone, George had worn his black tie no less than seven times, attending the funerals of four Sussex Lancers, a fella he'd met at Hazelpits, and Bill and Grant, the couple who owned the florists that supplied the hotel.

And then there were the ones who'd just disappeared into the night. Scooped up and shipped back to their hometowns before anyone knew what was going on.

Perhaps it was for the best if their families wanted to care for them. Though it seemed to George to be the exception rather than the rule. Especially with the older queens, for whom Brighton had been the place they'd escaped *to*, their family the thing they'd escaped *from*.

And, of course, there were the suicides.

The most recent being a young man who'd thrown himself off the cliff at Beachy Head, the note he'd left behind saying that the prospect of having to endure months of illness had been too much for him to bear.

Yet the horror of it all didn't always stop once a person died. Such was the fear surrounding the virus, lots of funeral parlours refused to handle the bodies of people whose deaths they knew to be AIDS-related. For this reason, Grace had begun making a directory of undertakers, up and down the country, who were willing to help. Anything to lessen the grief felt by those left behind.

At least more people were getting tested. And from the magazines Grace had been sent from the States, it seemed that scientists were beginning to look into treatments, something called AZT. But it hadn't been approved yet. And as for a vaccine? They were saying it could be years off. That the best we could do in the meantime was to try and contain the spread of the virus itself. A fact which even those laggards in Downing Street seemed to have finally grasped, with the launch of a new campaign that the papers had been full of recently.

And in just a few moments, George, Pete and Grace would be able to see it for themselves.

Someone not attending the 'premiere', however, was Odi, who'd decided to take his motorbike out for a spin instead. One of the few Sussex Lancers whose leathers actually got a taste of the open road, it was something he'd been doing quite a bit recently. Said it made him feel better than anything the doctors were able to give him. Certainly, he seemed to have more colour in his cheeks after speeding over the Downs or along the coastal road up to the Seven Sisters.

Which was especially good to see, considering the long list of unpleasant illnesses that had paid him a visit over the last few months.

Beginning shortly after he'd settled into Gracie's Palace, when the lymph nodes in his neck had become worryingly swollen, and George had feared the worst. Thankfully, after a fortnight of complete rest, Odi had bounced back, and by September, he'd been well enough to take a leading role in an AIDS benefit at the hotel.

Playing the part of Ronald Reagan to George's Mrs Thatcher, in a satirical sketch about the two world leaders' half-hearted response to the epidemic, the skit had had the audience rolling in the aisles.

And digging deep into their pockets.

On that occasion for the Sussex AIDS Centre & Helpline, which, with little still in the way of public funding, continued to rely heavily on the generosity of those most affected: gay men and their allies.

Indeed, in a bizarre twist of fate, the virus had managed to do something that the previous decade's political movements had failed to achieve: it brought the community together. The Ls, the Gs, the Bs and the Ts. People of all colours and faiths. Wealthy and not so. United as one in the fight against AIDS.

And with his medical knowledge, Odi had become a valued addition to the team of Helpline volunteers, too. Apart from in November when a bout of candidiasis had made it too dangerous for him to leave the hotel.

But by mid-December, he was up and about again, happily hanging baubles and stockings filled with condoms and lube on the bushes up at Duke's Mound.

In fact, despite the weight loss and pallor of his skin, as far as George was concerned, Odi was still the handsome Viking who occasionally popped down from Valhalla for a bit of earthly fun.

Remembering him in a winged helmet at the Heroes and Villains Party at Hazelpits, looking heavenly through the clouds of talcum powder billowing from Eeyore's coat, the vision in George's head was suddenly made more real by the peal of thunder which filled the room at that moment.

No. Not thunder, but what appeared to be a volcanic eruption.

The TV advert had begun.

Accompanied by a sober voice warning of an incurable disease that anyone could catch, the footage cut to a mechanical drill attacking the surface of a piece of rock.

Joined seconds later by the clanging bells of doom and a close-up of a hand-held chisel, the idea behind the ad started to reveal itself.

The rock was a granite tombstone.

And the letters being etched into its surface spelled AIDS.

But perhaps even more terrifying was a message which would strike fear into the hearts of every heterosexual in the land. That although the disease was currently only affecting 'small groups', it was spreading.

And then, as if to underline the fact that we were all in for some really heavy shit, over toppled the tombstone, followed quickly by the appearance of the leaflet which would soon be dropping through the nation's letter boxes.

Jesus! thought George, *not only was this thing gonna kill you, but when you die, they're gonna desecrate your grave and cover it in junk mail!*

Ending with the plea that everyone should read the information inside the door-drop, the thinking behind the campaign also became clear.

'Don't Die of Ignorance'

In short, failure to educate yourself about the disease could potentially lead to you having an early appointment with the Grim Reaper!

But wait, there was more. Just when he thought it was safe to come out from behind the sofa, a bouquet of lilies fell from the sky. More than that even. To add insult to injury, it looked like one of those bunches which had been picked up last minute from a petrol station.

Yet before George could share his artistic critique, Pete reached for the remote, turned off the TV and gave his own succinct review.

'Fuck!' he shouted, throwing the controls to one side.

'Fucking waste of money,' exclaimed George. 'Not a single mention of gay, bi or homosexual. And just think how much research could have been done with what they've spent on printing those *fucking* leaflets! It doesn't bear thinking about.'

'I know you're right, Georgie. But it's a start,' said Grace. 'Even if the only reason they're doing something is 'cos it's not just queers getting it anymore.'

'Yeah. Definitely no mention of the G word,' added Pete.

'Probably think they've got us covered under 'small groups',' suggested Grace.

'Small groups!' shouted George. 'I ask you! They know it's us lot who are most at risk, so why spend money on warning those least likely to get infected. It just doesn't make sense. Surely, they should be telling as many gay and bisexual men as possible how to be more careful. That's the only way we're gonna stop this fucking thing. The only way we're gonna save lives,' cried George, even more animated than before.

'You mean stop having sex?' asked Pete, incredulously.

'Unprotected sex. Yes, I do. For a bit at least,' confirmed George.

'Ha! Giving up something is easy when you don't do it in the first place,' sniped Pete.

'Oh, you can mock me all you want. I don't care if people don't like what I'm saying. But if I could save just one person from going through this hell, I'd stand at the top of the New Steine with a loud hailer and tell the whole of Kemptown to put a rubber on it,' said George. 'I mean, surely there's more to being gay than what you do with your willy!'

'You mean like opera and collecting antiques. Yeah, I'm sure that's what all the queens at the Stonewall Inn were rioting about! The reason Harvey got a bullet in his head!' countered Pete in Grace's direction, probably expecting that this reference to her old friend would cajole her into joining forces with him.

If that was his hope, he was to be sorely disappointed.

'Harvey was rather partial to opera, as it happened,' she said, smiling. 'And sex, for that matter. But I think he would probably have been with George on this one. Especially when the powers that be can't even bring themselves to say the words gay, trans or bi. Or have any idea of how to reach those most at risk. Which, don't forget, includes IV drug users, sex workers and haemophiliacs, too. And God knows how many people in Africa. But given that there's little in the way of targeted help, then yes, I do think the only way we're gonna stop this fucking thing is to protect ourselves better. And if that means staying away from the rumpy-pumpy room for a little while. Then I think it's a price worth paying.'

Was mention of the *rumpy-pumpy room* an oblique reference to Pete's accident? Certainly, it was one example of how dangerous casual sex with a stranger could be. But before George had time to decide, the discussion was interrupted by the telephone in reception.

Sitting closest to the hallway, Grace got up to answer it, leaving him and Pete to endure an uncomfortable silence until…

'Fucking cheek! Telling us not to die of ignorance when they've pretty much been ignoring it themselves for the last three years,' grumbled Pete after a few seconds.

'Couldn't agree with you more,' concurred George, eagerly grasping the olive branch.

'I mean, I hear what Gracie's saying about it being better late than never. But for a lot of our friends, it *is* too late!'

'Too late for Bill and Grant…' said Pete as Grace reappeared at the door.

'And Graeme and Robbie…' continued George, his voice petering out as he saw the tears rolling down his friend's cheeks.

'And Odi…' wailed Grace before collapsing to the floor.

But even before the words had left her mouth, George knew immediately the cause of her distress.

The agonising look on her face said it all.

'They found him about an hour ago. At the bottom of Beachy Head…' she said between sobs.

And for the second time that evening, the image of Odi against a backdrop of clouds shone brightly in George's imagination. Not dressed as a Viking warrior this time, but wearing motorcycle leathers and riding his beloved bike.

'They've taken him to the Royal Sussex,' added Grace as George rushed over to comfort her.

Looking deeply into those eyes which had already seen so much pain, he somehow managed a weak smile.

'No, Gracie,' said George softly. 'He's gone to Valhalla!'

Chapter Twenty-Nine

Mistaken identity

**Wednesday 27th May 2020 –
Kemptown, Brighton**

At about the same time that George was reliving the devastating moment he'd found out about Odi's suicide, and Drew and Ollie were running up St. James's Street as fast as their legs could carry them, the scene at Wyndham Street, was, by comparison, one of relative calm.

'I still think you should go to A&E and have it checked out,' said Alex, entering the lounge with a tray of tea things.

'I'm fine. Stop fretting, will ye?' protested Cameron, sitting on the sofa with a bag of frozen peas pressed to his forehead. 'And besides, can ye imagine what A&E will be like?'

'OK. If you're sure,' agreed Alex, resignedly, before adopting a less conciliatory tone. 'But just wait till Adam gets back. I'll have his bloody guts for garters. How many times have I told him not to leave his sports bag on the landing? Honestly, I feel like his mum, clearing up after him all the time. I've lost count of the number of times I've come across one of his sweaty jockstraps on the bathroom floor!'

'Mmmmm… I bet ye have!' laughed Cameron.

'Ha bloody ha. I'm being serious,' said Alex, pouring his husband a cup of tea. 'Isn't it about time we broached the subject of him returning to his own place?'

'Oh, he's no that baaad…' began Cameron, taking a sip from the cup which Alex had just handed him. 'Jeez! What's this pish you're giving tae me?'

'Sweet black tea. It's what they recommend for concussion,' replied Alex.

'Any sweeter and you'll be rushing me into A&E wi diabetes, n'er mind a wee bump on the heed. How aboot a brandy instead, dawl? Must be cocktail hour by now, surely,' said Cameron, looking at the clock on his phone and noticing a missed call from Ollie.

He was just about to see if his friend had left a message when there was a commotion at the front door.

'Cameron, Cameron, are you alright?'

The voice he recognised immediately, but why Ollie was mercilessly bashing their door knocker while simultaneously caterwauling through their letterbox, he couldn't say.

Ascertaining it was a matter of some urgency, he nodded to his husband to go answer the door and find out.

'Cameron! Thank God!' cried Ollie, pushing past Alex.

'We were so worried that something had happened to you,' added Drew, following on behind.

Blimey! thought Cameron. Even in a town where gossip could spread quicker than an outbreak of crabs, it was inconceivable that his friend could have known about him tripping up over Adam's sports bag. But before he could ask…

'Oh shit!' said Ollie, pointing at the plaster on Cameron's forehead.

'One of Adam's death traps!' interjected Alex, still fuming about their houseguest.

'Aye, fell o'er his sports bag on the landing. Nae harm done, mind. Just a wee cut, that's aw,' said Cameron, still trying to make sense of the unfolding scene before him.

Mebbes he was concussed after all!

'Fuck!' exclaimed Ollie. 'George was right!'

'What? The old man thought I'd tripped o'er Adam's bag o' jockstraps and running vests?' enquired Cameron.

'Not exactly. But he was worried, yes,' replied Ollie.

'After he saw the cards that Pete dealt this afternoon,' continued Drew.

'Same as the reading he did for Odi in Copenhagen all those years ago,' added Ollie.

Suddenly the clouds in Cameron's head began to clear.

'Of course. Odi's hanging tree!' he exclaimed, remembering one of the last things he'd thought about before he'd gone flying down the stairs.

Judging by the row of bemused faces that greeted his outburst, it seemed it was now the turn of Ollie, Drew and Alex to be confused.

Noting this, Cameron began to explain.

'The final card in the reading. *The Ash Tree.* The kind which Odin hung himself on. I thought I'd misheard Pete at first when he called it Odi's tree. But now I realise I'd heard right.'

'Yes!' confirmed Ollie. 'That's why we rushed around here. I did ring, but…'

'Aye, I saw…' began Cameron, brandishing his mobile. 'But why did it make you think something awful had happened tae *me*?'

Yet before anyone had time to respond, the answer to his own question popped into his head.

'Oh right,' he said. 'But it wasnae a proper reading. It was just a technical run-through,' explained Cameron. 'I didnae choose any cards. Pete just shuffled the pack and picked off the top seven.'

First the clouds cleared. Then came the bright sunshine of realisation.

'Fuuuuuck!' cried Cameron.

'Of course!' said Drew, next to see the light. 'It wasn't *your* reading. It was Pete's!'

But before Cameron was able to conjure up another weather-related metaphor, Ollie's mobile announced that George was calling him.

Assuming it had something to do with recent events, they all waited in silence while he listened to what his neighbour had to say.

'It's Pete!' cried Ollie after ending the call and returning the phone to his trouser pocket. 'He's unconscious. *According to George anyway.* Says he's tried to wake him, but he's not responding. I think we better get back pretty sharpish.'

Message relayed, minutes later, all four boys arrived at the old man's flat to find him utterly beside himself.

Pete, on the other hand, was a picture of serenity. Or so it seemed to Cameron.

Indeed, what he saw on entering the fortune-teller's bedroom was nothing more alarming than a pensioner having a siesta. But after his own recent dalliance with death, he wasn't eager to make its acquaintance quite so soon again and approached Sleeping Beauty with extreme caution.

Bending over the beatific face, he put his ear to Pete's nose. To be honest, he hadn't the foggiest idea what he was doing and prayed to god that the ambulance would arrive soon.

Thankfully for Cameron, his prayers were answered.

'Scuse me, gentlemen, can we have a bit of space, please?' asked a butch woman in a dark green uniform, closely followed by a bald man in the same attire.

As requested, Cameron moved to the other side of the bed while the paramedics carried out a few tests. Examination complete, and Pete still not responding, they lifted the old man onto a stretcher and carried him out of the room.

Cameron was about to follow when something on the bedside table caught his eye.

Hidden slightly behind a framed photograph of Pete in a leather waistcoat and sporting a thick black handlebar moustache was a small jar of dried mushrooms. No, not mushrooms. On closer inspection, Cameron realised that the bell-shaped bullets were, in fact, acorns.

Oh, my goodness! He hasnae, has he?

Cameron grabbed the jar and shoved it into his jacket pocket. Best let the medics know, he thought to himself.

Arriving in the street just in time to see the ambulance pulling away with Pete and George inside and Drew and Ollie preparing to follow on by motorcycle, he was about to make his way back upstairs when he became aware of a buzzing against the jar of acorns.

It was their lodger.

'Where is everyone?' asked Adam. 'It's like a scene from the Mary Celeste at your place!'

'Well…' sighed Cameron before bringing the Irishman up to speed with recent events. *Including the incident with the sports bag.*

Hardly surprising then that it was a very sheepish-looking Adam who entered George's kitchen half an hour later.

'I'm so sorry, mate…' he began before Alex jumped in with the case for the prosecution, which included everything from sports bags on the landing and underwear on the bathroom floor to cereal bowls in the kitchen sink and cruising in the bushes.

In fact, had Ollie not rung at that precise moment, it's likely that Adam would have been taken outside and shot for crimes against health and safety.

'Dead!' gasped Cameron, interrupting the episode of *Judge Judy* being played out in front of him.

Even though they'd only known the old fortune-teller for a few weeks, during lockdown they'd enjoyed a closeness that had made their connection seem much deeper. Suffice to say, the argument about discarded jockstraps felt rather trivial by comparison.

Accordingly, Alex and Adam waited in embarrassed silence as Cameron uttered a few helpful yeses and nos into his mobile before ending the call.

'Bless!' said Alex, after hearing that Pete had passed away en route to the hospital.

'Aye,' added Cameron, returning his phone to his jacket pocket.

Clink!

Oh fuck, the jar of acorns!

Pausing for a moment, he made the snap decision to keep the discovery – and his suspicions – to himself for the time being. *Wait to see what was what.* In any case, it appeared that the focus of attention had already moved on.

'Well… you know what else is dead then?' began Adam, standing over the kitchen table where only a few hours earlier Pete had told his last fortune. 'The Fellowship! Without our digital Druid, I'm not sure it will have the same cachet.'

'Aye, I guess you're right,' agreed Cameron, picking up *The Ash Tree Sigil* card. 'Poetic really, I suppose.'

'How so?' asked Adam.

'Oh, y'ken, the last card he dealt being the 'death' sigil – that auld tree where *Woden* died,' replied Cameron.

'The 'death' sigil?' repeated Adam with a bemused look. 'But that's not where he died. *Woden* just hung there for a few days to get wisdom from the gods. Look!' he added, handing his mobile to Cameron.

On the screen was the bit on the Fellowship website about the *Tree of Life*.

> *'According to the Poetic Edda, the famous collection of Norse poems, Odin (Anglo-Saxon, Woden) sacrificed himself with a spear and hung on the Yggdrasil – the sacred ash tree – for nine days and nights in order to learn the secrets of the runes. After descending into hell, he was then reborn with the knowledge of all the world.'*

'Oh, aye,' conceded Cameron. 'Shame about the site though.'

'Mmmm…' mused the Irishman, a wry smile spreading across his face. 'Unless…'

Chapter Thirty

A faerie tale funeral

Thursday 25th June 2020 – Izzy & Ken's garden – Bear Road, Brighton

Removing the foil from a plate of vol-au-vents, Izzy recalled the last time she'd hosted a wake, the disastrous 'post-funeral gathering' she'd laid on the previous October for Grace Davidson.

Not that she'd known the city's former MP personally.

Rather, the cremation at one of the chapels opposite her and Ken's house had presented Izzy with an opportunity to place herself at the centre of things.

On that occasion, she'd been thwarted by Cameron, who'd hosted a rival gig at his home, just down the road from the church where Ms Davidson's service had been conducted.

Thinking about Grace, it suddenly occurred to Izzy just how similar were the deaths and funerals of the former MP and the recently departed fortune-teller.

Both had died peacefully in their sleep. *There'd been a rumour circulating that Pete's death had been acorn-related.* But the postmortem had found the cause to be nothing more alarming than old age.

Both had had their services at St. Mary's, the Neo-Gothic church at the top of St. James's Street in Kemptown.

And both had been cremated at one of the aforementioned chapels.

Of course, having passed away before lockdown, there'd been standing room only at both church and crematorium for Grace. Something which rules still surrounding these events had made impossible for Pete to achieve. Although Izzy suspected that it was unlikely the old fortune-teller would have been able to pull in a crowd the size of Grace's anyway.

Even after his association with Sussex's only complete sarsen stone circle.

Yet the most important contrast of all – as far as Izzy was concerned – was that this time there would be no competing post-funeral event. She and Ken having the largest garden of all their friends – allowing for a degree of social distancing – it had been mutually agreed that after the cremation everyone should retire to their home at the top of Bear Road.

So, banishing thoughts of the last wake to the back of her mind, Izzy picked up the plate of vol-au-vents, stepped out of the kitchen and skipped up the crazy-paving path to the table which had been erected in the shade of the arbour at the end of the garden.

Catching her reflection in the patio doors of her summer house, she was pleased with what she saw. In fact, dressed in a stylish black silk dress and her hair bobbed and dyed the same hue, 'funereal' was a look that Izzy carried off with aplomb.

Despite having been mistaken for a drag queen the last time she'd worn the same outfit.

Being reminded of the embarrassing moment at the Rococo Piccolo caused her to shudder, a rare chill on what had so far been a scorcher of a day. So hot, in fact, that thunderstorms had been forecast. Fine for now though, Izzy thought to herself as she placed the plate down on the table and wafted back to the kitchen for more food, the guests from the crematorium being expected imminently.

'Ah, Kenneth! How are you doing, dear boy?' asked a voice in the hallway, signalling that the first two had done exactly that.

Followed immediately by the cry of 'Beniiiiiito! Noooooo!' there was no mistaking their identities: Stephen Tinsdale, the verger from St. Mary's, and the irascible force of nature, Mr Ben, his fox terrier, who was off the lead and on his way to the garden before Izzy could close the door.

'Ah, Stephen,' she said cordially as the ball of fur shot past her. 'So nice to see you. Lovely service, wasn't it.'

'Yes, charming. And so nice to get back into the church after all these months,' he replied, referring to the restrictions. 'Especially to oversee such an… err… interesting send-off.'

Given Pagan Pete's religious predilections, the thrust of the affair at the church and crematorium had been humanist in nature and led by elders from the local branch of the Radical Faeries, of which Pete had been a lapsed member. So much so, in fact, that it took Izzy a while to realise that the Little Acorn to whom one of them kept referring was Pete's Faerie name!

Entranced by their outfits, Izzy had also invited the Faeries to the wake. In fact, she'd even arranged for them to have a starring role. If nothing else, having 'Queen Hollyhox' and 'Enchanting Nightshade' in attendance at her event would add a little Druid magic to the proceedings!

Embracing them both as if they'd been long-lost siblings, after the Faeries came the Velociraptors, who, dressed in strikingly similar black suits and designer sunglasses, looked even more sinister than usual. And walking alongside

Adam was the cameraman whom she'd incorrectly diagnosed as having COVID-19 – and who it transpired was the Irishman's latest conquest. Sporting the same blue jeans and denim shirt he'd worn on the day of the TV interview, it was clear that Giles had not received the memo from the boys about the event's dress code!

Behind the dinosaurs and the cameraman were Ollie and Drew, the former in a dark polo shirt and the latter in a black zip-up Bomber jacket. And following them into the garden, a few seconds later, were Maria and Meena. Her sister dressed similarly to Ollie and her sister-in-law, wearing something more akin to what Izzy had chosen.

Last to arrive was chief mourner George, who, in honour of his dear friend, had accessorised his outfit with Pete's black leather waistcoat.

Josh, Kwan, and Ken were already present, having returned with Izzy to help set things up in the garden. And as it turned out, now also tasked with keeping Mr Ben away from the cheese straws, vegan sausages and ham rolls. At least until the highlight of the event had taken place: the part which had been deemed a little too Pagan for the cemetery across the road.

With that in mind, Izzy scanned the lawn for her Faeries.

Since it transpired that Pete's ashes would not have been ready in time for the wake, in lieu of a scattering, they'd decided to plant an ash tree in his memory instead. In all honesty, the delay in acquiring the urn had been a relief for Izzy, who'd not been especially keen on having the old man's remains getting caught up in her herbaceous borders. Especially when she'd discovered that, in a last show of defiance, Pete had requested that he was to be cremated in his Sussex Lancers gear – complete with studded cap, leather jacket, chaps, harness and nipple clamps!

Perennials saved from the remnants of charred fetish wear, Izzy happily clinked her glass with a fork and announced that Queen Hollyhox would like to begin Little Acorn's memorial speech.

Dressed in a sort of toga which reminded Izzy of *Bedwig,* the Saxon god of fertility – without the basket of fruit and the bushel of barley but with brightly painted fingernails and wearing a crown of twigs and flowers – the Master of Ceremonies stepped forward with Pete's tree.

As Izzy had hoped, nail varnish wasn't the only colour that Radical Faerieism was bringing to her party, and over the next few minutes, Queen Hollyhox invoked spirits with chants and spells while Enchanting Nightshade lit feathers and rang bells.

Deciding she'd got the gist of the act, after smiling serenely at the latter-day *Bedwig,* she moved onto the faces of her guests in an attempt to assess their appraisals of the performance so far.

She had to admit, it was rather a mixed bag, ranging from a good deal of eye-rolling from Stephen at one end to the respectful observance of Meena and Maria at the other. Also in her sights was a seagull circling overhead. Although the bird was probably more interested in the unattended buffet than the affair below. And finally, there was Mr Ben, who'd already taken advantage of Stephen's attention being on the Pagan ritual to steal a chicken wing from a plate that someone had left on a chair.

Distracted slightly by the dog's opportunism, Izzy suddenly realised that Queen Hollyhox had stopped chanting and was now holding aloft the tree sapling and saying something about the word 'radical' in Radical Faerie meaning both 'revolutionary' and 'root'.

Ah yes, from the Latin 'radix', thought Izzy to herself, as the baby ash tree was being lowered into the hole that had already been dug in the middle of the garden.

There was a communal raising of glasses and the customary 'To Pete!' and then it was back to the small talk and ham rolls.

All in all, the scene could not have been more pleasing to her.

After months of isolation, like a fabulous butterfly emerging from its pupa, she was finally at the centre of her adopted social circle.

And then there was the recent boost to her career.

Still bathing in the glory of her research into Brighton's queer past, the chance discovery at the tower had catapulted her academic reputation to dizzying new heights, with offers of interviews and TV appearances coming at her left, right and centre.

Though, of course, the thing that made it all so much sweeter was that, without Pete to front it, Cameron's website and his plans to corner the market in online Sarsenic Sigil fortune-telling was dead in the water, too.

Happy days indeed!

Never one to miss the opportunity to kick a man when he was down, she made her way over to where he was standing with his fellow Velociraptors under the arbour at the far end of the garden.

Bravo! Not just one man, but all three of them.

Noting how much like extras in a Sicilian mobster movie they looked in their dark suits, designer shades and black ties, Izzy decided it was time for her massacre.

'Such a shame about your website, darlink,' she began in Cameron's direction.

'Aye, I ken. He'd have loved tae have brought the magic of the Sarsenic Sigils tae more people around the world,' replied Cameron, not nearly as disheartened as she'd hoped.

Not even slightly injured by her first shot, it seemed.

And where was the cut on his forehead she'd heard about?

Despite the lack of an obvious wound, she reached for some of that idiomatic salt and prepared to start the rubbing.

'All that wasted time and effort,' she said, waiting for the expected sting.

Again, nothing.

Except, perhaps, the almost imperceptible sound of the Velociraptors' ruffs being raised in preparation for an attack.

Had she just walked into a trap?

'A waste? Well… not exactly,' interjected Adam, reaching into his shoulder bag.

'Just a bit of a rethink…' began Alex as the Irishman retrieved his tablet and fired it up.

'Artificial Intelligence!' announced Cameron as Pete's face appeared on the screen.

'Obviously, it involved a bit more faffing. But with all the recordings we'd made of him over the last few weeks, you know from the readings and video chats, it was relatively easy to create an avatar,' explained Adam gleefully.

'Of course, it's no' as guid as the real thing. And it won't be for everyone, y'ken. But as Pete always said, so much of fortune-telling is aboot how you interpret the cards. His avatar makes a few wee suggestions, and then it's doon tae the individual tae decide what the reading means tae them,' continued Cameron. 'And tae be honest, the online readings are only one aspect of the Fellowship. Mostly people want tae learn how tae di it themselves. Pete's book and Meena's cards are flying off the shelves. Cannae print 'em fast enough.'

'Brilliant, isn't it, dear,' said a new voice as George joined the chorus of approval. 'And best of all, Pete will live on for as long as the site exists. So clever.'

'And not just Pete, either. We all will. Immortalised by Meena's drawings,' added Alex.

That was something, at least, thought Izzy, reminded of the caricature of her as the leading witch on *The Wyrds Sigil* card.

A silver lining in the dark cloud that had just rained on her parade.

But before Izzy could process what she'd just seen and heard, she felt a spot of *actual* rain on her arm.

The promised thunderstorm was about to break.

'Aaaaargh! Quick! The buffet!' she cried, gesticulating to everyone to grab whatever they could from the table and take it indoors.

Seconds later, slightly bedraggled from the sudden downpour, Izzy glanced through the kitchen window at the lawn where the party had just been.

Empty, except for a solitary seagull pacing about amongst the detritus on the table.

And Mr Ben cocking his leg against the newly planted sapling.

A tableau vivant joined moments later by Stephen running towards him at speed.

'Beniiiiito! Nooooooo!'

Chapter Thirty-One

Turn up for the books!

Wednesday 1st July 2020 – Pete's flat – First Avenue, Hove

George's world felt rather empty the first few days after the funeral. It wasn't just that he missed his old friend. Further relaxations of lockdown rules meant that by the beginning of July, the boys hadn't been around as much either.

Oh well! At least he'd have time to sort out Pete's affairs.

Which, if the single sheet of paper that was his Last Will and Testament was anything to go by, wouldn't take very long.

Certainly, it seemed there were no fortunes to be had from telling people theirs!

And with no provision whatsoever for Pete's belongings, everyone had agreed it was only right that they should all go to his oldest friend.

This being the case, the morning after the reading of the will, George found himself in an area of town which, though always a little bit alien to Brightonians, after three months of lockdown, felt more like a foreign country!

Hove.

In fact, glancing at the headlines on one or two of the newspapers that had piled up in Pete's absence, opening the front door to the fortune-teller's flat was akin to stepping back in time!

And then there was the smell!

If the task of going through Pete's belongings wasn't off-putting enough, the thought of what might be the cause of the stench which filled his nostrils as he pushed back the snowdrift of letters and leaflets filled him with utter dread.

He paused for a moment. *Was it too late to change his mind?* No! He owed his friend that much.

So, covering his nose with Odi's mustard-coloured hanky, he braved his way to the source of the offending odour in the kitchen, which turned out to be the remnants of a cottage pie that had decided to become penicillin.

After depositing it in the outside bin, he moved onto the lounge, where he knew Pete kept most of his valuables.

As expected, it didn't amount to much, confirming his suspicion that being the sole heir to the fortune-teller's estate was somewhat of a poisoned chalice.

Ironic then that one item amongst the bric-a-brac was a pewter goblet.

Though whether it had ever been used to administer anything toxic, he couldn't say.

The occult and Pagan memorabilia – of which the chalice had been one of the classier items – George boxed up for Adam to drop off at The Sussex Beacon charity shop on St. James's Street.

Next up was Pete's collection of books.

Apart from a few classic novels, it mostly fell under the broad genre of fortune-telling, including a box containing about 50 copies of his friend's own tome on the subject. *Perhaps those nice Radical Faerie fellas would be interested in some of the titles?* Not much of a reader these days, after grabbing a copy of Pete's magnum opus, George moved on to sorting out his friend's clothes, which being as threadbare as his will, met the same fate as the cottage pie.

That is to say, shoved into a bin bag and thrown away.

But it wasn't all going to charity or landfill, though.

There was a crate of LPs and singles which George would gladly find space for in his gramophone cupboard. And there were quite a few old films on DVD and video cassette that he looked forward to watching again.

Yet most tantalising of all, after a few hours of sifting, sorting, recycling and binning, George's hard work was rewarded with the discovery of a shoe box of old photos.

'OK, you old rascal!' he said, looking over at Pete's favourite armchair opposite the TV. 'Let's see what you've got on us!'

Imagining his old friend grinning back at him through his grey beard, which in later years had joined the handlebar moustache he'd had since his days as a clone, George smiled and returned his attention to the box.

Of course, there were plenty of pre-moustache photos of Pete.

Black-and-white ones of him as a baby. Sepia ones of beach holidays in once glamorous locations like Leigh-on-Sea and Robin Hood's Bay. And technicolour photos of him in his school uniform against painted backdrops of clouds and sky.

After this, there were Polaroids of Pete in the bloom of youth, which, judging from the Marc Bolan perm, probably dated from the early 70s. As did the clothes. Most notably in one photograph, a pair of denim flares, fit-to-bursting at the crotch, the tell-tale sign of the serpentine monster that would later earn him the nickname Python Pete.

But most exciting of all, as far as George was concerned, were the round-cornered snapshots which dated from the 80s: the era of Hazelpits, the Sussex Lancers and Kelly Marie!

Boom boom… boom boom!

Surely there would be photos of himself amongst these.

Yes! There he was! As Lady Godiva at the Heroes and Villains Party. Stood next to Pete dressed as Victor Hugo, in shorts, knee-length socks, and not much else except for a gold medallion and a pair of silver roller skates!

Moving on, there were quite a few photos of the Lancers, including a large one of them all at some Christmas event. George cast his eye over the group of young men, who, aside from Pete and The Three Muskaqueers, had all succumbed to that other pandemic.

And then he saw something which properly made his heart beat loudly in his chest.

The photo he'd taken beneath that old oak tree in Frederiksberg Gardens.

Suddenly it struck him.

For the first time in over 30 years, his friends would be together again.

All, of course, except himself.

I suppose that's what the boys mean by FOMO! he mused, reminded of a phrase he'd heard Ollie and Drew use a lot.

'Not long now, my dears,' he said to the motley crew in the photo, lifting it to his lips and kissing the cracked and faded image. 'Not long now.'

After this particular snapshot, Pete seemed to have lost interest in photography, and when he and George next appeared together – at the opening of The Sussex Beacon in 1994 – they were both well into their 40s. Still smiling, but George knew that the intervening years had not always been happy ones. In fact, as far as he could see, there wasn't a single photo from 1986 to the early 90s.

Roughly the period in which they'd lost countless friends to AIDS.

Feeling a tingle in his nose, he was about to reach for Odi's handkerchief when he heard the sound of the telephone in the hall.

Who on earth could that be? Probably someone selling something or other.

Confident that was what it would be, George's decision to answer it was partially motivated by the chance to tell the person at the other end that unless they were expecting a nasty cold spell in hell this year, the flat's former resident would *not* be in the market for double-glazing.

Imagine his disappointment then when it turned out to be the woman from Pete's publishing company.

After a few minutes explaining why he was answering the phone, there was an uneasy silence at the other end until…

'I'm so sorry… it's just that… something extraordinary's happened,' said the woman.

'Extraordinary?' repeated George.

'Yes, it's about Mr Sissinghurst's book on Sarsenic Sigils,' she replied.

George knew that Cameron and Adam had organised an updated re-print, which could be ordered online. Now available as something called an e-book, too. So, it wasn't a total surprise that she was trying to get in touch.

What came next, however, was completely unexpected.

'It's number one in the non-fiction charts!' she gushed.

'Oh…' began George, not sure what to say next.

'And, of course, it's raising lots of money for that charity he mentions in the dedication. The Sussex Beacon, is it called?' asked the woman.

Well, I never, George thought to himself.

Intrigued by what she'd told him, after exchanging contact details and ending the call, he picked up the copy of Pete's book which he'd put to one side earlier.

Flicking to the front page, there it was in black and white.

I dedicate this edition to my dear friend Odi Olafson and all the other beautiful souls I knew whose lives were cut short by AIDS. In those early days of despair – when there was little in the way of medical treatment – I hope my readings helped in some small way. An entertaining diversion, at least! In memory of the ones we have lost, and those who continue to live with the virus, I donate all royalties from the sales of this book to The Sussex Beacon.

'What a turn-up!' said George out loud.

Returning to his spot opposite the armchair, George was about to start putting the photos back when he noticed an envelope lying flat at the bottom of the shoe box.

Emblazoned with the name of some long-gone photo-developing company, his heart began to race once again.

Were there more delights to be had? Another ticket-to-ride down memory lane?

Damn.

It was empty.

But wait.

On closer inspection, he realised that the folder did contain a strip of negatives.

Interest piqued, George unfolded the sheet of celluloid and walked over to the window.

Noticing a large seagull pecking at the bin bag containing Pete's clothes, he tapped on the glass until it got the message and flew off.

Alone once more, George held the strip of negatives up to the light.

'Good Lord!' he gasped as the brown blotches started to make sense.

But that wasn't all which revealed itself.

About halfway down, he saw something even more familiar.

Himself!

How old would he have been then? 26? 27? It was difficult to work out from the mottled plastic, but he seemed to recall that his hair – shoulder length as befitting the period – was still blond at the time.

And were they the platform shoes he'd worn for that Bowie gig?

Of course, the rabble of misfits and hippies pictured walking down Norfolk Square and onto the seafront in the early 70s was minuscule compared to the tens of thousands of people which now attended a similar event in the city each year. But judging by the slogans on the placards – it was clear that the reason for the gathering had changed little in the half-century which had passed since the missing photographs had been taken.

'Glad To Be Gay!' shouted one. 'Gay but not ashamed!' declared another. It was, of course, the Pride march organised by the Sussex branch of the Gay Liberation Front in 1973.

I wonder if any of them are still around.

How wonderful it would be if he could track one or two down.

Scanning the strip of negatives, he tried to recall the names of his fellow gay-libbers.

Sadly, none came to mind.

Ah well, he sighed, returning the strip to its envelope.

And that was when he saw it.

A roll call from his past, in a familiar hand.

On the inside flap, it seemed that Pete had made a list of everyone who'd been on the march that day.

'Oh my goodness!' cried George to the empty room.

Perhaps his old friend had left him something of value after all!

EPILOGUE

Fortune favours the brave

Wednesday 17th July 2020 –
i360 – Lower King's Road, Brighton

Why fortune-tellers are drawn to Brighton is almost as mysterious as the art itself.

But whatever the attraction, this far-from-quintessential coastal town has seen more than its fair share of them over the years.

One of the most famous was Gypsy Lee, who saw the future in the mists of her crystal ball and could list Edward VII amongst her clientele. In the 1950s, angling-mad palmist, Madame Binnie, would do readings on the Palace Pier while fishing for crab and plaice through a hole cut in the floor of her booth!

And more recently still, there are the clairvoyants, psychics and spiritualists who have occupied the cubby holes and arches that run along the promenade for as far as my beady eye can see. As much part of the city as fish and chips and amusement arcades, whether readers of tarot or tea leaves, I've witnessed them all.

But whatever the lure, none have been quite as intriguing as the old man who used to ply his trade on the seafront below where I perch today.

Seated at a table in the middle of this circle of rusty posts, a sort of seaside Stonehenge, his choice of location was no accident. That's because the tools of *his* trade were the cards inspired by the magical symbols carved into stone by the Pagan settlers after whom this stretch of land is named. Signs which represented the most important aspects of their world.

The minerals that formed the ground upon which they walked. The gods to whom they prayed. The forests which once covered their lands. And the animals that roamed therein.

From Steyning to Stanmer. Goldstone to the Old Steyne, the importance the Saxons placed upon the stones which littered their lands will be remembered for as long as the towns and villages named after them continue to exist.

But the endurance of the Sarsenic Sigils will be thanks to the old man who went by the name of Pagan Pete. And a group of people who proudly call themselves Brightonians.

The End.

(For now.)

TIMELINE of HIV/AIDS

(Some key dates and statistics relating to the period covered by the novel)

5 June 1981 – The U.S. Center for Disease Control (CDC) publishes an article in its *Morbidity and Mortality Report* (MMWR) which describes cases of a rare lung infection called Pneumocystis Pneumonia (PCP) in five young, previously healthy, gay men in Los Angeles. On the same day, a New York dermatologist calls the CDC to report a cluster of a rare and unusually aggressive cancer called Kaposi's sarcoma (KS) amongst gay men in New York and California. Like PCP, KS is associated with people who have weakened immune systems. (HIV.gov)

27 July 1982 – The term AIDS (acquired immunodeficiency syndrome) is proposed at a meeting in Washington, DC of gay-community leaders, federal bureaucrats and the CDC to replace GRID (gay-related immune deficiency) as evidence showed it was not gay-specific. The cumulative number of known deaths in the US by end of 1982 is 1,118 at which point US President Ronald Reagan had still not mentioned the word "AIDS" in public. (factlv.org)

4 July 1982 – Terry Higgins dies of an AIDS-related illness in the United Kingdom, prompting the foundation of what was to become the Terrence Higgins Trust. 10 persons

registered at Brighton & Hove HIV Clinic have been seen in the last 12 months and are alive at the time of this year's latest data. (Lunch Positive Timeline)

In 1983 the first AIDS-related death occurs in Australia, in the city of Melbourne. The Hawk Labor government invests in a significant campaign that has been credited with ensuring Australia has one of the lowest HIV infection rates in the world.

25 April 1983 – the BBC broadcasts "Killer in the Village" as part of its *Horizon* series. The documentary describes the illnesses affecting patients and looks at theories and early research into AIDS. (IMDb.com)

1984 – the first person from Brighton known as having died from AIDS is reported in the news. This was the 45th reported AIDS death in the UK. 22 people registered at the Brighton and Hove HIV Clinic have been seen in the last 12 months and are alive at the time of this year's latest data. (Lunch Positive Timeline).

1984 – the first public meeting on AIDS in Brighton & Hove is arranged by Graeme Wilkinson and Clive Stevens. (The Brighton AIDS Memorial remembrance project founded by Harry Hillery and archived on Queer Heritage South)

1985 – The Sussex AIDS Helpline is formed in the same offices as Brighton Gay Switchboard on Ditchling Road.

1985 – 54 persons registered at the Brighton & Hove HIV Clinic. (Lunch Positive Timeline) According to the current affairs series TV Eye, 58 AIDS-related deaths have been recorded in Britain by the end of this year.

17 September 1985 – President Reagan mentions the word "AIDS" in public for the first time in response to a reporter's questions. Number of known deaths in US by end of this year is 5,636. (factlv.org)

2 October 1985 – Rock Hudson dies of complications from AIDS.

24 March 1986 – the BBC broadcasts "AIDS: A Strange and Deadly Virus" as part of its *Horizon* series. The documentary looks at early work to identify the virus and experimental use of AZT (zidovudine), the first antiretroviral drug.

12 April 1986 – Sussex AIDS Helpline becomes registered charity Sussex AIDS Centre & Helpline. 49 persons registered at the Brighton & Hove HIV Clinic have been seen in the last 12 months and are alive at time of this year's data. (Lunch Positive Timeline)

January 1987 – the UK Government launches "AIDS: Don't Die of Ignorance", a major public information campaign. A leaflet about AIDS is delivered to every household in the UK, which warns that it is impossible to tell who is infected with the virus.

March 1987 – ACT UP is founded. After a demonstration by the group, the FDA announces a two-year shortening in the drug-approval process, enabling the use of AZT.

April 1987 – with virtually no mention made in the interim, President Reagan appears before the College of Physicians in Philadelphia to deliver his first "major speech" on AIDS, calling it "public enemy number one." Cumulative known deaths in the US by this year is 20,436. (factlv.org)

9 April 1987 – Princess Diana opens the Broderip Ward, a dedicated ward at Middlesex Hospital for the treatment of HIV patients. Notably she shakes the hands of AIDS patients without wearing gloves.

1987 – 67 persons registered at the Brighton and Hove HIV Clinic have been seen in the last 12 months and are alive at the time of this year's data. (Lunch Positive Timeline)

1 December 1988 – to mark the first World AIDS Day, Terrence Higgins Trust release 1,000 balloons – roughly matching the number of recorded UK AIDS cases in 1987.

Please note: statistics credited to Lunch Positive Timeline can be found at https://silo.tips/download/hiv-aids-a-local-history#

Timeline of COVID-19

(Some key dates and statistics relating to the period covered by the novel)

23 January 2020 – China reports 17 deaths linked to the coronavirus and imposes a lockdown in Wuhan.

29 January 2020 – British Airways suspends all flights to and from mainland China.

30 January 2020 – the first two cases of COVID-19 in the United Kingdom are confirmed, two Chinese nationals staying in York.

6 February 2020 – a third case of COVID-19 is confirmed in the UK.

10 February 2020 – the total number of cases in the UK reaches eight.

2 March 2020 – the government holds a COBRA meeting to discuss its preparations and response to the virus, as the number of UK cases jumps to 40.

3 March 2020 – UK supermarkets draw up plans to feed the nation as COVID-19 spreads.

5 March 2020 – first death from COVID-19 in the UK is confirmed, as the number of cases exceeds 114.

11 March 2020 – World Health Organisation announces COVID-19 is officially a pandemic.

16 March 2020 – UK death toll reaches 82, with the number of cases of the illness passing 1,500.

Prime Minister Boris Johnson advises everyone in the UK against "non-essential" travel and contact with others. Wherever possible, people are encouraged to work from home and avoid visiting social venues such as pubs, clubs or theatres.

20 March 2022 – Chancellor Rishi Sunak announces that the government would pay 80% of wages for employees not working, up to £2,500 a month. Prime Minister Boris Johnson orders all cafés, pubs and restaurants to close, except for takeaway food. All the UK's nightclubs, theatres, cinemas, gyms and leisure centres are told to close "as soon as they reasonably can".

23 March 2020 – Prime Minister Boris Johnson announces new strict rules applicable to the entire United Kingdom with the aim of slowing the spread of COVID-19 by reducing transmission between different households.

6 April 2020 – the death toll from COVID-19 in the UK exceeds 7,000. The total number of reported cases is nearly 53,000. Boris Johnson is taken into intensive care at St. Thomas' Hospital. It is announced that First Secretary of State Dominic Raab will deputise for him.

16 April 2020 – Dominic Raab announces a three-week extension to the nationwide lockdown measures. Number of confirmed COVID-19 cases in the UK surpasses 103,000. Confirmed deaths exceeds 16,000.

20 April 2020 – total number of recorded deaths rises to 20,223, making the UK the fifth country to pass the 20,000 mark, alongside the United States, Italy, Spain and France.

23 April 2020 – first human trials of a COVID-19 vaccine in Europe begin in Oxford.

30 April 2020 – Prime Minister Boris Johnson says the UK is "past the peak" of the outbreak.

5 May 2020 – the number of recorded deaths rises by 649 to 30,076, giving the UK the highest number of COVID-19-related deaths in Europe.

13 May 2020 – the re-opening of garden centres, sports courts and recycling centres. In addition to outdoor exercise, open-air recreation is also permitted with no more than one member of another household with whom social distancing must be practised.

18 May 2020 – the UK adds loss of smell and taste to the list of COVID-19 symptoms.

27 May 2020 – Matt Hancock, launches the Track & Trace system on evening update.

28 May 2020 – tenth and final Clap for Our Carers event is staged at 8pm.

1 June 2020 – gatherings of people from more than one household are limited to six people outdoors and are prohibited entirely indoors, with exceptions including education.

5 June 2020 – pubs and restaurants can utilise outdoor spaces such as terraces and pavements.

17 July 2020 – Prime Minister Boris Johnson announces a further easing of lockdown restrictions for England, with plans for a "significant return to normality" by Christmas.

Total deaths by this date: 45,273.

25 December 2020 – on Christmas Day the total number of deaths in the UK was 70,195.

Some historical notes

Chapter One – (i) The Sussex Lancers existed until the late 90s. The event at Whispers on Friday 3 August 1984 was, indeed, the first meeting of the club in that venue. (ii) Given the safe sex advice relating to lubricants, it is likely that the nickname Vaseline Alley was coined before the early 80s. (iii) the Lesbian and Gays Support the Miners (LGSM) was an organisation set up to raise money for miners during the 1984/5 strike. For more info visit www.lgsm.org

Chapter Five – The gay discos at Hazelpits Farm in Kent were the stuff of legend in the late 70s and early 80s. For more information about this and the antics of the Sussex Lancers, visit Alf Le Flohic's website at www.gayhistory.co.uk

Chapter Eight – For further information about Brighton's queer history, visit The Keep – in person or online at www.thekeep.info

Chapter Ten – (i) Sadly, there is no evidence of a Heroes and Villains themed party at Hazelpits. (ii) Common on the gay scene from the 70s, the hanky code is widely discussed on the internet.

Chapter Thirteen – (i) Full transcripts of the daily update – from which I have quoted here and in Chapter Twenty-One and Chapter Twenty-Seven – are available at www.gov.uk

Chapter Fourteen – (i) For examples of the sort of homophobic news articles that Adam mentions here and which Grace is reading out in Chapter Twenty-Four, one of the best places to start is www.bishopsgate.org.uk (ii) On 23 May 1988, the evening before Section 28 came into force, lesbian activists stormed the BBC News studio where Sue Lawley was midway through the Six O'Clock News. (iii) The virus causing the mystery illness which fatally compromised people's immune defences, that more and more doctors were seeing at the beginning of the 80s, is now believed to have originated in non-human primates in West-Central Africa at the beginning of the 20th-century – and passed on and spread to the human population as a result of dramatic changes happening there at that time, including the destruction of natural habitat and associated hunting, poor health care practises, such as the re-use of hypodermic needles, an increased movement of people in and out of the area, and new networks of sexual interactions. This being so, it is now clear that by the early 80s, many people had already died of what went on to be called acquired immunodeficiency syndrome (AIDS).

Chapter Sixteen – (i) After writing the chapter about a gay board game, I discovered that an unofficial gay version of Monopoly had been marketed in 1983, featuring the hanky code and leather boy imagery! (ii) Queer the Pier opened at Brighton Museum in February 2020.

Chapter Eighteen – Whitehawk is believed to be Saxon for 'holy oak' – and the area so called because of a wooden pole that stood on a hill there. As for the existence of an actual holy oak on Whitehawk Hill? Sadly, not to my knowledge. Certainly, it is unlikely that there would be one still growing that had been known to Saxon Pagans.

Chapter Twenty-Two – Whilst the letters J W and U do not appear in the Latin of the Romans, by the Middle Ages, they were more commonly in use.

Chapter Twenty-Seven – Opened on 23 November 1923, The Royal Suspension Pier was destroyed by a storm on 4 December 1896.

Chapter Twenty-Eight – (i) There is disagreement as to when the 'Don't Die of Ignorance' TV campaign first aired, but 12 January 1987 is one that appears a lot. (ii) Credits for ad: TBWA (agency) Malcolm Gaskin (designer) David O'Conner-Thompson (copywriter) Nicholas Roeg (director) John Hurt (voice) Sammy Harari (producer) COI (client).

Chapter Thirty – Founded in 1979 by gay activists Harry Hay and Don Kilhefner, the Radical Faerie movement is still going strong today. The ones mentioned in this chapter are entirely fictional and, as far as I know, not the names of any actual members, past or present.

Chapter Thirty-One – Photos of the very first Pride march in Brighton in 1973 were discovered by local historians in 2021.

Epilogue – Angling-mad clairvoyant Madam Binnie was a real person. To watch her in action, search www.britishpathe.com for clairvoyant-fishing.

Some more historical-*ish* notes

SPOILER ALERT!!! If you're reading this before finishing the book, then I softly advise you to stop and desist! As Alf suggests, come back to it later.

If, like me, that has only encouraged you to read on, then let me just say this.

Fact is often more fantastical than fiction!

Certainly, some of the stuff I came across when devising the Sarsenic Sigils, was pretty jaw-dropping.

So, let's begin with the sarsen stones.

As a quick surf on the net will verify, there are indeed hundreds of these across the country. That they are so-called because of their association with Paganism. Also, true. And whilst not necessarily sarsen, many Sussex towns do, in fact, owe their names to stones.

As for the sigils themselves, whilst essentially fictional, most have their roots in actual folk lore. Indeed, one of the joys of writing this book has been finding out more about the stories and myths associated with my own ancestry, which being a Northerner is most likely a mix of Celt, Viking and Saxon.

So much so, in fact, that for at least three months I happily lost myself in books about Viking runes, the Celtic ogham and pre-Christian Saxon history; a good deal of which is documented in the collection of Old Norse poems, the Poetic Edda, the Old English classic Beowulf and the

Anglo-Saxon Chronicle, excerpts, translations and interpretations of which are widely available online via several sources. And given that two suits of sigils represent trees and rocks, there was a good deal of research directed towards the natural sciences, too.

But it wasn't all gleaned from books and websites. Once the restrictions surrounding COVID-19 had been lifted I was able to explore some of the fascinating places in Sussex that have interesting connections with the Saxons, like Pevensey and Alfriston, to name just two.

So, whilst the Sarsenic Sigils are a figment of my imagination, the gods, animals, trees and rocks on which they are based are rooted in our rich pre-Christian heritage. Here and in Northern Europe.

Interest piqued? Grab your computer. Your rabbit hole awaits!

ABOUT THE AUTHOR & THE BRIGHTONIANS

Fags, booze and lard!

When people asked me what an advertising copywriter did, that's what I used to tell them I helped to sell. Though I could have just as easily said, 'trains, planes and automobiles'. Or even 'sex, drugs and rock 'n' roll'. The fact is that for just under 30 years, I wrote ads for anything and everything across every possible medium.

And for the most part it was fun.

Until it wasn't.

For me, anyway.

Which is why, in 2016, I jacked it all in and carved out time to write about the sort of things I wanted to write about.

So, it was goodbye margarine and men's body spray, and hello Brighton's vibrant queer present and past.

Inspired by an exhibition I helped to curate at the city's museum, called Queer the Pier, and my lifelong adoration for E F Benson's Mapp & Lucia series of novels, I refocused my passion for words and tried my hand at writing fiction. *(Not that a good deal of what I was writing before didn't require a sprinkle of make-believe dust, now and again!)* The result was *The Brightonians*, a queer tale of life beyond the picture postcards and candy floss of this far-from-quintessential seaside town, which draws a group of bitchy socialites back to the saucier side of 1960s Brighton.

Drag queens, gay porn, fancy-dress parties – what's not to love!

With over 70 reviews and an average rating of 4.5 on www.goodreads.co.uk and www.amazon.co.uk I'm happy (relieved) to report that quite a few people agreed!

For more information about both books please visit www.darenkay.com – where you will find radio interviews, press coverage and lots of stuff about Brighton's queer culture.

It's also where you can contact me by email.

Or, if you prefer, you can get in touch @darenkayauthor on Instagram.

'Daren Kay has the ability to draw you into his world with vivid and compelling characters. His work is funny, entertaining, moving and endlessly fascinating.'

Jill Nalder, actress, HIV/AIDS activist and fundraiser, author of 'Love from the Pink Palace', inspiration for Jill in Russell T Davies' 'It's a Sin' and patron of The Sussex Beacon.

Milton Keynes UK
Ingram Content Group UK Ltd.
UKHW010846280324
440101UK00001B/22

9 781803 817934